Ralph Compton

Nowhere, TX

Also by David Robbins
in Large Print:

The Return of the Virginian

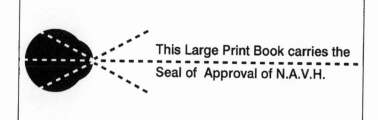

This Large Print Book carries the
Seal of Approval of N.A.V.H.

Ralph Compton

Nowhere, TX

A Ralph Compton Novel
by David Robbins

Thorndike Press • Waterville, Maine

Published in 2004 by arrangement with NAL Signet,
a member of Penguin Group (USA) Inc.

Thorndike Press® Large Print Western.

The tree indicium is a trademark of Thorndike Press.

The text of this Large Print edition is unabridged.
Other aspects of the book may vary from the original edition.

Set in 16 pt. Plantin by Ramona Watson.

Printed in the United States on permanent paper.

Library of Congress Cataloging-in-Publication Data

Robbins, David, 1950–
    Ralph Compton : Nowhere, TX : a Ralph Compton
novel / by David Robbins.
        p. cm.
    ISBN 0-7862-6923-5 (lg. print : hc : alk. paper)
    1. Outlaws — Fiction.   2. Texas — Fiction.   3. Large
type books.   I. Title: Nowhere, Texas.   II. Title.
PS3568.O22288R35 2004
    813´.54—dc22   2004054756

LP
F
Rob

Ralph Compton
Nowhere, TX

As the Founder/CEO of NAVH, the only national health agency solely devoted to those who, although not totally blind, have an eye disease which could lead to serious visual impairment, I am pleased to recognize Thorndike Press★ as one of the leading publishers in the large print field.

Founded in 1954 in San Francisco to prepare large print textbooks for partially seeing children, NAVH became the pioneer and standard setting agency in the preparation of large type.

Today, those publishers who meet our standards carry the prestigious "Seal of Approval" indicating high quality large print. We are delighted that Thorndike Press is one of the publishers whose titles meet these standards. We are also pleased to recognize the significant contribution Thorndike Press is making in this important and growing field.

Lorraine H. Marchi, L.H.D.
Founder/CEO
NAVH

★ Thorndike Press encompasses the following imprints: Thorndike, Wheeler, Walker and Large Print Press.

THE IMMORTAL COWBOY

This is respectfully dedicated to the "American Cowboy." His was the saga sparked by the turmoil that followed the Civil War, and the passing of more than a century has by no means diminished the flame.

True, the old days and the old ways are but treasured memories, and the old trails have grown dim with the ravages of time, but the spirit of the cowboy lives on.

In my travels — to Texas, Oklahoma, Kansas, Nebraska, Colorado, Wyoming, New Mexico, and Arizona — I always find something that reminds me of the Old West. While I am walking these plains and mountains for the first time, there is this feeling that a part of me is eternal, that I have known these old trails before. I believe it is the undying spirit of the frontier calling, allowing me, through the mind's eye, to step back into time. What is the appeal of the Old West of the American frontier?

It has been epitomized by some as the dark and bloody period in American history. Its heroes — Crockett, Bowie, Hickok, Earp — have been reviled and criticized. Yet the Old West lives on, larger than life.

It has become a symbol of freedom, when there was always another mountain to climb and another river to cross; when a dispute between two men was settled not with expensive lawyers, but with fists, knives or guns. Barbaric? Maybe. But some things never change. When the cowboy rode into the pages of American history, he left behind a legacy that lives within the hearts of us all.

— *Ralph Compton*

Chapter One

Out of the heat haze to the south came a rider. He drew rein when he saw the town. Pushing his low-crowned hat back on his mop of brown hair, he studied the dozen or so buildings and sheds, then clucked to his buttermilk.

Svenson the blacksmith was the first to see the rider. He was hammering a horseshoe on his anvil and only paused long enough to notice that the rider was young, and judging by the dust that caked his clothes, had ridden a long way.

Old Man Taylor was in his rocking chair in front of the stable, as always, whittling. He stopped slicing his knife when the clomp of hooves fell on his ears, and peered at the newcomer. He, too, observed that the rider was barely old enough to use a razor, and from where he sat, he plainly saw a pearl-handled Colt worn high on the rider's right hip.

Dub Wheeton was sweeping the boardwalk in front of his saloon. When the rider came to his hitch rail and dismounted, he greeted him with a friendly smile. "Howdy, stranger. You look like a man who could stand to wet his throat."

A lopsided grin split the young rider's tanned face. He had high cheekbones sprinkled with freckles and blue eyes that sparkled like a high mountain lake. Placing his hands on his saddle horn, he looked up and down the street. "I'd heard tell there was a town in these parts. What do you call this two-bit pile of planks?"

"Nowhere," Dub said.

"How's that again?"

"The town is called Nowhere." Dub gave the boardwalk a last sweep, then leaned on his broom. "We ain't got around to putting up a sign yet. There's no rush, since no one will claim us."

The rider cocked his head. "Do you always talk in riddles or is it just me?"

"Sorry." Dub pointed to the south. "That way is Texas." Dub pointed north. "That way is No Man's Land." He let out with a long sigh. "And here we are, smack in the middle."

"So you called your town Nowhere?" The rider snorted. "Are all the folks hereabouts naturally loco?"

"No, you don't understand. We thought

we were *in* Texas. But when they sent a surveyor out, he claimed we're twenty miles too far. And since No Man's Land ain't got a government yet, we're stuck in the middle of nowhere."

"Now I get it," the rider said. "You sure are in a pickle." Chuckling, he dismounted and looped his reins around the rail.

"They call me Dub," Dub said. "I ain't got a fancy place like you'd find up to Denver or down Dallas way, but my beer and my whiskey are as good as any."

"What say we put it to the test?" the rider proposed. Spurs jangling, he stepped to the open door. "Braden is my handle. Billy Braden."

"Right pleased to meet you, Billy."

Dub made for the bar. He saw Billy wait for his eyes to adjust, his right hand close to his Colt. "You're the only one here. My regular customers don't usually show up until about sunset."

"Got a lot of them, do you?"

"More than you'd think. We've got us twenty-three people in town. Then there are the punchers from the Bar J. And I get some from the outfit that rides for Chick Storm over to the Coldwater River country. But they only make it in about once a month."

"A right lively place," Billy said.

"Are you a puncher?"

Billy laughed as if that were the funniest notion ever. "You've got to be joshin'. Bust my rump day in and day out for thirty dollars and found? Life is too short to spend every wakin' hour breathin' cow piss."

"All work has its drawbacks," Dub remarked. "Take my job, for instance. You'd think that being around all this booze is a dream come true. But I can't guzzle my own stock, not if I want to make enough money to live on."

"Speakin' of drinks," Billy said, "some coffin varnish would do me right fine." He rested his left elbow on the bar. "Too bad you don't have a dove or two. Gents like me can always go for female company."

"I thought about importing a gal from St. Louis once," Dub mentioned. "But her upkeep wouldn't hardly make it worth the expense."

"Yes sir, I sure could go for a dove," Billy said, as if he hadn't heard.

At that moment into the saloon came Marshal Paul Lunsford. The dented tin star pinned to his vest was almost the same shade of grey as his hair. He ambled over, nodded at Dub, and said amiably to Billy, "I saw you ride in and figured I'd make your acquaintance." He offered his left hand to shake, and introduced himself. His right arm was bent at an odd angle against his side and his right hand was missing the thumb and two fingers.

Billy nodded at the arm. "What happened?"

"War wound," Marshal Lunsford said. "Gettysburg."

"Before my time." Billy glanced at the lawman's waist. "You don't go around heeled? What sort of lawman are you, anyhow?"

"The kind who believes in getting along with everyone. There's never been a difficulty that can't be talked out, I always say." Marshal Lunsford placed a coin on the bar. "Besides, it isn't as if Nowhere is overrun with outlaws and gun sharks."

"Lucky for you."

They both grinned. Billy's grin lasted longer, and then his expression became thoughtful.

"So tell me," Marshal Lunsford prompted. "What's the latest news from the outside world? A drummer passed through a while back and told us there's talk of turning Oklahoma Territory, Indian Territory and No Man's Land into a state."

"There are already more states than we know what to do with," Billy said. "Who needs another?"

"We do," Marshal Lunsford said. "Cut off like we are, the only laws that apply are the laws we make up ourselves."

"You don't say?" Billy accepted a glass from Dub and downed the whiskey in two gulps. "Not bad," he said. "Not bad at all. It's nice to know not every barkeep waters his liquor."

"So you haven't heard anything about statehood?" Marshal Lunsford pressed.

"I should hope to God I haven't," Billy declared. "No offense, but the fewer laws there are, the more I like it." Billy slid his glass toward Dub for a refill. "It's gotten so bad that in some places, a man can't spit without being arrested."

"Spit all you want in Nowhere."

"Will do," Billy said, and promptly did, right there on the floor. Then he cackled and slapped his thigh.

Dub rose onto the tips of his toes to see the wet spot. "If you're going to do it in here, kindly use the spittoon."

Billy stared from him to the lawman and back again. "I'm beginnin' to like this town of yours."

"We're glad that you do," Marshal

Lunsford said. "Next time you visit, bring your friends. We can always use the business."

Billy downed his second glass in just one gulp, paid for it, and announced, "I reckon I'll take me a little stroll. I've got a long ride ahead and I need to stretch my legs." Touching his hat brim, he sauntered out into the harsh glare of the afternoon sun and stood for a minute balancing on the edge of the boardwalk before he turned left and sauntered down the street with his thumbs hooked in his gun belt.

Old Man Taylor glanced up from his carving, and grunted. "As I live and breathe. A peacock on the loose."

Billy's eyebrows nearly met over his nose. "Old-timer, either you've got a powerful hankerin' for an early grave or you need spectacles."

"Or it could be I have a sense of humor and you don't," Old Man Taylor said. "What's a young, full-of-life gosling like you doing in a withered husk of a shell like Nowhere?"

"Is that any way to talk about the place you live?"

"Sometimes we live where we have to and not where we want to. I stumbled on Nowhere when I was bound for Beaver

City and saw that it's perfect for the walking dead." Taylor shaved off a sliver of wood. "Here I'll stay and here I'll die, and I hope when they plant me, they do as I've asked and give me a tombstone that reads, 'Here lies Thomas Taylor. He took the wrong turn straight into hell.' "

Billy's cheeks bloomed in a smile. "You're a cantankerous old cuss, aren't you?"

"And damned proud of it," Old Man Taylor bragged. "Someone has to set these misguided souls straight or they'll go through life thinking it's a bed of roses."

"Ever any excitement in these parts?"

"You mean, besides watching the weeds grow? Well, Saturdays are lively. That's when the punchers come in, and they like to raise a little hell. The most they ever do is get drunk and shoot into the air, but we did have us a real honest-to-goodness shooting affray about a year ago, if that counts."

Billy's interest was piqued. "Who was involved? Some nobodies, I bet."

Old Man Taylor cut into the wood. "I don't know how as I'd call Lin Cooley a nobody, you young quail. He's foreman for Chick Storm of the Circle C and not a gent to trifle with. He's also a top-notch gun hand."

"If he's so good, how come I never heard of him?"

"Because he's not one of those blowhards like Wild Bill and Buffalo Bill. He minds his own business and expects folks to do the same."

Billy waited a few moments, then said, "Well? Are you going to tell me about it or do I have to beat you with a rock?"

"Curious killdeer, aren't you?"

"Quit callin' me birds. I don't know as how I like it."

"Oh my. I wouldn't want to rile a hawk on the peck like you." Taylor snickered, then related, "Like I was saying, it was about a year ago. The Circle C boys came down for a night of drinking and cards. There was a gambler passing through. I can't rightly recollect his name but he made the greenhorn mistake of trying to cheat those cowboys out of their hard-earned wages."

"And?" Billy goaded when Old Man Taylor stopped and didn't say anything.

"I ought to charge you for all this gum-flapping."

"Did you see it?"

"Hell, yes. Soon as I'm done here every day, I mosey on over to Dub's and stay there until I can barely stand. That night was no different. I was there when Randy Quin accused the gambler of cheating and the gambler stood up and pulled his coat back and told Randy he'd better apologize."

"I thought you said it was some other jasper. Cooley?"

"Try to keep up, little sparrow. Cooley and Randy are partners. So when the gambler called the play, Cooley stepped in. He told the gambler he had two choices. Make good the money he cheated them out of or push up mesquite. The gambler made the wrong choice."

"Who drew first?"

"What difference does it make? The gambler's dead and Cooley isn't. That's all that counts."

"I'd like to know. I keep track of who's fast and who ain't."

Old Man Taylor set his knife and the block of wood in his lap. "You sure are peculiar. But just so you can sleep nights, it was the gambler who went for his six-gun first. I saw it with my own eyes. Cooley, on the other hand, I never saw draw."

"But you said Cooley shot him."

"When was the last time you cleaned the wax out of your ears? I didn't *see* Cooley draw. I never said he *didn't*. He drew so damn fast, no one saw it. His hand just sort of filled with his revolver, and just like that the gambler was as dead as you please, with a stupid look on his face."

"That fast?" Billy echoed, and smiled. "Lin Cooley, huh? Now there's a gent I'd like to meet some day."

"Whatever for? Are you fond of sticking your head in bear traps and kicking the backsides of mules?"

"Old-timer, you are just about the —" Billy stopped, his mouth half open, his gaze fixed on a figure up the street.

Old Man Taylor looked, and laughed. "Her name is Sally Palmer and her pa owns the general store. And don't be getting any ideas in that peacock head of yours. She's already spoken for."

"Says who?"

"Says Randy Quin. He's been sparking her for the better part of a year now, and everyone sort of takes it for granted he'll step into her loop before too long."

The girl in front of the store was shaking a blanket out. She had lustrous hair that gleamed like spun gold and a flowered dress that swirled when she moved.

"She's beautiful!" Billy breathed.

"Randy Quin thinks so. I might if I were forty years younger. But the only things

19

that get me excited nowadays are waking up in the mornings and making it through the day without my gout acting up."

"And you called me peculiar?" Billy saw the Palmer girl go back inside the store.

"Damn."

"Whippoorwill, take my advice. Light a shuck and forget her or they'll be planting you next to that gambler in our pitiful excuse for a cemetery." Old Man Taylor picked up his knife and wood. "Now go pester someone else. I can't carve and jaw at the same time."

"What are you carving, anyhow?" Billy asked.

"Nothing. I just like to cut up wood."

"Crazy coot." Billy crossed the street and jingled along the boardwalk until he came to the general store. He stared in the front window a few moments, then suddenly wheeled and walked to his buttermilk and was about to climb on when Marshal Lunsford stepped from the saloon.

"Leaving so soon? I thought you said you liked it here."

"Except for that old fart over to the stable, it's right friendly," Billy said, forking leather. "And don't you worry. I'll be back. I'll do like you want and bring some of my friends along. I have me a hunch they'll like it here as much as I do."

"We'll look forward to seeing you again," Marshal Lunsford said.

Billy Braden laughed and rode off.

Chapter Two

"What do you think?" Randy Quin asked while examining himself in the mirror above the washbasin in the Circle C bunkhouse. "Should I wear the red bandanna or the blue bandanna?"

"Wear them both," was Lin Cooley's reply. "That's the third time you've asked. Better yet, strangle yourself with either and put yourself out of our misery."

Two bunks down, Charley Lone tittered with glee. "That's tellin' the peckerwood, Lin! Land sakes, you'd think he didn't know how to dress himself, the way he carries on so."

"I just want to look my best when I see Sally," Randy defended himself. "If either of you had a girl you'd know how important it is."

"Why, you whippersnapper," Charley growled. "I've had more girls in my time than you have fingers and toes." He scratched his salt-and-pepper beard. "There was this schoolmarm once who took a fancy to me down near San Antonio. Have I ever told that story?"

Lin Cooley groaned. "Ninety-seven times."

Ignoring him, Charley said, "She was a right pretty gal. Big-boned, with a nose a buffalo would love, but she baked the best pies this side of creation. And once she got me alone, why, she about curled my toes. Big as chile peppers, those lips of hers, and a heap hotter."

"Enough!" Randy said. "I am not going to stand here and listen to another of your vulgar stories."

"What's vulgar about a man and a woman lockin' lips? Don't tell me you and your sweetheart haven't. I know better."

"Sally is a lady, I'll have you know."

"She still has lips and a tongue, don't she?" Charley shuffled toward the washbasin. "Now get your lovesick hide out of here so I can wash up. I've been polite and went last. But as much time as you're takin', it'll be Christmas before I get to head for Nowhere."

Lin Cooley, who was lounging against the wall, straightened and nudged Quin. "He's right. You're as lovely as you're ever going to get."

"Men aren't lovely, they're handsome,"

Randy corrected him. "And you should side with me, not this old cuss. I'm your pard."

The contrast they presented in the mirror was striking: Cooley with his broad shoulders and blond hair and grey eyes; Quin with hair the color of a raven and a lean build and brown eyes.

"Shoo, the both of you," Charley said. "Be sure to tell the boys to save me some bellyin' space at the bar. Tonight's the night I drink Old Man Taylor under the table."

"You've tried that more than once, as I recollect," Randy said, "and it's you we have to keep pickin' up off the floor."

"You have no respect for your elders, boy. And unless you want to eat burnt beans for the next month or three, I'd scat, were I you."

"Never argue with the cook," Lin Cooley advised.

"Got that right," Charley grumbled. "Us bean masters are the Almighty in britches, in case you ain't heard."

Cooley and Randy left the bunkhouse and strode toward the stable, but stopped when a big man came from the main house and intercepted them.

"Off to Nowhere like all the rest of the

boys?" Chick Storm asked. He was taller than both of them by a head and had a chest as broad as a steer's.

"They got a head start on us, boss," Randy said, "but only because half of them don't wash but once a year."

Chick Storm winked at Lin, then said to Randy, "Word is, son, you've been using more soap than all the rest combined. Why, Charley was saying the other day how he never saw anyone so godly."

Cooley laughed, and Randy blushed red.

"I've got a reason for wantin' to be clean."

"When I was your age I had the exact same reason," Chick Storm said. "So don't let their teasing get to you. I stuck with it, and look at where I am now. I didn't get this prosperous on my own. Behind every man who makes something of himself is a woman prodding him to do it."

Randy poked the ground with the toe of a boot. "I hope you won't mind my being nosey. But do ever you regret marryin' Mrs. Storm?"

Chick placed a hand on the young cowpuncher's shoulder. "Not once in seventeen years. Regrets are for those who are always looking back, not for those who look ahead."

Randy grinned. "Thanks, Mr. Storm."

"Before I forget," their employer said, "Mrs. Storm wants to know if you boys would mind picking up some things for her at Palmer's." He pulled a folded sheet of paper from a pocket. "Small things you can fit in your saddlebags. Here's her list." He also pulled out a twenty-dollar gold piece. "This should be enough to cover the cost. If not, have George Palmer charge the extra to the Circle C's account."

"Will do," Lin Cooley said. He pocketed the list and the money as Randy walked on ahead.

"Watch over our young friend," Chick Storm said. "He's as love-blind as a buck in rut, and we both know what that can do to a man."

Cooley frowned, then nodded.

"My apologies," Chick said quickly. "That was thoughtless. I didn't mean to bring her up. There's no one I think more highly of than you, and you know that."

Again Cooley nodded, and went to catch up with his partner. They saddled up and headed out.

Chick Storm was on the ranch house porch. He smiled and waved.

"Nice people, those Storms," Randy said. "Salt of the earth and then some. I've never been so proud to ride for a brand as I am to ride for the Circle C."

"Anyone who tries to harm them answers to me."

"That Mrs. Storm sure is something. Don't tell the big sugar, but I suspect she runs things more than he does."

"She's a special lady," Lin agreed.

Randy adjusted his blue bandanna. "I've given it a lot of thought. Tonight is the night I pop the question."

"Just like you were fixin' to do every month we go to Nowhere," Cooley responded. "That girl isn't going to wait forever."

Randy nodded. "I know, I know. I should have got down on bended knee months ago. But it's one thing to think about doing it and another to have the courage to go through with it." Although there was no one within a hundred yards of them, he lowered his voice. "Just between you and me, pard, I get so scared, I shake inside."

"Ever heard of seizin' the bull by the horns?"

"Hell, I'll tackle any bull alive. But a female critter is something else. When I look into those green eyes of hers, my throat won't work and my brain stops and it's all I can do to remember my name."

"Love does that," Cooley said.

"You were in love once, weren't you? Before we met?"

Cooley duplicated his earlier frown. "I don't want to talk about it. Not now. Not as long as we live."

"Sorry, pard."

After that they were quiet for many a mile, until they came to the southwestern boundary of the Circle C.

"What will I do if she says yes?" Randy abruptly asked.

"I'll take a wild guess and say you should marry her. Or run off to Argentina. Your choice."

"I'm serious. I've barely two hundred dollars to my name. I don't own any land, I don't have a house. Where would we live? What would we do?"

"Take the stairs one step at a time," Lin said. "First you get married, then you work out the rest."

"But her folks will be expectin' me to provide for her, won't they? And how would it look, Sally and me livin' in a tent in the middle of the prairie somewhere? With not even an outhouse to call our own?"

Cooley glanced at him. "Do you know why I like being your pard?"

28

"Because I'd back you to the death?"

"Because you're the silliest galoot who ever wore spurs. There isn't a day goes by but you don't tickle my funny bone."

"How nice for your digestion. But while you're makin' merry at my expense, my happiness is in shambles."

"There you go again," Cooley said, and laughed out loud.

Randy fluttered his lips and shook his head and made a sound that resembled a goose being strangled. "I don't mind admittin' this whole love business has me buffaloed. Half the time, I can't rightly figure out whether I'm doing the ropin' or I'm the one being roped."

"Females like it when a man isn't sure if he's comin' or going," Lin remarked. "It gives them an edge."

Randy gazed across the rolling prairie. "The way I see it, the Good Lord dipped into some tarantula juice the day he created fillies. They're the most exasperatin' creatures alive, and that includes rattlers and mustangs. Try as I do to figure Sally out, the more I try, the less I figure."

Lin Cooley reined his smoky dun to the right to avoid prairie dog holes. "I knew an hombre once who fell head over spurs for the prettiest gal that ever wore a ribbon.

29

She had hair as red as a sunset and a face that took a man's breath away. Every time he looked at her, his heart about burst out his chest."

"It's nice to know I have a common ailment."

"This hombre spent his every wakin' moment thinkin' about her, his every sleepin' moment dreamin' about her. He had it bad, real bad, and there was nothin' any of his friends could do."

"Sounds more and more familiar," Randy said. "Maybe sawbones should start callin' love a disease."

"That hombre would likely agree," Lin said. "He spent every cent he had on her. Buyin' her frilly things and such. Taking her to socials and off to Kansas City once with her sister along to chaperone. He lived, breathed and ate her. In the end, all it got him was more misery than you can fit in a bottomless well."

"What happened? Didn't she love him back?"

"She claimed she did. So when one of his friends mentioned seeing her in the company of another man, he knocked his friend to the ground and called him a damned liar. And when the girl's own sister warned him that he should give himself more breathin' space, he flattered himself she was jealous."

"Sounds to me like this hombre's head was too big for the biggest hat ever made."

Lin Cooley was silent a bit; then, "He learned the truth, though. One night he went into town when she wasn't expectin' him and caught her havin' supper with the man who owned the hotel. There they were, holdin' hands and makin' cow eyes. And what do you think that hombre did?"

"Went off and bawled his brains out. That's what I'd do."

"Only because you're so sissified," Cooley said with a grin. "No, the hombre we're talkin' about showed exactly how much jackass blood was runnin' through his veins by marchin' in on them and callin' the hotel owner out into the street even though he and everyone else knew the man never carried a gun." Cooley pulled his hat brim low against the bright glare of the early morning sun. "Stupidities are like rabbits. They breed faster than we can blink."

"Go on with your story. I'm interested in learnin' what happened to the poor fool."

"The girl stood up right there in front of all the people in the restaurant and did the worst thing she could have done. She laughed in his face. She laughed, and she told him that he was actin' like a boy who had never grown up."

"That must have stung."

"The worst was yet to come. She said that she was a grown woman and free to go out with any jasper she wanted, and from that day on she never wanted to see him again."

"How did he take it?"

"He felt like a Comanche had stuck a knife in his gut and was twistin' it back and forth. He was so upset, he couldn't think straight, and he blurted out about all the months they'd spent together, and all the good times they'd had. And she laughed some more, and told him the only reason she gave him the time of day was to have something to do. That in her eyes, he was never more than a dalliance. Her exact word. A dalliance."

"Dang. That girl had a tongue sharper than a saber."

"He mentioned all the things he'd bought her, and their trip to Kansas City, and how he took it for granted they would be hitched."

"Did she go on laughin'?"

"No. She got mad. Madder than he'd ever seen her. Madder than he'd ever seen any female. And she started pokin' him in the chest and going on about how men are always takin' women for granted, and how just because a woman goes for a buggy ride with a man doesn't mean they're joined at the hip, and how if he wasn't so pathetic, he wouldn't be actin' so immature."

"Were those her words too? Pathetic and immature?"

"Yep."

"Lordy. I'd have shriveled up and died right there on the spot. I embarrass real easy."

"The hurt was worse than the shame. He looked at her, really looked at her for the first time since he met her, and what he saw about tore him apart. He saw that behind her pretty face was a heart of stone. That all she ever cared about was herself. That she'd led him around like a dog on a leash, and now that she had found someone with more money, she was lettin' go of the leash."

Randy glanced at his friend. "What did he do then?"

"What else? I went to the nearest saloon and tried to drink it dry. By then the news was all over town. A sidewinder who never much liked me was at the other end of the bar and took to makin' comments about fools in love. So I walked over and insulted his mother and threw whiskey in his face and called him a coward, and when he went for his pistol, I shot him."

"Dead?"

"Through the shoulder."

"It's not like you to have a habit of going on the prod." Randy justified the deed, then stiffened. "Wait a second. You're not by any chance comparin' my Sally to the gal who did you wrong?"

"All I'm sayin' is that when it comes to females, don't take it for granted you can put your horse in her corral until you're sure the corral gate is open."

"Sally is nothin' like your gal," Randy insisted.

"I hope so, pard. For your sake, I truly do."

Chapter Three

Billy Braden rode north out of Nowhere thinking of blond curls and a shapely dress. He was still thinking of them, off and on, two days later when he spied a pale hump off across the plain to the northeast. He was heading northwest but he reined toward it and was glad he did.

A Conestoga had broken down. The team of oxen was dozing in the heat of the afternoon sun, while up on the seat sat a middle-aged woman, peacefully knitting. A burly, bearded slab of a man was at work fixing the wheel.

Billy plastered a smile on his face and trotted toward them with his hands in plain sight. It proved a smart move.

The instant the bearded man heard the buttermilk, he snatched a big rifle that had been leaning against the wagon and tucked it to his shoulder. "That's far enough, stranger!"

Drawing rein, Billy held his arms out from his sides. "I don't mean you no harm, mister. I just saw your wagon and thought you might need a helpin' hand."

"I can manage right fine on my own. Mosey along."

Billy smiled at the woman, who reminded him of a biddy hen without the feathers, and as was often the case, his smile had the effect he intended.

"He's just a boy, Hiram. We should be grateful he's a Good Samaritan and not a cutthroat."

The muzzle of the man's big rifle stayed fixed on Billy. "This is No Man's Land, Maude. I'm not taking chances." To Billy he called out, "We're obliged, son, but you go your own way. And keep in mind I can pick off a deer at half a mile with this here Sharps of mine."

"Hiram Bradshaw, I declare!" Maude indignantly declared. "You've got no more manners than a goat."

Billy kept smiling at her. "That's all right, ma'am. I understand. I just hope you folks are long gone if those Injuns happen by."

"Indians?" she repeated in alarm.

"Comanches, I think," Billy said. "I struck their trail about an hour ago. Weren't no more than nine or ten so maybe you can hold them off with that cannon. He reined the buttermilk around. "Good luck."

"Wait!" Maude hollered.

There followed a short but heated exchange that resulted in Hiram reluctantly lowering his Sharps and Maude cheerfully beckoning. "We'd be pleased to have your company. And don't you worry. My husband won't shoot you."

"That's nice to hear." Billy didn't like how Hiram kept fingering the rifle's trigger but he pretended not to notice and brought the buttermilk nearer. "It would ruin my day something awful."

Maude laughed and set her knitting needles on the seat. "I daresay it's nice to hear another human voice. We've been weeks on the trail and haven't seen another soul in forever."

"Surely you're with a wagon train?" Billy asked.

"Would that we were," Maude said. "But Hiram was confident we could make it all the way from Wichita to Amarillo on our own. He didn't want to pay the fee those wagon masters charge."

"Why pay for something you can do yourself?" Hiram interjected.

"You're mighty brave to do it on your own," Billy flattered him.

Their prairie schooner was the large model — a third again the size of those that routinely made the trek from St. Joseph to the Oregon Country. Rising in his stirrups, Billy saw that the bed was filled with scores of household items and tools, everything from a plow to a washbasin. "You're about to overflow in there."

"That's why our front wheel broke, I suspect," Maude said.

One of their spokes had split. A jack was under the axle, and Hiram had been turning the hand crank when Billy rode up.

"Anything I can do?"

"No." Hiram still had the Sharps in his hands. "I believe in doing my own work. Another half an hour and I'll have this done."

Maude wagged a finger at him. "There you go again. Can't you be civil? I swear, sometimes I suspect you were raised under a rock."

"I wouldn't be so hard on him, ma'am," Billy said. "It doesn't pay to be too trustin' in these parts. But to prove I'm not the scoundrel he thinks I am, how about if you hold this for me so I can lend a hand?" Unbuckling his gun belt, Billy kneed the buttermilk to the Conestoga and handed it to a delighted Maude.

"Now aren't you ashamed of yourself, Hiram? Treating this sweet boy as if he were Jesse James when he's more Christian than you are?"

"I won't apologize for being careful." But Hiram leaned the Sharps against the wagon and thrust out a calloused knob of a hand to shake. "If you really want to help, hop on down."

Billy had rarely felt such immense strength. He volunteered to turn the hand crank and had to use both hands to do so, the wagon was so heavy. "You carry spare spokes, do you?"

"Spokes and felloes and an axle too," Hiram said. "Always be prepared, that's my motto."

Maude had slid to the end of the seat and was observing. "So tell me, young man. Where are you from?"

"I was born in Indiana," Billy related. "My parents left when I was six and I don't recollect much about it other than it was green. My pa had a job lined up in Leadville but we weren't there a month when winter set in, and along about Christmas my folks were killed in an avalanche."

"Goodness gracious!" Maude exclaimed. "Who looked after you?"

"No one," Billy said, turning the crank harder.

"You were cast adrift all alone at that tender an age? It must have been terrible. How did you survive?"

Shrugging, Billy replied, "Any way I could. I learned early that we do what we have to in order to get by in this world."

"I must say, you've done your parents proud. Look at you now, going out of your way to help strangers in need. Why, any woman would be glad to call you her own." Maude's expression was kindness personified.

"You're an angel to say that, ma'am," Billy said, then devoted himself to finishing the repairs. He made sure to do as little of the work as possible, and stood by while Hiram slid the wheel off the hub bearing, loosened the iron rim, then removed two of the curved felloes to get at the broken spoke.

The whole time, Maude chattered with hardly a pause for breath about their farm in Wichita and how they had sold it so they could move to Amarillo and take up farming anew on property adjoining that of Hiram's brother. "Our new farm will be five times the size of our old one. Almost a thousand acres, all to ourselves!"

"Some ranches in Texas have over a hundred thousand," Billy mentioned to show her he was listening.

"So we've heard. Why, they say there's one ranch as big as all of Rhode Island. What a body would want with that much land is beyond me."

Hiram had removed the broken sections and was inserting a new spoke into a socket in one of the felloes.

"Cattle need more land than cabbages," Billy said.

"I suppose," Maude responded. "Say, you wouldn't happen to be hungry, would you? We have jerky to spare. Or how about a honey popcorn ball? I made a batch before we left and there are still some left in the tin."

"I don't believe I've ever had one."

"Then you're in for a treat. I'll just be a second." Maude ducked into the wagon, remarking, "Now where did I put that tin?"

"Go slow in there, woman!" Hiram shouted. "I don't want this jack tipping over on me." For the first time he grinned at Billy. "A word of advice, boy. When you get married, find yourself a wife with more common sense than a tree stump."

"I'm not the apron string kind," Billy informed him.

"That's what we all think until we're smitten. Then one day we look at a gal and our insides turn to mush and we're never the same again." Hiram began reassembling the wheel. "But don't let me fool you. I'd rather be nagged to death than single." A loud thump from inside the wagon caused him to glance up sharply. "What did I tell you about moving around in there?"

"Sorry, honey bunny."

"Honey bunny?" Billy chortled.

"Her pet name for me. Women do fool things like that all the time. Why, the stories I could tell you . . ." Hiram left the statement unfinished.

Maude reappeared on the seat clutching a tin box. "Here they are." She leaned down so Billy could take it. "Help yourself."

Hunkering, Billy pried the lid open and popped one of the honey popcorn balls into his mouth. He liked the sweet taste and how the ball crunched when he bit down. A second and third followed it down his throat. "Right tasty."

"I thank you, kind sir." Maude was delighted. "I hope they'll convince you to stick around for supper. It would be wonderful to have your company."

Billy munched on another honey popcorn ball and watched as Hiram slid the wheel onto the axle. When the wheel was secure, he replaced the lid on the tin and gave it to Maude. "Do you suppose I could have my pistol back now?"

Maude glanced at Hiram, who nodded, then gingerly picked up the gun belt. "You'll think this is silly of me but I've never been all that comfortable around guns. My grandfather lost half his leg in a hunting accident and I can never forget the sight of all that blood and his horrible screams when the doctor amputated it."

"Guns have their uses." Billy strapped on his gun belt and twirled the Colt from its holster. He spun it forward several times and spun it backward several times, then shifted on the balls of his feet, cocked the hammer, and shot Hiram Bradshaw through the right knee.

The burly farmer toppled, clutching his leg, his teeth clenched against the pain. Red mist spurted from between his fingers.

For a few seconds Maude was too shocked to speak or move. Then she let out with a screech and vaulted from the wagon with an agility and speed her years belied. "Hiram!" Dashing past Billy, she dropped to her knees. "Dear God, no!"

Billy saw the husband look at the Sharps

and he quickly took it and placed it on the seat, well out of their reach. "Now then. Suppose we get this over with."

Tears glistened on Maude's cheeks and her lips were quivering. Groaning, she gripped one of Hiram's hands in both of hers. "How could you do this after we were so kind to you?"

"Your husband was right, lady. You can't trust anyone in No Man's Land." Billy took a few steps to the left so he had a clear shot at the husband. "Fork over your money and I'll make this easy."

"We don't have any money," Maude said. "Whatever gave you the notion we did?"

"You sold your farm in Kansas, didn't you?"

"Yes. But we spent it all on this wagon and our new farm near Amarillo. We hardly have twenty dollars left to our name."

"Sure you don't," Billy said, and shot Hiram Bradshaw again, through the other knee.

Crying out, Hiram thrashed in torment, spittle dribbling into his beard. Suddenly uncoiling, he heaved erect and lunged, but his knees betrayed him and he buckled just as his outstretched fingers clawed for Billy's throat.

Again the Colt boomed. This time the slug tore through Bradshaw's left thigh. An artery or vein was severed, because scarlet gushed from the wound like scalding water from a geyser. Hiram howled in rage as much as in agony, and clamped his palms over the entry and exit wounds. "I'll kill you for this, boy! So help me, I'll send you straight to hell!"

"The money," Billy said.

Racked by sobs, Maude slowly rose and came toward him, her hands clasped in appeal. "Please, young man! I'm begging you! Leave us be and we'll never tell a soul."

Billy backhanded her across the face. "Some people just never sweat the fat off their brains."

Maude staggered back, more stunned than hurt, a red welt on her cheek. "You — you *struck* me!"

"This ain't no church social," Billy commented, then had to skip aside as an outraged Hiram, bleeding like a gut-shot buck, scrambled at him on all fours and tried to seize his legs.

"Don't you touch her! Do you hear? Don't you dare lay a finger on her again, or it will be the last thing you ever do!"

"I'm tired of your squawkin'," Billy said,

and shot him smack between the eyes.

The rear of Hiram's head exploded outward, showering brains and grisly bits, and Hiram sagged, his eyes frozen wide in astonishment. He oozed to the ground like melted wax, drool seeping from a corner of his mouth.

Maude was transformed to marble.

Calmly flipping open the Colt's loading gate, Billy began replacing the spent cartridges. "All he had to do was tell me what I wanted to know and he wouldn't have suffered near as much."

"You're an animal!"

"Woof, woof," Billy said.

"You're a vile, despicable beast!" Maude cried. "I pray to God I live to see the law throw a noose around your neck."

"You won't," Billy said. He shot her in the left leg.

Screaming, Maude toppled and flopped about in anguish, repeating over and over, "You shot me! You shot me! You shot me!"

Billy twirled his Colt into its holster and stood over her. "For the last time. Where's the money hid?"

Maude stopped thrashing and glared, her tears of sorrow now tears of fury. "It will be a cold day in hell before I tell you!"

Bending, Billy slid a double-edged knife from his right boot and held it so the blade glittered in the sunlight. "Want to bet?"

Chapter Four

Old Man Taylor grinned when the Circle C hands drew rein at the livery stable. He stopped whittling long enough to say, "Well, look at this. I wonder what brings you two cowbirds to Nowhere."

"I don't want to hear it," Randy Quin said.

"Could it be a certain golden thrush?" Old Man Taylor teased with a lopsided grin. "The kind that lives over behind the general store, maybe?"

Lin Cooley dismounted and handed the reins to Taylor. "There you go with the birds again. You sure that you weren't born a loon?"

"I happen to like birds. I like them more than most people, in fact." The stableman gave each of them a pointed look. "Truth is, at one time I had me a dream of becoming an ornithologist."

"An orni-what?" Randy said.

"An ornithologist. That's a bird wrangler, you ignorant lump. I could have spent my whole life studying birds and their habits."

"That would fit you like long under-wear," Cooley said. "Why didn't you?"

Old Man Taylor's features mirrored deep regret. "To be one you have to go to a university and that costs money. Money my folks didn't have. Money I couldn't rustle up short of robbing a bank. So I never became one. But I still love birds as much as ever."

Cooley gazed out over the prairie. "Then why settle here, where there aren't enough birds to fill a thimble? Why not go East or on to California or somewhere they have heaps of birds?"

"The pain, my fine eagle. The pain."

"He's addlepated," Randy declared.

"Every time I see one of our feathered friends, it sears me to the quick," Old Man Taylor explained. "I'd rather spare myself the pain, if you don't mind."

"So you live where there's hardly any birds?" Randy said. "I had no idea."

"I daresay there's a lot you don't know." Taylor stiffly stood and accepted their reins. "The thing to keep in mind is that sometimes we only get one chance at happiness and if it passes us by we spend the rest of our days waiting for dirt to be shoveled on top of our cold corpse."

"You sure have an inspirin' gift for gab."

"Mock me all you want, my young cowbird. Just so you don't end up like me." Old Man Taylor led their horses into the stable. "Is it a stall and oats for both or aren't you boys spending the night?"

"The night," Randy confirmed, with a hopeful glance in the direction of the general store, and nudged Lin. "Let's go wash down the dust."

Dub Wheeton was pouring red-eye for three Bar J punchers when Cooley and Quin entered the saloon, and one of the Bar J boys let out with a wild whoop.

"Well, lookee here! Chick Storm has let two of his swivel dudes come to town all by their lonesomes. Some day he ought to break down and hire himself some real cowboys." The speaker chortled and clapped his companions on the back. He was short and muscular and favored a brown leather belt decorated with silver studs, a high-crowned hat, and boots with heels an inch higher than most.

"You're a fine one to be calling us swivel dudes," Randy shot back, grinning as he shook the other cowboy's hand. "It's good to see you, Joe. Even if you do bray a lot just to hear your own voice."

"Drinks for my friends, barkeep!" Joe

Elliot bawled. "And that jar of pickled eggs while you're at it!"

Randy stuck a finger in his ear and jiggled it. "Do you always have to holler so? I swear, after an hour of your company my eardrums are fit to burst."

"Hell, hoss, I come from a family of fourteen kids!" Joe declared. "In our house it was always the loudest who got the most attention, and the most food at the feed trough."

"In that case," Randy said, "your folks must not have known they had thirteen others."

Joe chuckled. "Why, you're almost gettin' good at this. Are we on for poker tonight? I sure hope so! I feel lucky."

"Count me in," Cooley said.

"Not me," Randy said. "One drink, and I've got business to attend to."

Joe Elliot looked at Cooley and said in mock seriousness, "For the life of me I can't figure what that girl sees in this pard of yours. Why give him the time of day when she could be courtin' a handsome devil like me?"

"Sally has good taste," Randy said.

Dub came over carrying the jar of pickled eggs. "It's days like this that make me glad I set down roots here. Good

51

whiskey, good friends, and good times. Life doesn't get any better than this."

"I don't know," Joe said. "A ranch of my own, a wife who likes to give back rubs, and a pretty cook who will meet me in the root cellar every afternoon is my idea of the good life."

"If you like women so much, you should spend your free time in Beaver City," Randy said.

"It takes too long to get there," was Joe's reply. "I go when I'm so in need I can't stand still." He gulped a shot of whiskey. "I wouldn't have to go at all if Dub, here, would get us some females."

"How many times must I tell you boys?" Dub defended himself. "I've tried. Honest to goodness I have. But the only doves who would give this place consideration are too broken down to earn enough to make it worth my while."

Randy drained his glass and dropped a coin into it. "All this talk of females and such has me hankerin' for a stroll. See you gents later." Tilting his hat at a rakish angle, he hurried out and across the street to the general store. The door was open for ventilation and he stood in the doorway watching Sally Palmer rearrange merchandise. No one else was there. She stacked cans of peaches and tomatoes, then folded the top blanket on a pile of blankets, and turned.

"Oh!"

"You're so pretty you take my breath away."

Sally came around the counter and was about to throw herself into his arms when she glanced at a door at the rear and primly pecked him on the cheek, whispering, "He's in the back but he might come out any second."

"I savvy," Randy said.

"I've missed you," Sally stated. "Missed you something awful." She gripped both his hands. "Why do you only get in here once a month?" Her green eyes feasted on him as a starved woman's would on a plate of food. "The Bar J crowd are here every weekend."

"The Bar J is a lot closer to Nowhere than the Circle C," Randy reminded her. "They can get here in a couple of hours. With us, it takes most of a day."

Just then a roly-poly ball of energy came bouncing out of the back. "Randall! How good to see you again." George Palmer was carrying sacks of flour, which he deposited on a shelf. "My daughter has been pining away since your last visit."

"Daddy!" Sally squealed. "I have not."

George grinned and wiped his hands on his apron, then shook Randy's hand. "I take it you'll stay for supper? And maybe let me beat you at checkers later?"

"You always win fair," Randy said. "I wish I were half as smart as you. I wouldn't be nursemaidin' cows for a livin'."

"You never know," George said, and winked. "Maybe one day you'll marry into a respectable family and take up the mercantile profession."

"Daddy!"

"Why don't the two of you take a walk?" George proposed. "Helen won't have supper ready for an hour yet and I have inventory to do."

"Thank you, sir," Randy said.

The street was deserted, the rocking chair in front of the stable empty. From the saloon came Joe Elliot's loud voice and louder laughter.

Randy took Sally's hand and led her around to the side of the store. Next door to it was the feed and grain. But there were no windows. Pulling Sally to him, Randy kissed her full on the mouth, letting it linger as long as she permitted.

"I can't wait to do that every time I come here. I live for your lips."

"I hope you live for a lot more than that," Sally said, her green eyes twinkling. She cupped one of his hands to her bosom and kissed his square chin. "Do you have any idea how hard it is to go so long without seeing you?"

"I get in as often as I can." Randy touched her golden hair. "You always smell so nice. Like a flower in bloom."

"You always smell like a cow."

Randy stepped back. "I wash before I come. In clean water, too, unlike a lot of the rest." He plucked at his shirt and sniffed. "It must be my clothes. I never thought to wash them too."

"I don't care how you smell." Sally placed her cheek on his chest and snuggled against him. "The important thing is I can hold you again. Just like I dream of doing each and every day."

A lump in Randy's throat made him cough. "Girl, when you talk like that, you set me to tinglin' all over. You're the greatest thing that's ever happened to me."

"Am I, dearest? Am I truly?"

"How can you even ask? After all this time?"

"All this time," Sally said, and sighed.

"Let's walk." Holding her hand, Randy led her around to the back of the store. To the west the sun was setting and the sky was fire red. "Look at that." They strolled out across the prairie. It was just the two of them, alone amid the mesquite and sage-brush and scores of wild flowers.

Sally breathed deep and showed her white, even teeth. "I do so love it here. The only thing that would make it perfect would be to have a house and land of my own. And a husband to go with them."

"Houses and land don't come cheap," Randy noted. "I've been saving every cent I can but it'll take me years to scrape up enough."

"Men and women sometimes marry and save up together," Sally said.

"I wouldn't want any wife of mine workin' for a livin'," Randy replied as a lizard skittered away from them, moving almost faster than the eye could follow. "What would folks think?"

"My mother works. She helps Daddy in the store."

"That's not what I meant."

"And Chick Storm's wife is as good a rancher as he is. People say she can ride and rope and shoot as good as a man."

"That's different," Randy said. "Your ma and Mrs. Storm help their husbands at what their husbands do for a livin'. They don't have jobs of their own."

Sally let go of his hand. "That makes a difference to you, does it, Randy Quin?"

"Why are you usin' that tone with me? What have I done? All I'm sayin' is that I don't want any wife of mine to have to work. Folks would think I couldn't provide for my own."

"A wife isn't property."

"I never claimed she was."

"And what if the wife wants to work? What if she wants her own job so she can feel like she contributes to the marriage? Is there anything wrong with that?"

Randy bit his lower lip. "I don't know. I've never given it much thought." Stooping, he picked a handful of goldenrod. "For the girl I care for most in this world."

"How sweet." Sally accepted them, then asked, "How long have we been sparking now?"

"Going on ten months, I reckon."

"That's an awful long time, don't you think? My cousin Caroline was courted for six months when her beau proposed. And my other cousin, Abby, was proposed to after only four months."

"Some men rush things," Randy said uncomfortably.

"I wouldn't call ten months much of a

rush. More like a crawl. Why, I could have had a baby by now."

"Sally!" A red tinge crept from Randy's collar to his hairline. "If your pa heard you talk like that, he'd think we'd been misbehavin'."

"All I'm saying is that not every girl likes to spark half her natural life away. It's something you should ponder while you're out on the range singing to those cows."

After that neither of them had anything to say for a while. They stood admiring the splash of vivid colors the sunset presented, the breeze fanning their hair, the triple chirps of a field cricket the only sound.

"I suppose we should go in," Sally said. "Mother will have supper ready by now."

"I suppose." Randy held onto her hand. Twice he glanced at her and made as if to speak.

"When I was little I dreamed about the kind of man I wanted to be with," Sally reminisced. "For a short while I wanted him pudgy and bald like my father." She laughed at the memory. "Then I wanted a husband who was tall and broad-shouldered and rich."

"I don't make the grade," Randy said.

"Quit your fretting. That didn't last, either. I came to realize it's not how much money a man has, it's what's inside him that counts. I want a husband who is pure of heart, and who will always stand by me through anything and everything life throws at us." Sally squeezed his fingers. "That's not too much to expect, is it?"

"No."

"I also want a man who can make up his mind about things. Who doesn't dawdle when there's something to be done. Who seizes the bull by the horns."

"Where have I heard that before?" Randy muttered.

Sally slowed. "Pardon?"

"Oh, nothin'."

"I hope you're getting the point of all this. It's important, Randy. Patience is a virtue. But just like there is only so much water in a well, each of us only has so much patience. Sooner or later the well and the patience both run dry."

"You don't need to beat me with a skillet," Randy assured her. "I see what you're sayin'."

"You do? Good." Smiling, Sally pulled on his arm. "Come on. All of a sudden I'm hungry enough to eat an antelope, horns and all."

Randy, on the other hand, had just lost his appetite. Under his breath he said, "Lord, what do I do?"

Chapter Five

The Black Mesa country in No Man's Land was stark and remote and shunned by decent folk everywhere. Through its rocky canyons rushed hot winds known as the Devil's Breath. During the day the countryside baked; at night the land was black and foreboding.

Billy Braden whistled to himself as he came to the mouth of a particular canyon and waved to the lookout posted on the rim. The buttermilk's hooves rang loud on the stones that littered the canyon floor.

Reaching back, Billy patted one of his saddlebags. Then he placed his hand on his Colt and negotiated a series of bends that soon brought him to the hidden stronghold.

The canyon widened to encompass over ten lush acres of grass and trees. It was an oasis in the wasteland, nourished by a creek. The high canyon walls perpetually cast the canyon in shade and kept it cool even during the hottest part of the day.

Several cabins had been built at the base of the north wall along with a corral and a shed.

"Hey, Billy!" Dingus Mechum yelled from over by a pool under the trees. "Where in tarnation have you been? We'd about given you up for dead."

"I've been off to see the elephant," Billy hollered. He rode to the corral, nodding at others; sadistic Clell Craven; the Ellsworth brothers, backshooters from the hill country of North Carolina; bald Ben Towers, who always carried a double-barreled shotgun; and the undisputed deadliest of the bunch, Longley, kin to a famous killer and a famous killer in his own right, who wore a matched pair of Remingtons and could use either with uncanny ambidextrous skill. More than a dozen others were moving about.

As Billy climbed down, Dingus came from the creek toting a bucket full of water.

"Black Jack is a mite upset at you being away so long. Just last night he mentioned how you should have been back from your scout weeks ago."

"I don't hurry for anyone," Billy said, but not too loudly.

"Sure, kid, sure." Dingus bobbed his

grizzled chin. "Thought I would warn you, is all."

A cabin door opened and out strode a man-mountain wearing loose-fitting range clothes that made him seem even larger. He had unkempt black hair and a bushy black beard and hands the size of hams. For all his bulk, he moved with a fluid ease. "Did I hear someone say Billy was back?" His voice was like the rasp of quartz on metal, his eyes beady pits that glittered with inhuman vice.

"See for yourself," Billy said.

Black Jack scowled. "Don't get smart with me, boy. I don't take sass from anyone. Where the hell have you been?"

"Scoutin' the country to the south like you wanted. Lookin' for places we could hide rustled stock."

Some of the others strayed over; Craven, Towers, Longley.

"As long as you've been gone, you could have been to Mexico and back," Black Jack groused.

Billy locked eyes with him. "Do you think it's easy findin' a place to hide herds the size of those we rustle? Out on the open prairie? With plenty of water? Where no one is likely to stumble across them?"

"I get the idea," Black Jack said with a

dismissive wave. "So did you find us a spot or not?"

"I found something better but I need a drink before I tell you about it." Billy made for a cabin. Inside were three beds and a table, and three women at the table playing cards. All three wore skintight dresses. All three were pale from too much time indoors and all were tired from too much time spent making the beds creak.

"Billy!" the youngest and skinniest squealed. She wrapped her spindly arms around him and kissed his cheeks. "Did you miss me, handsome?"

"Get off me, Shasta," Billy said, prying her hands from his neck. "I came in for some bug juice, not to be slobbered to death."

"Be nice to her, kid," Belle James said. "She's been moping after you for weeks now. About drove the rest of us crazy."

Susie Metzger nodded. "I came close to boxing her ears. The way she prattled on, you'd think you were the handsomest galoot since Adam."

"He is," Shasta said lovingly.

Black Jack and the others had filed in after Billy and now Black Jack kicked the table and declared, "I want you females out of here. We have us some men talk to do."

"This is our cabin," Belle James objected. "Why don't you hold your stupid meeting in yours?"

Gripping her chin, Black Jack gave it a violent shake. "Need I remind you who pays you far more than you're worth to do as I damn well tell you to do?"

Belle wasn't intimidated. "And need I remind you that we're the only girls dumb enough to live in this godforsaken hole, and that if you rile us, you and your peckerwoods will have to ride a hundred miles to frolic under the sheets?"

Black Jack glowered. Belle James glowered right back.

"Damn it, woman! Why can't you ever be reasonable? All I want is to hear what Billy-boy has to say."

"Why don't we all hear it?" Belle James said. "We haven't had any word of what's going on in the world in weeks. Black Mesa is so out of the way, even Indians never come here."

Billy poured himself a glass and drank half. All eyes were fixed on him as he sat on the edge of one of the bunks. "So you ladies are as tired of livin' in the middle of nowhere as the rest of us?"

"It's worse for women," Susie Metzger said, swatting at a stray bang of red hair.

"We like to have our hair done up now and then, and to shop, and to walk down a street just seeing what there is to see."

Black Jack stirred. "Forget these stupid females. What did you find that might interest me?"

"It will interest all of you," Billy predicted, and leaned back. "Answer me something, Black Jack. Why do you keep us here at Black Mesa?"

"What kind of question is that? We're outlaws, you idiot. We rob, we rustle, we kill when we have to. We need a hideout from the law. A place where we can hold the herds we rustle until I find a buyer." Black Jack's tone hardened. "Which is why I sent you into Texas. We need a relay spot somewhere south of here."

"How would you like your own town instead?"

Ben Towers laughed. "Oh, sure. We'll buy us a ton of lumber and build us five or six buildings and call it Stupidville."

At that, Black Jack guffawed. "Ben, you come up with the darnedest notions. But he's got a point, kid. Your idea is plumb stupid."

"What if the town was already built?" Billy poured a refill. "What if all we had to do was ride in and take over?"

"Where is this place?"

"Nowhere."

Black Jack's hand drifted to the Smith and Wesson he wore on his left hip. "You're testin' me, boy. You truly are. You do it all the time and I'm gettin' tired of it."

"Nowhere is the town's name. Hardly thirty people live there, but it's got a saloon and a general store and a feed and grain and a livery. It's also got a crippled marshal who doesn't tote a six-gun." Billy paused. "And it's twenty miles north of Texas, in No Man's Land."

"Nowhere?" Black Jack repeated. "How come I've never heard of it?"

"The town hasn't been there that long," Billy said. "Which is good or there would be more people, and we couldn't make it our own."

"Since when do you decide what we do?" Black Jack snapped. "It sounds risky to me. A crippled lawman is still a lawman. And the other townsfolk aren't about to welcome us with open arms, are they?"

"That depends on how we cozy up to them, doesn't it?" Billy retorted. "They sure made me feel right to home. Why, the marshal invited me back and asked me to bring all my friends."

Black Jack's beady eyes glittered brighter. "You know, maybe you're not as loco as I thought. You could be on to something."

"I figured you might like the idea." Billy grinned and started to raise the glass to his mouth.

With a swift bound, Black Jack knocked the glass to the floor and leaned down so they were nose to nose. "Do you know what else I think, boy? I think that maybe you've got yourself a notion you're smarter than me. I think maybe you have a hankerin' to take over. To put me out to pasture, permanent-like."

"I never said any such thing!" Billy was shaking from head to boots, he was so mad.

"You didn't have to say it," Black Jack snarled. "I've had run-ins with your kind before. Wet-nosed snots who figure I'm too dumb to know which end of my britches to stick my feet into. The last one who thought that is buried across the creek." Black Jack unfurled. "So any time you want to let the coon dogs loose, you give a holler."

Billy glanced around the room. Clell Craven had a hand on his revolver. Ben Towers was nonchalantly pointing his

67

shotgun at him. Longley stood relaxed and at ease but his hands were near those nickel-plated Remingtons of his. "I ain't fool enough to ever buck you, Black Jack."

Black Jack moved to the door. "You're clever, boy. Too damn clever for your own good. But clever don't make you fit to lead. To do that you need savvy and grit."

"I've got plenty of grit!" Billy said resentfully.

"Oh? When was the last time you bucked someone out in gore without havin' an edge? Without their backs being turned or them not havin' a gun? When was the last time you went up against an hombre man to man?"

"Killin' is killin'."

"You hear that, Longley?" Black Jack said. "You hear that, Ben?"

Ben Towers didn't try to hide his disgust. "I've never backshot a man in my life, boy. I'll blow anyone to kingdom come and back again. But I'll give them their chance before I do."

"The Ellsworths have backshot plenty!" Billy declared.

Black Jack snorted. "Jed and Jeb are hill trash. They live for the feud. They don't care how they kill because they were raised to think people are no different from coons." He opened the door. "Killin' *ain't* just killin', boy. We don't go around shootin' folks for the hell of it. That's outright murder, and will earn us an invite to a hemp social as quick as you can blink." He went out, Longley and Ben Towers on his heels.

"I could use some fresh air," Belle James commented. "How about the rest of you girls?"

"Count me in," Susie Metzger said.

Billy glowered after them.

"I'll stay with you," Shasta offered, smiling. "I've missed you so much, I don't ever want to let you out of my sight."

Smacking the bed, Billy stood. "The nerve of him! Talkin' down to me like that! Lecturin' me on killin' and such!"

"Black Jack just likes to keep us all in line," Shasta said. "He carped at me once for not taking enough baths."

"We're outlaws, for cryin' out loud! I kill what I want and take what I want, and the rest of the world can go to hell."

"Does that include me?"

Billy was pacing and smacking his right fist against his left palm. "Maybe hookin' up with this outfit wasn't such a bright idea. All we ever do is sit around twiddlin' our thumbs."

Shasta had grown glum. "That's not true. You stole that herd four months ago, remember?"

"And had to go all the way to Kansas to do it," Billy complained. "Then we had to drive all those cow critters clear down into Texas to find a buyer. That's a lot of work for a piddlin' three hundred dollars for each of us."

"Why are you always like this?" Shasta touched his arm. "Forget about Black Jack. Sit down. Relax. Have a couple more drinks. Later we can fool around if you'd like."

"Quit clingin' to me." Billy walked to the door, which had been left open, and glared out. "I'm sick of him. Sick of Black Mesa. Sick of being treated like an amateur. And I'm sick of you."

"You don't mean that."

"Find someone else who tickles your fancy. Jeb Ellsworth thinks you're a ravin' beauty. Pick him."

"I don't like Jeb. I like you." Shasta came up behind him and wrapped her arms around his waist. "Why are you so mean to me when I care for you so? Don't you know how much it hurts?"

"You should be more like me. Don't ever let anyone or anything get a hold on you."

Billy smacked the wall. "I should show him. I should start my own outfit and steal and kill until I put him to shame."

"Forget about Black Jack." Shasta stepped toward the table and tugged at his shirt. "Have a seat. I'll pour you another drink."

Suddenly whirling, Billy pushed her. "I said to stop clingin' and I meant it! If you want to do something useful, get in bed and take your clothes off."

"For you, anything."

Billy slammed the door, then kicked a chair and sent it skittering across the floor. "The more I think about it, the madder I get. Here I do him a favor by tellin' him my brainstorm, and what does he do? He treats me like I'm fresh off the stage from New York City."

"I was raised there, you know," Shasta mentioned. "We left when I was twelve. My father thought he could strike it rich panning gold. But when he fell on hard times, he sent me to work in a bawdy house and —"

"You talk too damn much." Billy came to the bed and began undoing his belt. "Why don't you have blond hair instead of brown? And get yourself a flowered dress instead of that sack you wear."

"You never complained about my dress before." Shasta grasped his hand. "I wish you wouldn't talk like that. I love you so very, very much."

"That's your problem," Billy Braden said.

Chapter Six

Chick Storm was an early riser. A rancher had to be. There were never enough hours in the day to do all that needed doing.

This particular morning Chick was up and dressed before his wife stirred. He went down the hall and out the front door and stood on the porch, breathing deep of the crisp air. To the east a yellow sliver framed the eastern horizon. To the west the sky was still dark.

Light gleamed in the bunkhouse windows. Chick smelled cigarette smoke and heard voices when he was still ten feet away. Inside, the smoke was heavy, his punchers in various stages of undress. A few were still in bed but wouldn't be for long.

"Mr. Storm," Lin Cooley said. "You're up with the robins today."

"I wanted to be sure you boys made it back," Chick said. "The wife and I turned in early and I didn't hear you ride up."

"We made it, as always," Cooley said in

that Texas drawl of his. "We're about ready for breakfast. Then I'll have the men head out."

Chick saw Randy Quin down at the other end of the bunks, talking to Kip Langtree. "Did he pop it yet?"

Cooley shook his head. "From what he told me, she tried to pry it out of him but he got cold feet."

"That's a shame," Chick said. "Dixie is looking forward to the wedding. She thinks they're a handsome couple."

"He's afraid he won't measure up," Cooley said. "Afraid he'll take her for better or worse and it'll turn out worse."

"We all go through that. I was certain I would ruin Dixie's life. I even said as much, right to her face, and she laughed at me and gave me her word she wouldn't let me fail no matter how hard I tried."

A deep chuckle rumbled from Cooley's chest. "That sure sounds like Mrs. Storm, all right. You branded a fine heifer, boss, if you don't mind my sayin' so."

Now it was Chick who shook his head. "There isn't a man alive could brand that woman. The best I can do is try my damnedest to keep up with her and hope she never tires of me." He straightened. "Well, enough chitchat. That's a minute

I've wasted and the day hasn't hardly begun. Were you able to pick up those things my wife wanted?"

"Yes, sir. They're in a burlap sack up on your porch, to the left of the door."

"I walked right by them and never noticed. When you have as many grey hairs as I do, you're not as observant as you used to be."

"Hell, boss. You can still lick any man here with your bare fists," Cooley said. "There's plenty of bark on the old tree yet."

"Any news from Nowhere?" Chick asked. "Any gossip I can pass on to Dixie? When it comes to that, she's as female as any woman ever born."

"Sorry. It's been as peaceful as ever except for a kid passin' through who didn't think too highly of the place. Old Man Taylor thought the kid might be a gun hand but all he had to base it on was the kid's pearl-handled Colt."

"Hell, half the kids on the frontier tote fancy hardware," Chick mentioned. "They think it makes them more of a man." His mouth curled ruefully. "Funny, isn't it, the stupid things we do when we're young?"

"It takes a heap of experience before we learn which side our bread is buttered on,"

Cooley agreed. "I figure at the rate I'm going, I'll be halfway smart by the time I'm one hundred and sixty-three."

Chuckling, Chick walked out. He wasn't quite to the ranch house when he spied several riders approaching from the northwest. Instinctively, he tensed, then walked faster. His Winchester was on pegs above the fireplace. Taking it down, he verified it was loaded, a precaution he learned to take back in the days when Indian raids were a constant threat, and returned to the porch just as the tip of the sun crowned the world and dispelled the lingering gloom.

Lin Cooley, Randy Quin, Kip Langtree and four other punchers had also seen the riders and were crossing the yard. Langtree's eyes were the best in the outfit, and he was the one who exclaimed, "Why, it's Mr. Jackson! What's he doing here so early?"

"It's none of our business," Cooley said. "Let's get to eatin'. We have a lot of cows to round up."

Now that Chick knew who it was, he cradled the Winchester and leaned against a porch post. From inside the house came the clang of pots and pans.

"Chick!" Seth Jackson called out when he was still a good distance out. "I was hopin' I wouldn't catch you in bed." He was a heavyset man with more muscle than fat and a swarthy face sprinkled with pimples.

"Dixie doesn't cotton to layabouts," Chick said. "You must have been riding all night to show up with the crow of the cock."

"I spent a few days up to Beaver City," Seth said. "Left Joe Elliot lookin' after my spread and can only hope he hasn't accidentally burned everything to the ground."

"Joe is a good man, a good foreman."

"But almighty loud." Seth reined up at the hitch rail and wearily swung down. "You boys light and rest a spell," he said to his men. "I need to talk to Mr. Storm." Swatting dust from his clothes, he came up the steps. "I don't suppose I could wrangle a cup of coffee?"

"You can wrangle a whole pot. What else are neighbors for?" Chick held the screen door for him, then led Jackson to the dining room. "Dixie!" he shouted as he took his seat. "We've got us a visitor. Can you bring us some coffee?"

The door to the kitchen opened and Dixie bustled in. She was wearing a man's shirt and a man's pants and her reddish brown hair was done up in a bun. "You're not a moose, Chickory Storm, so I'll thank you not to bellow like one in my house. Next time, come into the kitchen and tell me proper."

"Yes, ma'am," Chick dutifully said.

Dixie smiled sweetly and bustled back out.

"I wish my Clara were still alive," Seth Jackson said. "I miss how she used to boss me around like Dixie bosses you."

"That's not bossing. She calls it 'correcting.' She says I was born an Eastern gentleman and I should behave like one whether I want to or not."

Seth grinned. "That's what you get for being from Ohio. Me, I'm Texas born and bred and damn proud of it." He added, "Not that there's anything wrong with being from back East. More than half the folks out here are."

"I read a newspaper article once where the editor went on about how America is a melting pot of people from all over," Chick related. "He said that one day it won't matter who we are or where we're from. We'll all be one great nation."

"I don't have much time for readin'," Seth said. "And I don't much know as I like the notion of being thrown into a pot with redskins and greasers."

The kitchen door opened again and Dixie brought in a tray with two brimming cups of coffee, two spoons, and cream and sugar. "Here you go. Try not to spill any on my table or you'll mop it up."

"We'll mind our manners," Chick said, and received a kiss on the cheek. He watched her go back in.

Seth chose a cup and took a loud sip. "Nice and hot. Just how I like it." He ran a finger around the cup's edge. "I have a favor to ask."

"Ask it."

"This doesn't come easy. A man has his pride, you know."

"We've been neighbors going on ten years," Chick said. "We've helped each other out more times than I can count."

"You're a good friend," Seth said, "which makes this all the harder. I've never had to stoop to askin' for a handout, and it rankles."

"You're taking the long way around the barn. Come right out with it."

"I reckon that's best." Seth took a deep breath. "I'd be obliged if you could see fit to loan me two thousand dollars."

Chick put down his cup.

"I know, I know." Seth gestured. "It's just that I'm in a bind and I don't know where else to turn. If I don't scrape up the money I stand to lose my spread. You see" — he stopped and averted his gaze — "you see, I went and did something stupid. So stupid I can't believe I did it."

"Gambling?"

Seth sat back. "You know?"

"Secrets don't stay secrets for long in these parts," Chick said. "Poker, the word is. Several high-stakes games a year."

"High stakes is right. But I've never lost so much before. I've always been able to stop before I got in over my head. This time I lost all the money I took with me, then was dealt a hand I was sure was a winner. So I signed a note for two thousand dollars, with my ranch as collateral." Seth paused. "I'll pay it back as soon as I can."

"I don't have that much handy," Chick said. "The last few years have been lean, what with cattle not fetching as much as they used to and the cost of my new barn and the like."

Seth closed his eyes, then opened them and shrugged. "Oh well. I'm a grown man. I'll take my medicine without complainin'."

"Your ranch is worth a lot more than two thousand," Chick said. "Your cows alone would bring twice that much. Why not sell some off?"

"I can try, but this is a poor time of the year to sell. And if I don't come up with the money in two months, Merney will come and take my place."

"Titus Merney?" Chick made a clucking sound. "You played against a professional cardsharp? I thought you knew better."

"My greed got the better of my judgment. I had four tens, the best hand I'd had all night, so I went for broke and he broke me."

"Damn."

"If I have to, I reckon I can go to Amarillo and ask the bank for a loan. They already hold my mortgage, so what's another two thousand?" Seth abruptly stood. "It's best I be going. Thanks for hearin' me out."

Chick followed him to the porch. "If there's anything I can do to help tide you over, let me know. We have about four hundred saved, and I'm sure I could talk Dixie into letting you have most of it."

"That's kind of you," Seth said as he climbed into the stirrups. "But don't worry. I'll figure a way."

Chick watched his friend recede into the distance, then turned. "How long have you been standing there?"

"Since he left," Dixie said. She linked

her arm with his. "I couldn't help but over-hear when you were in the dining room. He only has himself to blame for the tight he's in. Gambling is a surefire road to the poorhouse."

"There aren't any of us saints."

"Granted. But like he said, he's a grown man, and a grown man shouldn't let him-self be fleeced by a card slick."

"Seth has had a hard time of it since that bull gored Clara," Chick reminded her.

"It was her own fault, walking into that pen like she did," Dixie said. "But Clara had raised it from a calf and still treated it like one. I tried telling her a bull is temper-amental but she was as headstrong as I am."

Chick squeezed her arm. "No one is that headstrong."

They laughed, and Dixie said, "We don't get ahead in this world by sitting on our thumbs. Those who want to make their mark need more than a small amount of pigheadedness."

"In which case you and I should go down in the history books as plumb fa-mous," Chick quipped. He gazed to the south but Seth Jackson had vanished into the early morning haze. Shutting Seth's plight from his mind, he went about his morning chores, including a midmorning ride to the east a few miles to check on one of his herds.

Lin Cooley and Randy Quin happened to be there, and when Chick found himself alone with the young puncher, he casually mentioned, "There's been some talk you haven't asked the question yet."

Quin blushed and seemed to be trying to shrink into his saddle. "Let's just say I wouldn't hold my breath, were I you, boss."

"I only mention it because Mrs. Storm has offered to have the ceremony here, instead of in Nowhere," Chick disclosed. "We're also willing to put the two of you up in one of our guest rooms until you find a place of your own."

"I don't take charity."

"That was uncalled for," Chick said sternly. "You have to learn to tell the difference between a helping hand and an insult. My wife and I would take it as an honor. We don't get many guests, and it's been ages since Mrs. Storm enjoyed the company of another woman."

"Females are as scarce as hen's teeth in these parts," Randy allowed.

"Talk it over with your cow bunny if it ever reaches that point." Chick raised his reins to ride off.

The young puncher quickly said, "Mind if I ask you a question, Mr. Storm?"

"Not at all. So long as you don't mind if I don't have the answer. Dixie is the one who knows all there is to know."

Randy looked to see where Lin and the other hands were. None were anywhere near them. "She's the one I want to ask about. How did you know Mrs. Storm was the one for you? Out of all the women in the world, what made you pick her?"

"I don't know as I did. It was more a case of her picking me. Lord knows why." Chick was partly joking but Randy failed to appreciate the humor. "There was something about her, Randall. Something I can't describe. When we were apart I couldn't stop thinking about her, and when we were together, I was so happy, I thought I'd died and gone to heaven."

"You weren't scared when you proposed?"

Chick grinned. "I'll be honest. I was never so afraid in my life. A herd of long-horns were stampeding in my stomach and my knees had changed from bone and muscle to mush."

"Yet you asked her anyway?"

"I figured I might as well after all the suffering I put myself through." Chick waited for another question and when there was none, he said, "We don't get many chances for lasting happiness in this life. When one comes along, grab it or you're liable to spend the rest of your days miserable."

"Thanks, Mr. Storm," Randy Quin said, and rode off deep in thought.

Chapter Seven

The sun was at its zenith. Nowhere lay as still as a cemetery under its burning rays, her buildings as squat as tombstones. Svenson the blacksmith was kindling his forge. Over in the saloon, Dub Wheeton played solitaire. The Palmers were having their midday meal. Robert Renfro was wiping off the sign to his barbershop.

Marshal Paul Lunsford stepped from the jail, adjusted his white hat so the brim shielded his eyes, and strolled to the livery stable. "It sure is a hot one."

"Then why in hell are you out and about when you should be inside out of the sun like everyone else?" Old Man Taylor baited him.

"I don't see you inside."

"I'm old. The only time my muscles and joints don't ache is on really hot days like this one. I can even move my fingers without them hurting." Taylor wriggled his right hand to demonstrate.

"I know what you mean. On hot days I

sometimes think I can feel this." Lunsford patted his twisted right arm. "For a little while I can half convince myself it's not completely useless."

"A man's worth isn't measured by what he can do but by what he is," Old Man Taylor said.

"Better be careful. The heat is bringing out the human being in you, and you wouldn't want to spoil your reputation."

"At my age it's my privilege·to go around with a broomstick shoved up my ass if I want." Taylor resumed whittling. "It's the only other amusement I have."

"Heard the latest?" Marshal Lunsford made small talk.

"About the Palmers getting in a shipment of Saratoga chips and an icebox? I don't much care for the chips but I like to buy a glass of ice and suck on the pieces. No water or juice or anything in it, just the ice."

"Not that. About Dub maybe leaving Nowhere."

Taylor sat bolt upright in his rocking chair. "Tell me you made that up. A town can do without a lot of things but not its watering hole. Where in hell would we get our drinks?"

"Dub says he's tired of barely squeaking by. He says he's thinking about moving to

Kansas City or Denver or wherever there are enough people for him to show a profit."

"What's this world coming to when all anyone thinks about is how much money they make?" Old Man Taylor spat in disgust. "If he leaves, there goes our last bastion of life."

"Well, he's only thinking about it. And you know Dub. It takes him a century to make up his mind and then he wonders if he's doing right."

"Still, he's talked about it, and that's upsetting enough." Taylor jabbed his knife into the block. "Damn. Now you've gone and ruined my day. You realize, don't you, that if Dub goes, the Palmers and Renfro and his wife might soon follow. Then where would we be?"

"We'd still have you."

"I'd kick you but it's too hot."

"We'd still have Svenson and his missus, and Lafferty over to the feed and grain, and Wilson and some of the others."

Old Man Taylor swore. "You can't drink horseshoes and oats."

"Maybe you can get Wilson to sell liquor in his restaurant," Marshal Lunsford suggested.

"In case you've forgotten, Agnes is a teetotaler, and a Bible-thumper, to boot. Wilson isn't about to rile her and have to sleep on the settee until the Second Coming."

"I guess you're doomed, then."

"Make light of this calamity all you want, but you like a nip as much as I do. Or are you fixing to head for greener pastures too?"

Marshal Lunsford patted his arm again. "With this clipped wing? Nowhere is as green as my pastures get."

"I should go have a talk with Dub." Old Man Taylor placed his hands on the arms of his chair to push to his feet, then froze. "What the hell? Am I seeing things, or are we being invaded?"

Over twenty riders were entering town from the north. In the lead was a brawny bearded man who was studying the buildings as if he found them intensely interesting. At the rear was a Conestoga, driven by a scrawny character in a floppy hat.

"There's that kid!" Old Man Taylor exclaimed. "Billy Braden." Suddenly Taylor shot erect. "My God. Look! Three of them are women." He took several steps, his astonishment growing. "*Painted* women!"

The visitors angled toward the saloon, and Marshal Lunsford did the same.

"Hello, Billy," he greeted the younger man as they dismounted. "This is a surprise."

Up and down the street people were appearing out of doorways and poking heads from windows.

"Marshal!" Billy said, thrusting a hand out. "You told me to bring my friends, remember?"

Lunsford flicked his eyes from one to the other, taking their measure. "You sure have a lot of them."

The big man with the bushy beard stepped up to shake. "That he does. I'm Jack Shelton. When he told me about this place, I had to come and see for myself."

"You've never seen a town before?"

Shelton had a rumbling laugh. "That was a good one. Why don't you join me and my boys for a drink? We'd like to get acquainted."

"You don't need to twist my arm where whiskey is concerned," Marshal Lunsford said.

Jack Shelton roared once more. "I guess not, when it's all busted up like that." He steered the marshal toward the door. "From the war, I hear? I never did enlist, myself. Couldn't stand to take orders."

Lunsford was sensitive where his stint in the military was concerned. "I believed I was fighting for a worthy cause."

"Was that cause worth your arm?"

Then they were inside and Dub Wheeton was gawking in dumbfounded disbelief. Within moments his saloon was more filled than it had been in a month of Sundays. Scooting behind the bar, Dub embraced them with a warm smile. "Welcome, all of you! I don't know what the occasion is but I'm right happy to meet all of you."

While the men bellied up to the bar, the three women took seats at a table. Marshal Lunsford was trying to recall if he'd ever seen them before when the oldest grinned at him, and winked. He looked away. "So, Mr. Shelton. Might I ask where you folks are bound?"

"This very spot," Shelton said.

"You're staying the night?"

"This night and maybe a lot more besides. I'm thinking of settling here. Of starting up a ranch a few miles outside town." Jack Shelton accepted a whiskey bottle from Dub. "Is the land west of here spoken for or can I stake a claim?"

"Claim all you want," Lunsford said, "but there's not much there. Not in the way of good grazing land. Nor much water."

"Oh, we'll manage," Jack Shelton said confidently. He filled a glass from the bottle and emptied the glass in one swallow. "That would put hair on a nail! My compliments, barkeep. Don't forget the ladies yonder."

Dub went around the end of the bar to the table. "What can I get you gals?"

"I'm Belle James," the oldest said, "and Scotch is my poison. Remember that, because I drink a lot of it." She looked him up and down and fluttered her eyes. "My, aren't you a fine figure of a man. And you own this saloon, too? Your wife must be considerably proud."

"I'm not married, ma'am."

"All the better," Belle James said, and ran the pink tip of her tongue across her cherry red lips.

Dub's throat bobbed. "Forgive me for askin', but what is it you girls do?"

"Anything and everything, sugar," Belle James said. "But we'll talk about that later."

Marshal Lunsford leaned his good arm on the bar. Some of the men had drifted to tables, among them a tall man who favored a shotgun. He broke out a deck of cards and began shuffling. "How long will you be in town before you head off to start your ranch?"

"As long as it takes," Jack Shelton said.

"This is a nice, quiet place we have

here," Lunsford said. "I'd like to keep it that way."

"Makes two of us, lawman," Jack Shelton said. "Anyone who acts up will have me to deal with me as well as you." He poured another glass and gulped, heedless of the whiskey that sloshed over his chin and down his beard. "You should be grateful. In one day we've pretty near doubled the population."

"It's just that this is my home. I like these people."

"Good for you. I hope I grow to like them, too. I'm all for gettin' along. You want to get along with me, don't you, Marshal? Billy told me you make it your life's work to get along with everyone."

"Excuse me," Lunsford said, and left the saloon. Laughter rang in his ears but he didn't look back. He went straight to the restaurant and sat at a corner table and ordered a coffee, black.

Mrs. Wilson brought it. "Why, Paul, is it me or are you glum today?"

"The eclipse doesn't agree with me," Lunsford said.

"We had an eclipse?" Mrs. Wilson gazed out the window. "I didn't notice everything go dark."

"You will."

"I declare, you're talking less sense than that crotchety Taylor." Mrs. Wilson began wiping off the next table. "Him and his silly birds. The last time he was in here, he called me a speckled hen. Can you imagine?"

Deep in thought, Lunsford nursed his cup. He had a decision to make, a decision that could affect everyone in Nowhere. But after half an hour he was no closer to making up his mind than when he came in.

That was when the door opened and in clomped Hap Evans from the Bar J. Evans was the oldest puncher on the spread, his exact years a mystery because he refused to say.

"Howdy, Hap," the lawman said. "Delivering another cow to the Wilsons?" It was Evans's job to make the weekly run from the Bar J so the restaurant had a fresh and steady supply of beefsteak.

"Marshal!" Hap sank into a chair and grinned his toothless grin. "Have you heard the news?"

"Nowhere has been overrun by locusts?"

"What? No." Hap scratched his chin. "I just stopped off at Dub's and found out he's hired himself some girls. Three of 'em, as pretty as you please."

"They worked fast," Lunsford said. "I

didn't think he could afford the extravagance."

"The way I hear it," the old puncher revealed, scratching his leg, "Dub struck a special deal with a fella by the name of Shelton. Dub doesn't pay those girls a cent. They pay *him* ten percent of their earnin's. Is that shrewd or what?"

"Shrewd as a tree stump."

"Dub is tickled. Why, he was buyin' drinks for everyone and crowin' about how he doesn't have to leave Nowhere." Hap scratched at his shirt. "I can't wait to go to the saloon this evenin' but I'd best take a bath first. I saw a flea on me yesterday, and females can be right fussy."

"Two baths would be better," Marshal Lunsford said. He paid for his coffee and walked out. Down the street the Conestoga was parked in front of the general store and George Palmer was talking to the man who called himself Jack Shelton. With Shelton were Billy Braden and several of the hard men they rode with. Lunsford came up on them quietly.

". . . whole wagon load?" George was saying. "But what about the ranch you plan to start? Won't you need the stove and clock and the rest?"

"I need money for other things right now

95

and this is the only way to get it," Jack Shelton answered. "So do we have a deal or not?"

Lunsford had to find out. He stepped past the team, asking, "What deal would that be?"

George Palmer nodded at the Conestoga. "Mr. Shelton is offering to sell me the wagon and all its contents, the oxen included, for four hundred dollars. I could resell it for ten times that much."

"It sounds too good to be true," Marshal Lunsford said. "And you know what people say when that's the case."

Jack Shelton gave him a sharp glance. "You've never known anyone to sell something for less than it's worth just to get rid of it?" He thumped the Conestoga's bed. "I don't have any use for this prairie schooner anymore so I'm willin' to part with it for less than it's worth."

"Your offer is tempting," George Palmer said.

"Quit straddlin' the fence or I'll change my mind," Shelton warned. "Then you'll be kickin' yourself for not jumpin' when you had the chance."

George turned to his Helen, who nodded. "All right. Four hundred it is. Just don't come back later wanting everything back because you realized you made a mistake."

"I can guarantee that won't happen."

"Come inside. I have to get the money."

Everyone entered the general store except Lunsford. He made a circuit of the wagon, noticing little things he hadn't noticed before. The team, for instance, was gaunt and haggard. Gripping the seat with his good arm, he pulled himself high enough to see under the canopy. Possessions were piled high, among them a grandfather clock that alone had to be worth seven hundred dollars. He had seen one just like it once in St. Louis.

Climbing down, Marshal Lunsford walked past the front wheel, then stopped. The spokes and the rim were spattered with red drops. Drops so bright, they had to be recent. Squatting, he touched one, and noticed a hairy gob stuck to the underside of a felloe.

He pried it off with his fingernails. Holding it up, he recognized it for what it was and dropped it as if it were a red-hot ember.

Rising, Lunsford hastened to the jail. He locked the door, pulled the blinds, and slumped into the chair behind his desk. "This is bad. This is very bad." From the

97

top drawer he took a silver flask, opened it, and glued it to his mouth. When he had enough, he bleakly asked the darkness, "What do I do now?"

Chapter Eight

When Hap Evans came back from Nowhere and told Seth Jackson there was a man in town who wanted to see him about important business, it pricked Seth's curiosity. Next morning, Seth instructed Joe Elliot to look after things while he was gone. Then he had his horse saddled and hit the trail to Nowhere.

Seth reckoned the newcomer might want to buy some stock. The word being bandied about was that Jack Shelton intended to start a ranch, and that took cattle.

Normally the ride took about two hours but Seth dragged it out so it took almost three. He had a lot to ponder. His gambling was foremost. All these years, he had managed to keep from getting in over his head. Not this time. Chick was right. It had been unbelievably stupid of him to pit his skill against Titus Merney. Professional gamblers were in a class by themselves. Everyone knew that.

The prospect of losing the Bar J frightened Seth no end. Clara and he had put everything into the ranch. It was a testament to their love. Losing her had been the worst calamity of his life. The long, lonely nights since had been unbearable. He hated to think his addiction to cards would cost him all they had achieved.

Maybe Shelton was the solution, Seth reflected. If the man bought enough cattle from him, his problem was solved.

Usually not much was going on in Nowhere that early in the morning, but when Seth arrived George and Helen Palmer were busy unloading a Conestoga and Svenson was shoeing a horse and there were more horses lined up at the rail in front of the saloon and in front of the restaurant. Whoever was in Dub's was having a high old time, if the whooping and hollering was any indication.

Tying his zebra dun at the rail, Seth pushed through the door. Right away he saw the three doves Hap had mentioned. At another table sat a dark-haired man with a goatee, all by himself. His boots propped on the table, he was rolling the makings. Strapped around his waist were a pair of nickel-plated revolvers.

"Is there a Jack Shelton here?" Seth asked loud enough to be heard.

A bearded mountain turned from the bar. "Who wants to know?"

"Seth Jackson from the Bar J."

"Mr. Jackson, I'm plumb delighted. I'm your man. Join me, would you?" Jack Shelton carried a bottle and two glasses to a corner table and shoved a chair out. "Have a seat. I'd like to get to know you before we talk business."

"What more do you need to know other than I'm a rancher?" Seth saw a slab-faced man with a shotgun come to the end of the bar and stand where he could watch them and the door, both.

"I need to know how much you like money."

"There's like and there's need and I need a lot," Seth commented.

Shelton opened the bottle and poured drinks for both of them and slid a glass over, the whole while eyeing Seth as if Seth were a horse he might buy. "What would you say if I could earn you thousands of dollars a year more than you're earnin' now?"

"Is this money that falls from trees or the kind that drifts down out of thin air?"

Laughs came easy to the bearded man. "It's the cut I'll pay you for holdin' cattle for me until I sell them. Twenty percent of every herd."

Seth didn't bother to hide his disappointment. "So you already have all the cattle you can use?"

"Cows are like grass. You find them just about everywhere."

"True, but most of those cows belong to someone else. You wouldn't be proposin' something illegal, would you?"

"One man's illegal is another's bread and butter. I'm not askin' that you steal. All I want is the run of part of your range now and then. You keep your hands and your cattle away, and after I make a sale, your bank account grows."

The full scope of what Shelton was proposing hit Seth like a club between the eyes. "In case you ain't heard, rustlers are hung in these parts."

"But you wouldn't be rustlin' anything. You'd be rentin' me the use of your land and water, that's all. If anyone asks, you can say you never knew anything shady was going on."

Seth sat back. Part of him was tempted but part of him had scruples. "You've got sand, Shelton. I'll give you that. I could go to the marshal and have you run out of Nowhere. Or I could go to my ranch, collect all my punchers, and come back and run you out myself."

"You could," Jack Shelton said. "But my pards and I don't run easy." He spread his big hands. "And why spill blood when there's no need? What would you get out of it? Nothin'. But if you use your head and let me use your land, six or seven weeks from now I'll give you four thousand dollars."

"That much that soon?" Seth's temptation grew. He could pay off Titus Merney and have enough left to make some improvements on the ranch. Or go to Beaver City and sit in on a few games.

"That soon or sooner. What do you say? Are you interested?"

Seth hedged. "I need time to think about it."

"I need to know today. I'm leavin' later on to get the cattle." Shelton rose. "Let me know in an hour, why don't you?"

Seth sat there a while absently turning the glass over and over in his hands, then he rose and went out. He was so absorbed in thought that he crossed the street without realizing it and drew up short when he heard his name mentioned. "How's that?"

"It's a fine day, wouldn't you agree?" Helen Palmer asked. She had her hair done up in a fashion that reminded Seth of

Clara, and wore a dress like one Clara had bought in the Palmers' store.

"We're still breathin'," Seth said.

"My, my, aren't we cynical today?" Helen reached up to grab the strap on a trunk her husband was sliding out the end of the Conestoga.

George poked his head past the canvas. "Is that you, Seth? Thought I heard your voice. Did you hear about the great deal I struck with Jack Shelton?"

Seth nodded.

"That man is going to be a boon to this town. Wait and see. Wilson was saying how he's done more business since Shelton's outfit arrived than he usually does in a month. Svenson has been making horse-shoes around the clock. And every stall in Taylor's livery is taken."

"How does Chick Storm feel about him?"

"Chick? I don't know as they've met yet. Why should that matter? Chick doesn't live here." George hopped down and lifted his end of the trunk. "You should stop by in a few days. Once we've catalogued all the contents, we're having a special sale."

"Maybe I will," Seth said, and walked on to the feed and grain. Lafferty was behind the counter, sorting through a bin of seed packets. "Jim, I need to place an order for more oats."

"You haven't paid for the last one."

Shocked and a little angry, Seth responded, "Since when hasn't my credit been good enough?"

"Since you've taken to paying your account off later and later." Lafferty was pencil thin, with bushy eyebrows and a hawkish nose. He was from Illinois and had drifted West after the Civil War and somehow or other ended up in Nowhere. Seth knew little else about him.

"I've always made good, haven't I?"

"That was yesterday. We're talking today." Lafferty's nose crinkled. "Yesterday you were dependable. Today you spend a lot of time in Beaver City."

"Where I spend my time is none of your damn business," Seth said angrily.

"I beg to differ. It is when your behavior reflects on how you pay off your bills. Don't look at me like that. Your fondness for cards has become common knowledge. So has a rumor that you recently lost big against a professional gambler." Lafferty uttered a few *tsk-tsks*.

Dumbfounded, Seth struggled to collect his wits. "How did you hear about that?"

"My sources, to quote you, are none of

105

your damn business. Now, are you going to pay what you owe and clear your account, or aren't you?"

"I don't —" Seth clenched his fists. "I don't have the money at the moment."

"When you do I will gladly sell you more supplies. Until then, kindly refrain from gracing my establishment." Lafferty turned back to his seeds.

"I really need the oats."

"I really need a lot of things but I'm sensible enough and thrifty enough to save for them and not squander my income on frivolous pursuits like poker." Lafferty sniffed as though he had caught the scent of an offensive odor. "You'd never catch Chick Storm doing anything so reckless. Now there's a man who knows how to run a ranch."

Lafferty would never know how close he came to being shot. Seth was furious. Whirling, he stormed out and tramped along the boardwalk, not knowing where he was going and not really caring. He heard someone call his name but he didn't answer them.

Then a tiny bell jangled, and Seth looked up to discover he was at the restaurant. He opened the door and the bell tinkled again. Tim Wilson was in back in the kitchen, cooking. Agnes was cleaning a table.

"Mr. Jackson! We don't see you often enough," she warmly greeted him. "Would you care for some coffee?"

Svenson was there, devouring a plate heaped with steak and potatoes. He nodded at Seth and indicated an empty chair at his table. "How are things at the Bar J, Mr. Jackson?" He said "things" as if it were "dings", his accent thick enough to cut with a dull butter knife.

"Fine. How are things with you?"

"They could not be better. I have had more business than I know what to do with." Svenson's "have" was more like "haf" and his "with" more like "vith."

"The new bunch, I gather," Seth said.

"Yes. All their horses needed new shoes. And they pay with cash and coins." Svenson forked a fatty piece of steak into his mouth and hungrily chomped.

"So like everyone else, you think they're the greatest thing since spurs were invented?"

Svenson talked while chomping. "I don't know about that. Some of them have hard eyes. The one with the shotgun. And the twins who talk funny." Svenson stopped chewing. "But the worst is the man with the two shiny guns. In my country we say people like him have dead souls and want everyone else dead, too."

Agnes Wilson brought a coffeepot and a cup and saucer. "Here you are, Mr. Jackson. It's fortunate you've come when you have. Not fifteen minutes ago we were so busy, I could scarcely catch a breath."

Seth poured himself a cup and blew on the steaming coffee to cool it. "You've been busier than usual too."

"I should say we have. The new people eat and eat. Why, that Mr. Craven and Mr. Shelton are bottomless pits. I've never seen grown men down so much at one sitting in all my years." She grinned. "Except for Mr. Svenson, of course."

Svenson guffawed and stuffed half a baked potato into his mouth. "You are a most funny lady, Mrs. Wilson."

"I love the way you say 'funny' as if it were 'vunny.' " Agnes smiled and left them.

"Nice lady," Svenson said.

"Salt of the earth," Seth said testily, and drank some coffee.

"What do you think of the new people?" Svenson inquired.

"The same as I think of apples."

"I am sorry. Apples?"

Seth set his cup down. "How do you get a mule to go when it doesn't want to move? You tie an apple to the end of a stick and hold the apple in front of its face."

"I do not understand," Svenson admitted, eating lustily. "If they are the apples, who is the mule?"

Seth didn't answer. He finished his coffee in silence, paid and headed for the saloon. Two nearly identical young men with curly mops of hair and boyish grins were on the bench out front. They wore the exact same clothes, down to their short-topped boots. Both had the same model revolver tucked under their belts, and wore the same big knives on their hips.

"How do, neighbor," one said. "I'm Jeb Ellsworth."

"And I'm Jed Ellsworth," parroted his twin.

"You wouldn't happen to be from the South, would you?" Jeb asked.

"Texas," Seth said, passing them.

"That's good enough for us," Jed said.

The saloon was as busy as before and Dub was pouring drinks nonstop. Jack Shelton sat at the same corner table, the man with the shotgun and the man with the two Remingtons beside him. They rose when Shelton said something to them. "Mr. Jackson! You're back! Have you made up your mind about my offer?"

Seth claimed a vacated chair. "How will it work, exactly?"

"I've been doing some askin' around. I'm told that the northwest part of your ranch has plenty of water but it's rough country and you don't use it much." Shelton bent forward on his elbows. "Once every few months or so my boys will bring a herd in and keep them there. It won't be for long. Once I sell the cows, you get your cut. How much you get will depend on how much I get."

"You said something about four thousand dollars."

"I already have a sale lined up. Some of my boys leave tonight to collect the cows. The herd will be a big one. Soon as I'm paid, you get the four thousand."

Seth glanced over his shoulder. "And this will be our little secret? No one else will know?"

Jack Shelton had an oily smile. "It's to my benefit as much as yours not to say anything."

Indecision knifed through Seth, and he hesitated.

"Look. I'll be straight with you," Shelton

said. "I like Nowhere. It's just what I've been lookin' for, and I plan to stick around. The people here will be makin' a lot more money than they ever did. Why not dip your hand in the pie and come out ahead like everyone else?"

"What about the Circle C?"

"What about it?"

"Chick Storm can't be bought, broken or sweet-talked. If he learned what I was doing, he'd brand me a rustler and have me hung."

"He'll never find out. And even if he did" — Shelton indicated the man with the Remingtons and the man with the shotgun — "I take care of my friends."

"I don't like talk like that," Seth said. "The Circle C is a salty outfit. Tangle with them and you'll know you've been in a fight."

"I told you before, why spill blood when there's no need?"

Seth bowed his head, then looked toward the bar where Dub was grinning and talking to the oldest dove. A man in a floppy hat slapped a dollar on the bar and Dub scooped it up and gave him a bottle.

"Well? Do we have a deal or not?"

"We have a deal," Seth Jackson said.

Chapter Nine

Billy Braden came out of the saloon with a whiskey bottle in his hand. He tilted it, gulped the last of the red-eye, then dropped the bottle on the boardwalk and started across the street. He changed direction when he saw Marshal Lunsford coming up the other side. "Well, look who it is. Folks were beginnin' to think you'd died. It's been over two weeks since anyone has seen you."

The lawman came to a stop and swayed slightly. "What would you know?"

"Sheath your claws. I'm only being sociable."

Marshal Lunsford's shirt was splotched with stains and the top of a flask poked from his vest pocket. "When I want your company I'll ask for it."

Billy put his hand on his pearl-handled Colt. "You'd better climb down a few rungs, cripple. I don't take that guff off anyone."

"What would your boss say?" Lunsford smirked. "You're supposed to make nice."

"Make nice, yes, but not eat crow. And the boss ain't here. He and most of the boys had business elsewhere. But I suspect you know that or you wouldn't be pokin' your head out of your hole." Billy looked the marshal up and down and shook his head. "What have you been doing? Suckin' down coffin varnish and wishin' you had courage?"

Lunsford's lips became thin slits.

"You know, don't you?" Billy asked.

"It's my job to know."

"But you haven't told anyone. You haven't called the sheep together and demand we be run out. Why not?"

Pulling the flask from his pocket, Lunsford uncapped it and took a swig, then replaced it. "They're good people. I don't want them hurt."

"Is that all? Or could it be you don't feel up to leadin' the charge? It was easy to be the law when there wasn't any lawin' to do, but now that there is, all that badge is good for is target practice."

"I'm still the marshal here and don't you forget it."

Billy put an arm around the lawman's stooped shoulders. "Truth is, we like you wearin' the tin. You're so useless, it's the same as havin' no law at all. So you go on being marshal for as long as you want, you hear?" Laughing, he went into the general store.

Sally Palmer was behind the counter seated on a stool, reading a book. She heard his spurs and glanced up with a smile but when she saw who it was she frowned and went back to her reading.

Billy strutted to the counter and leaned on it. "If I didn't know better, I'd swear you're not glad to see me."

"My folks are over at the restaurant," Sally said without lifting her eyes from the page. "They'll be back in an hour. If you have business to conduct, conduct it with them."

"That's not very neighborly of you," Billy teased. "And I know where they are. I was watchin' and waitin' so I could talk to you alone."

"Why do you keep doing this?"

"Why do you think?" Billy plunged his hand into a jar and helped himself to a gumdrop.

Lightning danced about Sally's blond head. "You're despicable. Day after day you come in here and bother me, and day after day I tell you to leave me be."

"When I want something I generally don't back down until I have it." Billy hopped up on the counter and leaned toward her. "Goodness, you smell nice. Better than Belle and all those others ever could."

"I'll thank you not to mention me in the same breath as those hussies." Sally slammed her book shut, slid off the stool, and came around the counter. "I want you out of here. I want you out now. Or so help me, I'll scream."

Billy sucked on the gumdrop, making a slurping noise. "And then what? Your pa would come runnin' and get all mad and maybe try to throw me out and I'd have to unravel some cartridges."

"You wouldn't!" Sally exclaimed.

"Not unless you force me, no." Billy opened his mouth and showed her the gumdrop on the tip of his tongue, then closed it and grinned. "I wish this candy was you."

Flushing, Sally raised the book as if to hit him with it. "You are the lowest of the low! How you think I could ever be interested in someone who treats me so poorly is beyond me."

"Poorly?" Billy slid off the counter. "I just paid you the highest compliment a man can pay a female and you're ready to bean me?"

"You call that a compliment? Decent ladies don't like having tongues wriggled in their faces."

Folding his arms, Billy smiled his most dazzling smile. "I'm sorry. I admit I don't have a lot of experience with ladies of your caliber. But all I wanted was to make you grin."

"Just go."

"Have you ever seen a waterfall?" Billy asked her.

"What?"

"I did once, up in the mountains. Hundreds of feet high, it was. The water tumblin' and sparklin' and as beautiful as anything that ever was until I set eyes on you." Billy paused. "How can you blame me for comin' back every day to talk to the loveliest girl in this territory or any other?"

"Now you're poking fun," Sally said. She had lowered the book and was holding it close to her bosom.

"Look at me. At my face. At my eyes. I've never been more serious since I was in diapers." Billy reached out and touched her fingers. "The day I first set eyes on you, you took my breath away. And you've been takin' it away every day since."

"I've told you before. I'm spoken for."

"By that Circle C puncher? How much can he care for you if he keeps comin' around month after month and doesn't do more than hold your hand and eat your ma's cookin'?"

"I won't stand for you insultin' Randy. He's the nicest boy I've ever met." Her back as stiff as an ironing board, Sally returned to the other side of the counter and reclaimed her stool.

"There's the problem right there. He's a boy when what you need is a man."

"I suppose you qualify?"

"Why not? I'd never let a pretty girl like you go to waste. Why, if you favored me like you're favorin' him, I wouldn't let a day go by that I wasn't over here baskin' in your beauty. Which is more than can be said about your puncher. How often does he make it in? Once a month?"

Sally opened her book. "I will never favor you."

"Why? What's wrong with me? I've got all my teeth." Billy flashed his smile. "I take baths regular, and I splash on some smell-good every time I come over."

"I told you. It's your manners. You look just fine."

"Do I, now?" Billy chuckled. "Then there's hope yet."

"There is not. I was being polite. Now go away. I'm reading."

"What is that book you're holdin' upside down, anyhow?"

Sally looked, and blushed, and reversed the book so she was holding it correctly. "You get me so flustered, I don't know what I'm doing."

"Another good sign," Billy declared. "My pa always said when a girl is flustered it's a sign she's interested."

"I can't imagine you having a father," Sally jousted. "I figured you hatched from an egg like most lizards."

Billy laughed and slapped his thigh. "Dang, girl. You're good. But you're right. I did hatch from an egg. That's why I shed my skin once a month."

A grin blossomed on Sally's face but she immediately wiped it off. "There's a sight folks would pay to see. You could join a circus and be famous."

"How would you like to go for a stroll with me later? Say, about sunset?"

"And how would you like to jump off the tallest building in town, headfirst?"

"What, and put a hole in the street?" Billy shook his head. "The marshal might arrest me for my head makin' a nuisance of itself."

Again Sally grinned. Again she fought it. "I'll say one thing for you. It's hard to stay mad at a man with a velvet tongue."

"You noticed when I showed you that gumdrop, did you?" Billy opened his mouth again. The gumdrop was almost gone.

"You're hopeless," Sally said, and bent to her book.

Billy scrunched up his face, then tapped the counter. "What's this you're so all-fired interested in, anyhow?"

"*Ben-Hur* by Lew Wallace."

"That's a peculiar name. What's it about? Horses and such?"

Sally tittered. "No. It's about a man who becomes a slave back in Roman times after a great injustice is done him."

"Romans?" Billy thoughtfully stroked his chin. "Weren't they the ones who went around in dresses and rode in big wooden horses?"

"You're thinking of the Greeks." Sally set him straight. "The Romans wore togas and were famous for their laws and their roads. Didn't you study them in school?"

"I never went."

"Not once your whole life? What sort of parents did you have that they didn't see to your education?"

"My folks died when I was young," Billy revealed. "I've been on my own ever since. Anything I know, I've picked up from others. That Greek business I heard from an old codger who always carried around a book called the" — Billy's brow furrowed in concentration — "*The Iliad*! That's what it was."

"I read that years ago," Sally said. "Along with *The Odyssey*." She paused. "Do you read and write?"

Billy sheepishly stuck his hands in his pockets. "I can scribble my handle when I have to, and I can wrestle with a menu pretty fair. But I ain't never read a book all the way through, if that's what you're gettin' at."

"Have you ever wanted to?"

"When I was younger, sure. I'd see other kids readin' and see the *Police Gazette* in the barbershop and I'd get a hankerin' to practice readin' until I got good at it." Billy shrugged. "But nothin' ever came of it."

"Why not?" Sally asked.

"Life."

A minute went by, with Sally reading and Billy waiting, and then she said, "I could help you if you wanted. To read, I mean. Since you already know the basics, you would pick it up in no time."

"That's the kindest offer anyone ever made me."

"Don't make more of it than it is. We'll do it on my terms, and if you so much as give me a lick of trouble, I'll stop."

Billy beamed. "When do we start, teacher? Now?"

"I'm working, you chucklehead. Come back about sunset and we'll sit out back and I'll read to you from *Ben-Hur* and then let you read to me. How does that sound?"

"Like all my wishes have come true." Billy opened the jar and popped another gumdrop into his mouth.

"That will be five cents," Sally said.

"Five cents, nothin'." Billy pulled a wad of bills from his pocket and peeled several off. "Here's thirty dollars." He shoved the money into her hand.

Sally blinked. "Are you insane? All you had were two pieces of candy."

"The rest is a tip."

"No, no, no." Sally shoved the money at him but he stepped back. "I can't accept this. It wouldn't be right."

"Says who?"

"What would my parents think? What would —" Sally stopped.

"How will anyone find out if we don't

tell them?" Billy jangled toward the door. "Sunset it is."

"Hold up," Sally said.

Billy swung around, his thumbs hooked in his gun belt, the pearl grips to his Colt glittering in the sunlight streaming in the doorway. "For you, my lovely, anything."

"You'll behave? You won't take liberties or do anything to make me regret my decision?"

"I've never taken a liberty with a woman in my life," Billy said. "But I'm not a boy, neither." Whistling, he bent his boots to the saloon.

Dingus was at the bar. Ben Towers was huddled with Susie Metzger at a table. The rest of the gang were off with Black Jack, laying claim to cattle that belonged to someone else.

"Hey, kid!" Dingus hollered. "How's your store filly?"

"Drinks for everyone, on me!" Billy said, and whooped. "Does that answer your question?"

"Ain't love grand?" Dingus said.

Shasta Cunningham was the only one who frowned.

"You better watch yourself, kid," Belle James cautioned him. "Those prim and proper types have a way of changin' a gent."

Billy did not favor either of them with a reply. Marching to the table where Shasta and Susie sat, he grabbed Shasta's wrist. "Come with me." He hustled her toward the hall at the rear.

"Again?" Shasta said, without resisting. "Why is it every time you go see her, you want to bed me?"

"I'm not here to listen to you nag." Billy came to one of the special rooms Black Jack had set up. Formerly a storeroom, it now contained a bed and a small table with a pitcher of water. He closed and bolted the door.

Shasta was a downcast statue.

"What are you waitin' for? An engraved invite? Shuck those clothes."

"Has it ever sunk in how much I love you?"

Billy began undoing his belt buckle. "Has it ever sunk in how much I don't care? You're a whore, damn it. You do it with everybody. So quit actin' like I'm something special."

Shasta slowly undid a button, saying softly, "To me you are."

Chapter Ten

The prairie lay quiet under the mantle of night. Other than the occasional yip of coyotes the only sound was the sigh of the wind and the thud of hooves as five punchers from the Circle C neared their destination.

Lin Cooley rose in his stirrups and spied lights in the distance. "Half an hour more and we'll be there," he announced.

"I can't wait." A red bandanna was around Randy Quin's throat, his clothes were as clean as if they were brand new, and his boots were shined to a sheen. "It's been over a month this time. Six whole weeks, in fact."

"It ain't like Nowhere is a stone's throw from the Coldwater," Kip Langtree said. His straw-colored hair poked from under his hat giving him an untamed look that befit his wild and woolly eighteen years.

"Some of us have more cause than others," said Moses Sikes, his teeth white against his black face.

Amos Finch, the fifth cowhand and by

far the oldest of the entire Circle C outfit spoke up. "You snotnoses and your romances. I've been in love more times than I have fingers. You ain't about to catch me all cow-eyed."

Randy shifted in his saddle. "This ain't no romance, you old coot. Tonight is the night I ask her."

"You'll excuse me if I don't hold my breath," Amos said. "Human beings ain't supposed to go around lookin' purple."

The guffaws caused Randy's jaw muscles to twitch.

"You can hardly blame them, pard," Lin Cooley said.

"No, he can't," Amos said. "If willpower were oatmeal, Randy would have it comin' out his ears."

"Now, now," Moses said. "He can't help not being able to make up his mind. I heard he fell on his head when he dropped out of the womb and he's been tryin' to scrape his brains back together ever since."

More guffaws caused more tweaking of Randy's jaw. "You can all go to hell," he declared.

"I'll remember that when I'm buyin' drinks for everyone," Amos said.

"The way you carry on," Randy grumbled, "you'd think being in love was dumb."

Amos brought his horse up next to Quin's. "It ain't that at all, pup. We're just jealous. There ain't one of us but wishes we were in your boots. Human nature being what it is, since that won't happen, we'll settle for makin' your life miserable."

"That's a fine how-do-you-do," Randy said.

"It's not personal. It's life. I've been over the range and back more than a few times and I've learned a few things. We are who we are and we do what we do and that's that."

Randy wouldn't let it go. "Well, friends shouldn't poke fun because a man is head over spurs for a girl."

"But then we'd miss out on a heap of belly laughs. And laughter is one of the best tonics this dreary life has to offer."

"Why, Amos, you old faker, you," Lin Cooley commented. "You never let on that you could think."

That ended their conversation for a while. Hats were adjusted and belts were hitched and they regarded the glittering lights in eager anticipation. But when they were a hundred yards out, Lin Cooley reined up and the rest followed suit.

"Do my old ears hear what I think they hear?" Amos asked.

Clear as crystal on the cool night air came the high, tinny notes of a piano, and bursts of raucous mirth.

"Maybe we came to the wrong town by mistake," Moses said.

"It's the right one," Randy responded. "I can see Old Man Taylor sittin' in his rockin' chair out front of the livery."

"Can you imagine Dub springin' for a piano?" Kip Langtree marveled. "He must of struck it rich."

"What I'm wondering about," Lin Cooley said, "are all those horses at the hitch rails."

Nowhere had become somewhere. More mounts than any of them had ever seen in the town at any one time filled the hitch rails on both sides of the street, with surplus animals tied to overhang posts and the windmill. Every window glowed with light and people were moving about on the boardwalks.

Moses said, "So much for a quiet night of drinkin' and poker."

"Fine by me!" Kip perked up. "I'm a curly wolf from the Washita and I love to howl!"

On they rode, a wariness in their posture

that had not been evident before. Cooley had his eyes on the saloon; Randy was only interested in the general store.

"I see Joe Elliot's sorrel yonder," Kip Langtree said.

"A lot of the Bar J boys are here," Amos observed, "along with cayuses from other outfits."

The saloon door had been replaced by batwings which now opened, and out staggered a booze-blind cowhand pawing a slightly overweight woman in a too-tight red dress who smacked one of his hands and said, "The groping comes later. You promised me a piece of pecan pie first and I aim to hold you to it." Her elbow locked in his, she steered him toward the restaurant.

"A dove, by God!" Amos exclaimed in breathless astonishment. *"Here?"*

The merry laughter of another pealed inside.

"So that's the attraction!" Kip exclaimed. "We'd best get in there, boys, and lay our claim before they're all taken." He started to climb down.

"First we put up our animals at the stable," Cooley said. "Then you can paint your tonsils all you want."

For once Old Man Taylor wasn't whittling. His hands were folded in his lap, and he gloomily nodded as they came to a stop. "Howdy, boys. Welcome to Sodom. Or is it Gomorrah? I never can get the two straight."

"What in blazes has happened here?" Amos Finch asked. "I just saw a female critter with Toby Gill of the Bar J."

"That's right. You boys haven't been to town in a coon's age. There have been some changes. Mighty big changes. But I expect you'll find that out for yourselves soon enough."

Cooley held out his reins. "Can you put up our horses for the night as usual?"

"Would that I could," Taylor said. "I'm plumb full inside. But there's room in the corral if you don't mind them being outdoors. Strip them and put them in yourself. I'm too depressed to move."

All but Lin Cooley hurried to take the suggestion. The Circle C's ramrod hunkered beside the rocking chair. "What's the matter? Has there been trouble?"

"Depends on your definition," Old Man Taylor answered. "No one's been planted yet, if that's what you're thinking. But it's only a matter of time. You and your boys be careful. A longhair by the name of Shelton has taken things over, lock, stock and barrel."

"How's that possible?"

"He's got a passel of gun tippers with him. As snake-eyed a bunch as you'll ever come across. That they haven't curled anyone up yet can't be for lack of meanness." Taylor paused. "There's one in particular you should be on the lookout for. A cat-eyed gent with nickel-plated pistols slung low."

"This cat have a handle to go with his whiskers?"

"He hasn't let it be known but I've a hunch it's Longley."

"*Ike* Longley?"

Old Man Taylor nodded. "I mentioned it to Paul, figuring Paul would arrest him, but nothing ever came of it." Taylor glanced toward the jail, the only dark building in town. "It's a shame."

Cooley unfurled his long legs. "They say Longley has fourteen to his credit, not countin' Mexicans and Indians."

"He's no one to trifle with. And he's only one of many. There are wolves on the loose and they have sharp teeth."

Cooley led his horse to the rear of the stable and met his friends coming the other way. "Wait for me," he said.

"Not on your life." Randy was practically skipping. "If I don't see Sally soon, I'll bust."

Kip Langtree smacked his lips. "And I can't go another minute without a beer. My throat is so dry, it's a desert."

"Me, I want to make the acquaintance of one of those doves," Amos Finch said. "Maybe both if my money holds out."

"You reckon they do charity?" Moses asked.

Cooley stripped his horse and hurried to catch up but they were out of sight when he reached the street. He passed Bar J punchers and men he knew from other spreads a lot farther away. At the batwings he paused and was wreathed in a drifting cloud of cigarette and cigar smoke. When it thinned, he shouldered his way inside.

The saloon was crammed. Customers were shoulder to shoulder, wall to wall. Every chair at every table was filled. Men lined the bar from end to end and spilled around the corners. Dub Wheeton was filling glasses as fast as he could but one man couldn't keep up with demand, which explained why he had hired a helper for the first time since he owned the place — a kid of fifteen, the son of Robert Renfro, the town barber. Poker and faro games were in full swing, the clink of chips constantly in the background.

Cooley headed for the bar, nodding to

cowpokes he knew. For every one he recognized there were four or five he didn't. He noticed others, too, men who clearly weren't punchers, hard cases whose faces bore the stamp of violent natures: a pair of twins over by the north wall, their clothes as grimy and greasy as they were; another with a floppy hat who wore a constant cockeyed grin and fingered a long knife at his hip.

Two women were working the room, a redhead who flounced about in wanton glory, teasing and enticing and never objecting if a customer happened to smack her fanny, and a skinny girl who was having a rough time of it. She appeared tired and sad and if anyone slapped her backside, she would glare.

A lusty howl diverted Cooley to a table where Joe Elliot was raking in the pot and being his usual humble self about winning.

"Wahoo! That'll teach you tinhorns to play cards with your betters! The night's still young and I'm two hundred ahead!" Joe spotted Cooley and beckoned. "Lin, you handsome devil! Wait for one of these sheep to vacate a chair and join us! It's easy pickin's tonight."

"No thanks," Cooley said. "If I go broke, it won't be by linin' someone else's pocket."

"You're no fun. What's money for, if not whiskey, women and cards?" Joe piled his chips and grinned at the other players, who weren't nearly as pleased by his winnings.

Cooley reached the bar. He had to holler to get Dub's attention, and as his drink was poured, he commented, "I thought maybe I'd wound up in Dallas by mistake."

Dub mopped his sweaty forehead. "I'm about worn to a frazzle. I almost miss the old days." He had more to say but a bellow down the bar required his attention.

Careful not to be jostled, Cooley raised the glass to his lips and sipped. Perfume tingled his nose and slender fingers pulled at his sleeve, and he turned to find the redhead attached to his arm. "How do you do, ma'am?"

"Aren't you polite? I'm Susie. Susie Metzger. I saw you come in and thought we should get better acquainted."

"I bet you say that to all the cow crowd."

"Be nice," Susie said, and squeezed in closer, her breasts nearly oozing up out of her dress. "I'm only doing what I'm paid to do."

"You'd be wastin' your time," Lin informed her. "I'm not lookin' to cuddle, just to drink."

"I haven't asked you to take me into a

back room, have I?" Susie challenged. "I could go for a Virginia fancy, if you'll buy me one. The boss doesn't mind me standin' still for a minute or two if he sees me drinkin'."

Lin did as she wanted and the Renfro boy brought it to her.

"Mmmmm. You can't imagine how good these taste after you've been on your feet for hours." Susie surveyed the bedlam. "Each weekend has been wilder than the last. Another month, and every Saturday night will be a party from dark until dawn."

"Some folks might not like that."

"Once an avalanche starts, there's no stopping it," Susie said, appraising him. "So who are you and where are you from?"

"Lin Cooley of the Circle C."

The redhead gave a start but instantly recovered her composure and drained her glass in a long swig. "A pleasure meetin' you, ramrod. Maybe we'll talk more sometime. Right now I have to mingle." The crowd swallowed her.

Lin hadn't mentioned he was the Circle C's ramrod. Something strange was going on, he thought, and he marked her meanderings as she drifted from customer to customer and table to table until she came to one and whispered in the ear of a man wearing a wide-brimmed black hat and a pair of nickel-plated Remingtons.

Longley looked up, and Lin met his gaze.

Just then there was a thunderous oath and the *thud* of a fist striking a table, and Joe Elliot reared with one hand on his six-shooter and the other pointed accusingly at a player with a zigzag scar across his left cheek. "I saw that, you four-flusher! You dealt the last card from the bottom!"

The man with the scar had the deck in front of him, and the most chips besides Elliot. His clothes were not puncher clothes and he wore a revolver slantwise across his hip. "You're mistaken, cowboy."

"Like hell! You're a damned cheat!"

Bar J hands were moving to back Joe Elliot. Longley and the twins and the man with the floppy hat were on the move, too — to back the player with the scar, who picked up the deck and said, "You're welcome to redeal the hand yourself if you'd like. Just to prove I'm honest."

"That doesn't prove anything," Joe snapped, "except that you're a weasel. Now on your feet!"

Men were pressing toward the walls to give them room.

"I won't tell you again!" Joe Elliot bawled, and poised his hand to draw.

Chapter Eleven

Randy Quin floated on air the last ten feet to the general store. It had been so long since he saw Sally, he tingled with pure pleasure. But her parents were the only ones there, and from the look of things were about to close up. "Mr. Palmer, Mrs. Palmer." He removed his hat. "It's a pleasure seein' you again."

George and Helen looked at one another, and George said, "Randall! This is a surprise. Where have you been keeping yourself?"

"Where else? The Circle C." Randy stared at the door to their living quarters. "How have things been?"

"Hectic," George said. "Busier than you would believe. Business has never been better in all the time we've been here."

"That's nice. You've always said you wanted more." Randy moved toward the door. "Mind if I step on back and see Sally?"

Helen Palmer was there before him. "I'd

rather you didn't. The place is a mess. Let me fetch her." She ducked through the doorway and closed the door after her.

George was rubbing his palms together and rising up and down on the balls of his feet. "It's a shame you had to stay away so long."

"It couldn't be helped," Randy said. "Mr. Storm wanted all the strays accounted for. We had to cover the whole ranch, and you know how big it is."

"You're a good worker," George said. "No matter what else, no one can ever say you don't pull your weight."

"I do my part."

Then, for no reason that Randy could fathom, George Palmer commented, "Where women are concerned, there's no predicting." George had the CLOSED sign and was moving to the front door. "A man can never take them for granted. He might as well swim in quicksand."

"You and your wife get along fine," Randy said, puzzled by the trail their talk had taken.

"That we do, son. But only because Helen isn't one of those women who holds grudges. She doesn't carp a man to death over every little thing she thinks he's doing wrong." George hung the sign, aligning it so it was straight. "I can't say as my daughter is quite as forgiving."

"Sure she is." Randy defended his love. "Sally is the nicest girl who ever drew breath."

George was behind the counter again. "She was hoping you would ask for her hand, you know."

Randy kneaded his hat as if it were bread dough. "A man has to be sure the timin' is right."

"Women won't wait forever, Randall. Some things in life just can't be put off." George smiled. "I've always liked you, though, for what that's worth."

Now Randy was worried. Severely worried. The door to the living quarters opened and Sally was there, her golden hair as lustrous as ever, her eyes the same marvelous emeralds. Randy reached her before she could blink and clasped her hands in his. "At last! Let me drink in the sight of you."

"You're finally here." Sally glanced at her father, who excused himself and shut the door.

The instant he was gone, Randy enfolded her in his arms and breathed deep of her fragrant scent. "I'm sorry it's been so long. I've thought of you every minute. You can't know how much I've missed you."

"There have been some changes," Sally said.

It dawned on Randy that she was not returning his hug. "So I saw. Nowhere is livelier than Beaver City and that takes some doing." He kissed her forehead. "I reckon nothin' ever stays the same."

"All too true."

Randy stepped back to admire her. "I've been doing a lot of thinkin', and you and I have some serious talkin' to do."

Sally stepped to the vinegar barrel and perched on top of it. "That's for sure."

"This is one of the happiest days of your life," Randy said. "Your wish is about to come true."

"All that praying finally paid off?" Sally bowed her chin and her hair fell across her face. "Who would have thought it?"

"That's right," Randy said. Sinking onto his right knee, he gently took her right hand. "I don't rightly know how it's supposed to be done but this is how my pa proposed to my ma, so here goes." He cleared his throat. "Sally Ann Palmer, will you do me the honor of becomin' my wife?"

"No."

"I ain't much to brag on but give me time and I'll prove I can —" Randy stopped. "What did you say?"

"I decline your offer, Mr. Quin," Sally said formally.

Randy thought she must be teasing. He *prayed* she was teasing. "But you've wanted me to propose for months. Now you're sayin' you want me to hold off askin' after I finally get up the gumption to do the deed?"

"I'm saying I shouldn't tie myself to one man. I'm young yet. I'm fairly pretty. I should keep my prospects open."

Randy went to stand but his legs nearly gave out from under him and he had to grip the vinegar barrel for support. "I must be havin' a nightmare. How can things go from rosy to awful so sudden?"

"What's so sudden about it?" was Sally's tart rejoinder. "I wasted pretty near a year of my life waiting for you to show some backbone."

"You call our love a waste?" Randy had gone as white as snow.

"If what we had was love, it was the most peculiar love since Romeo and Juliet," Sally bluntly replied, then softened. "The blame isn't all yours. I was too patient. Too caught up in how a lady is supposed to behave."

"But you *are* a lady," Randy said softly.

"In some respects. But being a lady is only half of it. There's also being a woman."

"I've lost your trail," Randy admitted. His legs were steady enough for him to let go of the barrel and he stood staring down into her incredibly lovely face with his heart breaking into shards and bits.

Sally gripped his hand. "Goodness, your fingers are cold." Her eyes bored into his as if plumbing to the depths of his soul. "I'm truly sorry. The last thing I wanted is to hurt you. You've always been a sweet dear. Most any girl in the territory would be glad to have you court her."

"I waited too long? That's what this is about?"

Sally slid off the barrel and walked around the counter. "It's about feelings, Randy. They change. If you had asked me to marry you six months ago, I'd have said yes before the words were out of your mouth." She bit her lower lip. "Now I'm not so sure it's for the best."

Randy was desperately trying to make sense of the disaster. "You're ashamed of how I make my livin', is that it?"

"No, no, it's not that."

"I've been savin' every dollar I can —"

"It's not that, either," Sally said, with more than a trace of exasperation. "Haven't you been listening? It's about *feelings*. My feelings. I thought they were chiseled in rock but I've learned different."

"You don't care for me as much as you did?" Randy couldn't keep the hurt from his voice.

"Yes. No. I don't know!" Sally suddenly covered her face with her hands, then just as quickly lowered them again. "You're making this terribly difficult. Yes, I still care for you, but not in the way I cared for you before."

"How can it change? Just like that?" Randy snapped his fingers.

"It's been six weeks. A lot can happen."

Randy moved to the counter. "What can have happened to bring on *this*? One month you say you love me more than anyone has ever loved anyone, the next you're throwin' me out with the dirty dishwater." He halted, the shock beginning to register. "That is what you're doing, isn't it? Cuttin' my tether?"

A tear formed under Sally's left eye and trickled down her cheek. "We need to be apart for a while, is all. To give us time to think about things."

"I don't think with my heart."

"Randy . . . ," Sally said, and now a tear moistened her other cheek. "You have no idea how hard this is for me."

"You have no notion of how hard this is *on* me. I've never loved anyone before. Not this way. Not this deep."

"Please. No more."

"I feel like you've stabbed me in the gut with a knife made of fire." Randy reached for her but she stepped back. "Can't we at least talk this out?"

Sally wouldn't look at him. Shaking her head, she said, "There's nothing else to talk about. Go, and don't make it worse."

Slowly turning, Randy shuffled like a man bound for the gallows. His legs felt like wooden sticks. "I never thought —" he said, but he didn't come out and say what it was he was thinking. He fumbled to open the door and at last succeeded. Then he looked back. "I love you so much."

"Go."

Randy quietly shut the door and stood blinking blindly at the busy street. Several punchers passed him on their way to the restaurant and gave him peculiar looks. Pulling his hat brim low, he crossed to the barbershop and stood under the overhang. Shoving his hands in his pockets, he stared forlornly at the general store, at the window and the golden-haired beauty inside.

Sally stood with her head down for the longest while. Then she turned and took a few steps toward the front. She stopped when her mother came out of the back. They embraced, and Sally's body shook, as from weeping. They began talking.

Randy headed back over. His legs were in motion before his brain stopped them at the edge of the boardwalk. He waited for Helen to go into the back so he could be alone with Sally.

At length the mother did. Sally stepped to a mirror and dabbed at her eyes. Randy was in motion again when someone else came from the back hallway, and an icy chill rippled down his spine. Without consciously doing so, he clenched his fists so tight, it hurt.

Another man had moved up behind Sally. She turned, and they hugged. Her head fell to his shoulder and he stroked her hair, the whole while grinning.

Randy heard a roaring in his ears that came from inside of him, from his blood boiling in his veins. He grew as hot as a burning brand. A heavy sensation in his chest made it difficult to breathe.

Sally stepped back and was saying something to her suitor.

To Randy, it was as if blinders had suddenly been slipped over his head. He saw Sally and the other man, and that was all he saw. The rest of the world, the rest of Nowhere, the street and the punchers and the townsfolk moving about, were blotted out as if they didn't exist. It was like looking down a long tunnel, with the general store at the other end. He willed his legs to move.

"Watch where you're going, you lunkhead!"

The shout barely registered. The same with the whinny of a horse and a muttered oath. Randy came to within ten feet of the store and stopped, waiting.

Sally and her suitor were talking. The other man made a comment that brought a vigorous shake of her head. He reached for her arm but she shrugged his hand off and headed for her living quarters. Over her shoulder she made a last comment.

Grinning broadly, his gaze on the floor, her suitor strolled to the door. He opened it and stepped outside and raised his head. "Well, what have we here? You must be Quin."

In a rush of insight Randy realized he hated this man. Hated as he had never hated before. "Who are you?" Randy's

145

voice sounded strange even to him, a cross between a growl and a hiss.

"You don't know? I would have thought you'd have heard by now." The other man planted his legs wide and hooked his thumbs in his gun belt. "I'm Billy Braden, cowpoke. Sally's new beau."

"What have you done to my girl?"

"*Your* girl?" Billy scoffed. "I didn't see your brand on her anywhere. Nor no ring, neither."

Randy took a step. "You've been seein' her behind my back."

"Hell. You think I'm too yellow to court her in the open? Everyone in these parts knows I've been payin' my respects these past weeks. Everyone except you, because you weren't here." Billy laughed. "Maybe you ain't heard the old sayin'. Leave the henhouse open and a fox is bound to get in."

"I had plans," Randy said.

"It's what a person does that counts, cowpoke. Or, in your case, what they don't do. You sparked her for months and made no more headway than a bog-stuck wagon."

Randy was silent.

"Don't blame me for your faults," Billy said. "And now that she's given you the boot, don't let me catch you triflin' with her."

The roaring in Randy's ear grew louder. "Be careful."

"Or what? You'll pull on me?" Billy Braden lowered his hand to his side. "I hope to hell you do, you lump of stupidity. I'm under orders not to kill unless I don't have a choice, so please, don't give me a choice."

Randy's hatred overwhelmed his reason. A fierce determination seized him, and he tensed to draw. Suddenly both his arms were seized and he felt himself being hauled down the street. "What the hell!" he fumed. "Let go of me!"

"Simmer down," Amos Finch cautioned. "You wouldn't stand a prayer against that gunny."

"You're just lucky we happened by," Moses Sikes said.

"Let go, damn it!" Randy saw that Billy Braden was sneering at him, and he fought harder.

Moses had a calloused hand on Randy's wrist so Randy couldn't draw. "Not now, boy. Not when you're like this."

Randy sought a final time to shake them off but his strength inexplicably evaporated and his limbs went limp. A groan escaped him, and he was glad his friends were holding him, because without them, he would have fallen in the dirt.

"If you promise to behave, I'll go fetch Lin," Amos offered.

At that very instant, from inside the saloon, came the blast of gunfire.

Chapter Twelve

Lin Cooley felt a tug on his sleeve and Kip Langtree whispered, "Shouldn't we side with Joe?"

"It's his to do," Lin said. "An hombre throws his own rope in this country. You know that."

"Damn etiquette all to hell," was Kip's response.

Joe Elliot and Hap Evans and seven more Bar J punchers were on one side of the poker table. On the other side stood Longley and the twins and the scrawny man in the floppy hat. The player accused of cheating was still in his chair, holding the deck of cards. Everyone else had pressed to the sides of the room.

"On your feet, card cheat!" Joe Elliot commanded.

"The name is Craven. Clell Craven. And I'll thank you not to bellow."

"I'll shout if I damn well want to!" Joe retorted. "Now get up! The boys and me are about to show everyone what we do to card slicks hereabouts."

Clell Craven set down the cards and slowly rose. The pistol he wore slantwise across the front of his belt was a Merwin and Hulbert open top model, and judging by the worn grips, had seen a lot of use. "You've had too much to drink, cowboy. You only think you saw me deal from the bottom."

"Like hell," Joe Elliot growled. "I could drink all night and all day and still not be that booze blind. Shuck your artillery. We're fixin' to run you out of town."

"Go to hell," Craven said.

Joe gestured. "Maybe you're the one who is booze blind. Or can't you count? I've got plenty of friends."

"I've got friends of my own."

The two sides took each other's measure. Some of the Bar J hands were nervous, and rightly so. They were cowpunchers, not shootists.

Joe pounded the table again and jabbed a finger at Craven. "Hidin' behind your pards won't help! This is your last warnin'!"

Longley spoke for the first time. "And this is yours. Back off, cowboy. I can take you and your pards by myself."

Joe Elliot glanced at Longley's nickel-plated Remingtons. "Who the hell are you and why are you buttin' your nose in where it can be stomped?"

"I'm his partner," Longley said, with a nod at Craven. "Anyone who goes up against him goes up against me."

"That suits us just fine," Joe declared. "Make a play for those fancy guns and you'll be pushin' up weeds."

Ike Longley smiled grimly. "If that's what you think, you loudmouthed sack of pus, quit spewin' hot air and show us what you're made of."

Cooley saw Joe Elliot's eyes narrow. Joe was calculating the odds and maybe trying to figure out who he was up against. Another few seconds and Joe would probably sheath his claws to spare his friends.

But then one of the younger Bar J punchers, whose name Cooley couldn't remember, cried out, "Let's teach these polecats!" and clawed for his revolver with all the finesse of a two-year-old.

Twin streaks of lightning flashed and Longley's Remingtons were clear of their holsters. He fired both simultaneously, sending a slug into the young puncher and another into Joe Elliot. The young puncher was rocked off his boot heels. Joe twisted to the impact, then drew his own pistol and fired from the hip, rushing his shot.

He missed Longley and hit the man in the floppy hat, who clutched at his right shoulder and howled.

"No more shootin'!" Hap Evans cried, but he was ignored.

Clell Craven had drawn his pistol and now he fired at a Bar J cowboy leveling a Colt. The Merwin and Hulbert boomed, belching lead and smoke, and the cowboy folded like a collapsed house of cards.

Longley fired again, into Joe, who had taken hold of his revolver with both hands and was trying to steady his aim. Again Longley's twin pistols spoke. Joe was jolted but somehow stayed on his feet, somehow tried to get off a shot even though his shirt was stained scarlet and he couldn't lift his arms higher than his waist.

"Enough, damn you!" Hap Evans shouted at Longley as Joe Elliot collapsed. "You've shot him to pieces!"

"He brought it on himself," was the killer's rebuke.

Clouds of gun smoke hung in the still air above the three prone figures. Longley trained his revolvers on the rest of the Bar J crowd and demanded, "Anyone else want some of these pills?"

There were no takers.

"Then drag your friends out of here,"

Longley demanded. "And be damn sure you don't start any more trouble." With a flourish, Longley twirled the Remingtons into their holsters, then stalked away, supremely confident he would be obeyed.

Lin hurried over to where Hap Evans was cradling Joe Elliot's head in his lap. "How is he?"

"Breathin'. But barely."

"Tom and Woolsey are dead," someone said.

The Bar J boys lifted their fallen and carried them out. Cooley and Kip Langtree trailed along, Cooley holding Joe Elliot's hat.

"Did you see that fella with the fancy hardware draw?" Kip said. "He's greased lightnin' and then some."

Hap Evans had taken charge of the Bar J punchers. "Deke, go see if Old Man Taylor has his buckboard handy so we can get the bodies back to the ranch. Sam, you go ask Svenson if we can put Joe in that shed he has out back of the blacksmith shop. It's big enough and quiet enough."

"Quiet enough for what?" a puncher asked.

"So Joe can die in peace."

Onlookers were gathering. From out of them strode Marshal Lunsford, a Colt jammed under his belt. He was in need of a shave and part of his shirttail was hanging out and his hat was on crooked. "What's going on here? I heard shooting down to the jail."

Hap Evans briefly detailed the gunfight.

"So the Bar J boys drew first? You're positive of that?" Lunsford asked when the old cowboy was done.

"It was that hothead Woolsey," Hap said. "He had more green than earwax between his ears."

Lunsford regarded the batwing doors. "There's nothing I can do, then. The other side was within their rights."

"Rights, hell!" another Bar J hand exclaimed. "We should round up the rest of the boys and march back in there!"

"Let it go," Marshal Lunsford said. "Two bodies are enough for one night."

"But Joe swore that son of a bitch with a scar was cheatin'," the cowpoke said. "We let Craven get away with it once and he'll think he can get away with it all the time."

"It's not Craven you have to worry about. It's the one with the Remingtons. There aren't any five of you who could tangle with him and come out ahead. He's more gun wise than your whole outfit combined."

"Hell, you make him sound like John Wesley Hardin."

"You don't know how close you are," Lunsford said, and left chins wagging in his wake.

Cooley turned to Kip Langtree. "Find Randy and the others and have them meet me at the livery." He quickly caught up with the lawman. "You know who he is, don't you, Marshal?"

Lunsford kept on walking. "I knew who most of them were the day they rode in. Longley. Ben Towers. Craven. They all have reputations. And last I'd heard, they were all riding for Black Jack."

Cooley broke stride. "The outlaw who's been murderin' and robbin' for ten years or better? The one who operates out of the mesa country?"

"One and the same. Jack Shelton is Black Jack, or I'll eat my hat. No one ever knew Black Jack's last name, and I doubt Shelton is it. But he fits the description. All those gunnies clinch it."

"Then why haven't you done something?"

Lunsford had reached the jail. "Care for a drink? I talk better when my throat is lubricated."

"I'll hear you out," Lin said.

The place was a sty. Empty whiskey

bottles, newspapers and trash littered the floor. Blankets were heaped on a cot. Marshal Lunsford sat behind his desk, swept a pile of papers off it, and produced a half-full bottle. "Sorry about the mess. I don't often have company these days."

Cooley accepted the whiskey but didn't drink. "It's your job to keep this town safe, isn't it?"

"The people of the town, yes," Lunsford said. He polished off his glass in two gulps and immediately poured another. "But in case you haven't been in town long enough to notice, the good people of Nowhere have taken a shine to Black Jack and his curs. They think Black Jack is the best thing since pickled eggs."

"That can't be."

"It can when they're making money hand over fist. You should hear them. The Palmers, the Wilsons, Svenson and Renfro, they all sing Shelton's praises."

"Have you told them who he is?"

"No. And I'm not about to." Lunsford imbibed more rotgut. "The situation is complicated."

"What's so hard about deputizin' every man in town and every rider at the Bar J and the Circle C and roundin' up these owlhoots?"

"For one thing, I don't have the legal authority to arrest them. Yes, Black Jack is wanted in Texas, and yes, he's wanted in Kansas, but this is No Man's Land, smack between the two. Federal and state laws don't apply. So long as he doesn't step out of line, my hands are tied."

"Why not contact the Texas Rangers?"

"Because they'd have the same problem I do. No authority. Extradition papers don't apply here."

"There must be something," Lin insisted.

"Sure. I could try to throw them out on general principle but is that worth all the lives it might cost?"

"So they're free to ride roughshod? To do as they please with no regard for who they trample?"

"That's just it." Lunsford refilled his glass. "Black Jack is playing this smart. He's being downright nice to everyone. Lining their pockets while lining his own. And keeping a tight leash on his curly wolves."

"Damn," Cooley said.

"Damn is right," Lunsford echoed. "There's nothing I want more than to bring Black Jack down."

"Maybe someone will do it for you," Lin

said. "Once Seth Jackson hears about to-night, he's apt to ride in here with the Bar J hands and clean house."

"Maybe," Marshal Lunsford said, but he didn't sound confident. "The big question I need answered is where does the Circle C stand in all this?"

"I can't speak for Mr. Storm."

"I know. But you can pass on what I've told you. Tell him that if the Circle C will back me, I'll run Black Jack out. Your outfit is twice the size of the Bar J."

"We're all loyal to the brand," Lin said. "But few of our boys have ever shot anything bigger than a rattlesnake."

"You have."

"I'm not in Longley's class."

Lunsford wagged his glass, spilling some of the whiskey. "Don't sell yourself short. I've seen you draw. You can hold your own with any pistolero born."

Cooley moved to the window and tried to open it but it was stuck. "Stuffy in here, don't you reckon?"

"I really need to know."

"I'll ask Mr. Storm. That's the best I can do for now."

"Ah, well." Marshal Lunsford dispensed with his glass and drank straight from the bottle. "I suppose I could always shed this tin star and head East, maybe land a job as a clerk."

"What's keepin' you here?"

"Pride. I'm next to worthless but I'm not completely worthless and until I am, I'll discharge my duties as best I can." Lunsford grinned. "Which, for the past month or so, has meant pretending I'm a turtle."

"I never took you for one to booger easy."

"From the bottom of my heart, I thank you for the compliment. Some in town think I'm down in my boots. I'm not. I just don't want to get killed if I can help it until I'm ready. I'd like to pick the time and the place, and have it mean something."

Lin stepped to the door. "Keep your eyes skinned, hoss."

The night air was refreshingly cool after the stifling confines of the jail. Up the street a crowd milled in front of the saloon. Several Bar J hands were carrying a plank toward the blacksmith's; on it lay Joe Elliot.

Lin walked the other way. Old Man Taylor hadn't left his rocking chair but had stopped whittling. Near the stable were his friends. Amos and Moses were holding on to Randy, for some reason. Kip was

159

hanging back, unwilling to take part.

"What's this about?"

"A sidewinder named Braden is courtin' Sally!" Randy Quin raged. "I want to splatter his brains all over creation but they won't let me."

"You can tell me all about it on the way back to the Circle C."

"We're leavin' already?" This from Kip Langtree. "I had my heart set on triflin' with that skinny dove. I like gals with more bone than blubber."

"I've news for the big augur that won't wait." Lin placed a hand on Randy's shoulder. "I need you to calm down, pard. We'll get this girl business sorted out as soon as this other is tended to. My range word on that."

A growl escaped Randy, but gradually he deflated. "I reckon I could use some time to think."

It was a sober and solemn fivesome who rode out of Nowhere ten minutes later. Only once did Lin look back. The twinkling lights looked much the same as they had earlier but he wasn't fooled; nothing would ever be the same again.

Chapter Thirteen

Chick Storm was troubled. His ramrod's report weighed heavily on his shoulders. He mulled it over for several days, and that evening, at supper, he announced, "I'm thinking I should take our punchers and go run that gun crowd out of Nowhere. All I need is your blessing."

"Which you won't get," Dixie informed him, and speared a carrot.

"Mind telling me why? We have a stake there, don't we? We shop there. It's where our boys indulge their vices."

"We do more shopping in Beaver City," Dixie said. "And when it comes to vices, Beaver City has Nowhere beat all hollow." She set down her fork. "It's the principle of the thing. Our principle. Namely, we never meddle where it doesn't directly concern us or the Circle C."

"And this doesn't?"

"Dub Wheeton owns the saloon. Not us. If he wants to hire floozies and allow gunplay, it's his funeral."

"Seth Jackson is a friend and I know Joe Elliott well. I've met a lot of the Bar J hands, besides."

"Male logic," Dixie said in reproach, and bestowed what Chick liked to refer to as her "wifely look." "Men are living proof the Good Lord saved all the smarts for Eve."

"That's a bit harsh."

"Is it? You've always been a better friend to Seth than he's been to you. And all you ever did with Joe Elliot was share a few drinks. As for those others, if a body went around protecting everyone they met, they'd never have a life of their own." Dixie resumed eating. Her attitude suggested the matter was closed.

Chick poked at his steak. "I should go see Seth, at least."

"Is it Christmas and no one told me?"

"Dang it, woman. He's not plumb worthless," Chick said. "And in case you've conveniently forgotten, he and I were the first to bring cattle into this part of the country."

"So you're *twins* and no one told me?" Dixie said facetiously. "Go see him if you want. But don't pretend it's anything more than your silly male dander." And here she lowered her voice even though no one was around to hear. "He's not the man you are. He doesn't have your moral fiber."

"All this because he gambles?"

"All this because you can't wring gold out of coal. Don't commit us to anything unless you talk to me first. Promise?"

"I always do what you want, don't I?" Never once, in all the years of their marriage, had Chick struck his own course.

"That's good enough for me," Dixie said. "Be sure to take Lin with you."

"I'm not in diapers, thank you very much."

"You're not a pistolero, either. You told me yourself that Longley is a tie-down man, and I doubt those others tote lead for bluff or ballast." Dixie jabbed her fork in his direction. "Lin is a first-rate leather slapper, and the toughest hombre on the Circle C. He's the only one I can depend on not to let you down. You'll take him or I'll bolt the bedroom door for six months."

Chick was appalled. "This is serious enough for that?"

"Where your life is at stake, I can fight dirty as hell." Dixie caught herself, and blushed demurely. "I meant, dirty as the dickens."

"Sure you did. And I saw a heifer fly yesterday."

That night she didn't bolt the door, and

next morning Chick was up before the sun, feeling frisky and young again. He told her to sleep in, to not bother getting up on his account, but she pooh-poohed the notion and insisted on making breakfast and a pot of fresh coffee.

Chick had sent word to Lin the night before. There was a light knock on the door just as Dixie was setting out their plates. She admitted their foreman, and brought him back to the kitchen despite his protests that he was content to wait out front.

"Nonsense," Dixie said, pulling out a chair. "Plant yourself and prepare your stomach. It's in for a treat."

"I don't want to impose, ma'am."

"If you were, you'd have my boot up your backside."

Chick chuckled at Cooley's perplexity. "There's no modesty in her family. She grabbed it all. You might as well give in."

"I'll take some coffee then, ma'am," Lin said.

"You'll take eggs and bacon and toast and a sticky bun or three," Dixie said. "No man leaves my table hungry." She winked. "You forget, Lin Cooley. I've seen you eat. It's like watching a starved wolf."

"My ma always said a man should never be ashamed of his appetite."

"And mothers always know best." Dixie was bustling about the stove. "Why, if it weren't for us, half the people in this world would turn out more worthless than they already are."

"You'll have to forgive her," Chick said. "She thinks I'm making a mistake so she's taking it out on those around me."

"She could be right," Lin said.

Dixie stopped cracking eggs. "A rider stopped at the bunkhouse last night. I saw him from our window. Who was he?"

"Toby Gill from the Bar J," Lin confirmed. "He was askin' whether we need a new hand."

"No one told me he was here." Chick looked pointedly at his wife.

"You had turned in early to rest up for your ride," Dixie reminded him. "I wasn't about to wake you." She motioned at Cooley. "Go on, Lin. Why was he looking for work? He's been with the Bar J a few years now, hasn't he?"

"Yes, ma'am. He hasn't quit yet but he'd like to. Things aren't so good. A lot of their punchers are ready to cut tethers. It seems Mr. Jackson has lost their respect."

"What?" Chick forgot about his coffee. "That can be the death of a ranch, the first step from a top-notch outfit to a siwash outfit. Seth Jackson is too smart to let something like that happen."

"I'm only repeatin' what Toby Gill told us," Lin said. "There have been whispers of strange goings-on at the Bar J. And it hasn't helped that Mr. Jackson won't let his men pay those polecats in Nowhere a visit for what they did to Joe and the others."

"It's good we're going, then," Chick said. "It sounds like Seth can use my help."

Dixie looked at Lin Cooley. "My husband comes home safe, you hear? He's got more honor in his little finger than most have in their whole bodies, and he thinks his friends are the same even when they have more holes in their sombrero than a moth-eaten coat. You understand me?"

"Yes, ma'am."

"I wish I did," Chick complained. "You make it sound like I go through life with blinders on. I ain't no horse."

"*Aren't* a horse," Dixie corrected his grammar. Coming around the table, she tenderly took hold of his chin. "What you are, Chickory Isaiah Storm, is the most decent man alive. I thank God every day you were deluded enough to want to share breakfast with me the rest of your life."

Chick grinned. "I always take pity on loco fillies."

His volley brought a laugh from Lin, who quickly coughed and became intensely interested in the salt and pepper shakers.

After breakfast Dixie walked with them onto the porch and hugged Chick, then kissed his cheek.

"You'd think I was leaving for China."

Dixie snagged Lin's wrist as he walked past. "Remember what I said. I'm counting on you. You're the only other man in this world I trust besides him."

When the ranch was behind them, Chick let it be known, "Being married to her is never boring, I'll say that, but she does ride a man powerful hard."

"Most punchers would give anything for a gal who would dote on them like Mrs. Storm dotes on you," Lin said. "We've got one in the bunkhouse right this minute who can't hardly eat or sleep."

"Randy is taking it hard?"

"Any harder, and he'd be like that egg that fell off that wall. In more pieces than we could put back together with all the glue ever made."

"Young love is always a trial," Chick remarked. "Then again, so is anything involving females."

Lin grunted. "Which is why I've sworn off."

"Is this a temporary insanity or do you plan to go to your grave without ever having been in harness?"

"I won't kid myself. I talk big, but the first pretty filly who shows interest, I'll probably make a fool of myself."

"Got to admire an honest man." Chick grinned.

After that, conversation was sparse. They rode until sunset and made camp on the open prairie. Lin gathered brush and kindled a fire but it was Chick who made coffee and treated them to beans and biscuits Dixie had packed in his saddlebags.

Stars bloomed like flowers in the spring, filling the firmament with shimmering petals of light.

Sitting back against his saddle, Chick commented, "Lord, I do so love this life."

"It has its attractions."

"The sun, the mesquite, the wind, the night sky," Chick recited. "A good horse under you and a good woman waiting for you to come back. Life doesn't get any sweeter than this."

"You've got it licked, big sugar," Lin praised him.

Chick grew thoughtful. "No one ever

holds high trump on life. The best we can do is keep the varmints at bay until our string plays out."

"Why, boss. I had no notion Old Man Taylor and you are related. You're as cynical as he is."

"I call it being realistic," Chick said. "Life is hard. Anyone who thinks different can't see the thorns for the roses."

Sleep came easily. Chick listened to the crackle of the fire as it died down and the distant wail of lonesome coyotes and eventually succumbed to slumber. By nature he was an early riser but Lin Cooley was up before him and already rekindling the fire. They drank coffee for breakfast and were in the saddle before a golden halo crowned the rim of the world.

By the third morning Chick regretted being so impetuous. He disliked being away from Dixie. Her smile, her touch, the feel of her at night, so warm and so wonderfully soft, were the tonic that put zest in his step.

The more Chick thought about it, the more he realized she had been right, as always. He *was* a better friend to Seth Jackson than Seth had ever been to him. Seth would never do what he was doing, were the situation reversed. But he was committed, and he would see it through to the end.

Lin seldom spoke unless Chick brought something up. It wasn't in the foreman's nature. Except when joking with his pards, Lin was a man of few words, and Chick respected that. The best ones, in his estimation, were always on the silent side.

Dixie would have talked Chick's head off. She could gab the ears off a spinster, and the funny thing was, Chick never minded. Most talkative types had him hankering for earplugs, but not Dixie. He could listen to her chatter for hours and it would roll off him like drops of water off a duck. Why that should be had always been a mystery — especially since, in his younger days, Chick could never abide a person who ran off at the mouth. It was amazing what love could do.

Lin was a dozen yards ahead when he unexpectedly drew rein and hung low off his saddle to study the ground.

"Found a prairie dog hole you admire?"

"Take a look at these tracks, boss."

Chick had been so preoccupied he hadn't noticed the hoof prints. "Cattle? Way out here? What do you make of it?"

Lin ranged in a wide circle that brought him back to Chick. "Five hundred head, or

170

thereabouts. They came from the north-west and were driven southeast." Lin pointed. "Toward Mr. Jackson's spread."

"It can't be strays," Chick said.

"Not likely it's his own beeves at all."

"Maybe he bought a herd up Kansas way," Chick suggested, "and his boys were bringing it in."

"Maybe," Lin said.

It bothered Chick. Bothered him a lot. The next afternoon, when they spotted several riders, he reined toward them and Lin instantly reined to his side. The riders saw them and stopped to wait.

Lin's eyes were better. "Bar J hands. That old cuss is Hap Evans. The block of gristle is Deke Scritch. I don't know the third."

Chick had met Evans a few times, a crusty goat who could hold his own with the Circle C's own crusty goat, Amos Finch, any day of the year. "How are things, gentlemen?" he greeted them.

"I declare!" Hap cheerfully exclaimed. "This is a surprise, Mr. Storm. And Lin, you rascal. It's been a spell since you visited."

"Is your employer to home?" Chick inquired.

Hap spat a stream of tobacco juice and

wiped the dribblings with a badly stained sleeve. "Sure is. He's been keepin' to himself a lot the past couple of months, more so since Joe and the boys were shot."

Chick leaned on his saddle horn. "How is Joe Elliot, by the way? Lin was telling me he was shot to ribbons."

"Pretty near," Hap said. "I never saw anybody take so many slugs and keep on breathin'. The doc took enough lead out of him to sink a steamboat. But Joe's on the mend, believe it or not. Another month or so and he'll be up and about. And rarin' for revenge, if I know him. He'll give that gun crowd their lumps. You wait and see."

Deke Scritch had a comment of his own. "How about it, Mr. Storm? Are you here to talk Mr. Jackson into showin' some backbone?"

"Sheath your tongue," Chick said sternly. "Seth Jackson never showed yellow his whole life. You shouldn't slander your employer like that."

Deke held both hands up. "No offense meant. But I'm not the only one who is wonderin' where his grit went. Five of our punchers have taken their pay and skedaddled just in the past week and there's talk more will do the same."

"It's as bad as that?"

172

"Worse," Hap Evans declared. "I've never seen Mr. Jackson so down at the mouth. If his missus were still with us, she'd have him chewin' nails in two shakes of a calf's tail. But . . ." Hap fell silent.

"Then it's good I've come when I have," Chick Storm said.

Chapter Fourteen

Lin Cooley didn't like it. He didn't like it one bit. An invisible storm cloud hung over the Bar J threatening to unleash a downpour at any second. Lin saw it in the tense faces of the Bar J punchers.

Seth Jackson had a reputation for being hard but fair. Everyone who rode for him was expected to do their full share of work, and then some. Lazy lie-a-bouts weren't welcome, the same as on the Circle C. Today, though, most of Jackson's hands were standing around doing nothing, something they would never do were their boss his usual self.

"I don't like this," Chick Storm said. "I don't like it at all."

Lin had seen a few outfits go to seed in his time. Top-notch outfits, too, with a sharp big augur and punchers who were weaned on cow's milk. As a general rule, once the slide started, it took an act of Nature to restore a ranch to its former glory.

"I need to talk to Seth alone," Chick said. "Occupy yourself as you please."

"How long will you be?" Lin asked. They had parted company with Hap at the corral, and now they came to a hitch rail near the broad porch that bordered three sides of the squat ranch house.

"I shouldn't be more than an hour, I should think. Then we'll head back."

"We're not staying the night?" Lin was surprised. They always had before, in order to be rested up for the start of the long ride home.

"We'll see," was all the further Chick would commit himself.

Lin was averse to parting company but he drifted to the bunkhouse to look in on Joe Elliot. The curtains had been pulled, and the other Bar J punchers were fighting shy of the ram pasture to give Joe the peace and quiet he needed.

Once Lin's eyes adjusted, he ambled to the far corner and roosted on the edge of the next bunk over. Joe was breathing heavily, a blanket pulled to his chin. Lin eased the blanket up high enough to see that Joe was one huge bandage from neck to crotch. As he lowered the blanket, Elliot's eyes snapped open.

"Damn. For a second there I thought

you were one of those French maids they have in New Orleans."

"You've been drinkin' alkalied water again," Lin said.

"It was a dream, you knothead. I was in a big white mansion with marble columns, and I was being waited on hand and foot by this maid who thought I was the handsomest cuss who ever put on britches."

"Was she drunk?"

Joe Elliot snorted, then coughed, then aired his lungs. "Damn you, Cooley! Don't you know better than to make me laugh? The sawbones warned I could rupture something if I wasn't careful."

"Other than your brain?" Lin said. "What were you thinkin'? Going against Ike Longley and that pack of short-trigger artists?"

"Longley?" Joe was flabbergasted. "Why am I always the last to know these things? I'm lucky to be kickin'."

"All your nine lives rolled into one," Lin agreed. "I feel bad about not throwin' in with you."

Joe's features were hard to read in the murk. "Don't go weak sister on me. I lit the wick. It was mine to do. Mine and those shot down with me." His voice faltered. "I'm too damn mouthy. I got those boys killed."

"You called it like you saw it." Lin let his friend compose himself, then commented, "There's talk that once you mend, you're fixin' on bellyin' up to the trough for a second helpin'."

"Not on their terms, I'm not."

"On *any* terms would be like grabbin' a riled painter by the tail and holdin' on for dear life. I'd be obliged if you wouldn't get rambunctious without notifyin' me first."

"Oh? You my nanny now?"

"I'm Chick Storm's nanny, whether he knows it or not. And this business will involve the Circle C if it gets worse."

"It might already," Joe said.

When the other foreman didn't explain, Lin asked, "Is this a private puzzle?"

Elliot turned his face to the wall. "I've blabbed too much as it is. Just don't let your guard down."

Lin stood to go. "You worry me."

"I aim to." Joe weakly raised a hand. "Thanks for stoppin'. I'll think about what you said but I ain't makin' any promises."

The sun was doubly bright, its glare doubly jarring. Lin squinted and moseyed to the corral where Hap Evans and half a dozen other cowpokes were frittering the time away. "Is hard work forbidden here?"

No one cracked a grin.

"Mind your own ranch, we'll mind ours," Deke Scritch said.

Lin resented being talked down to, and let it show. "I mind Mr. Storm's just fine, thank you."

Deke started to say more but Hap Evans slapped his arm and barked, "Behave yourself! Don't you know to be polite when company comes callin'?"

"I ain't lazy," Deke said. Hopping down from the top rail, he led his sorrel toward a water trough.

"You've got to excuse him," Hap told Lin. "He's afflicted by leaky mouth and there's no known cure."

"Short of a bullet," Toby Gill commented.

Lin turned to the cow prod. "So you're stickin' around after all?"

"Only until I get wind of something better or lead hornets take to buzzin' too close for comfort," Toby Gill said. "Cows are my life, not gun fannin'."

"I mentioned your visit to my boss," Lin informed him, "but we're full up. Could be a few of the boys will drift after the next roundup but I won't dangle an apple in front of your nose."

Hap Evans gripped Gill's arm. "Not you too, Toby? You're thinkin' of leavin' us in the lurch when Mr. Jackson needs every hand?"

"I repeat," Toby Gill said. "My life is cows. I don't hire out to gunfight and I won't look the other way when sunflowers migrate south."

"Hush," Hap said.

Toby Gill did no such thing. "We're not supposed to air our gripes. But maybe we should. We both know what will happen, and I don't care to be here when it does."

Lin had not been a cowman for so long for nothing. "Are you sayin' what I think you're sayin'?"

Hap Evans scowled. "Since when do you make it a habit to leap to conclusions? We're not sure. Not to where we would swear on the Bible. And to be honest, we'd rather not root around. We might not like what we find."

"Damn," Lin Cooley said.

The change in Seth Jackson was something to behold. He hadn't shaved in days. He hadn't combed his hair, either, and it stuck out at all angles. His clothes had been slept in, his shirt was unbuttoned. On the table in front of him was a bottle of whiskey, three-fourths empty, and a glass. He filled it to the brim, lifted the glass in salute, and said, "Here's to friends who show up out of the blue."

"I was worried," Chick said. "I heard about Joe."

"So you came all this way? I'm touched." But Seth did not sound touched. He drained the tarantula juice and poured another.

"A little early for that, don't you think?"

"Early?" Seth chuckled. "Hell, I had some for breakfast with my pancakes. Only I forgot to make the pancakes. You should try it. Starts the day with a real kick in the gut."

"What's gotten into you?" Chick had never seen his friend like this.

"They call it *life*." Seth gulped the refill dry and smacked his lips. "It snuck up on me when I wasn't lookin'."

Chick hadn't been asked to take a seat but he sat anyway. "No one will think less of you if you don't lead a charge into Nowhere. But if you do decide to even accounts, I'm here to let you know the Circle C will back your play all the way."

"Dixie gave her consent, did she?" Seth asked, and laughed.

"I don't much like bringing my wife into

this. I'll thank you to show a little more respect."

"Oh, please." Seth filled his glass again. "You don't sneeze without her say-so. I'm not sayin' it's wrong. I was the same way when Clara was alive. I loved her so much, makin' her happy made me happy."

Mollified, Chick reached for the bottle but Seth slid it out of his reach.

"No, you don't. You're not spoilin' my fun. If my company offends you, light a shuck for the Circle C."

"That was rude."

"Damn it, Chick. Can't you take a hint?" Seth was becoming mad. "I want to be alone. I want to wallow in my mistakes. I want to make myself as miserable as I can so when I look in the mirror I'm as miserable on the outside as I feel inside."

"Which mistake is this we're talkin' about? The only one I know of is your fondness for cards."

It was a mistake. Seth bristled and smacked his glass down on the table so hard, he spilled half of it. "Bound to bring that up, weren't you? The great man doesn't have weaknesses like the rest of us! Oh no! But he's sure not above grindin' our noses in the ones we have."

"Great man?" Chick said.

"Don't be modest. The Circle C is one of the best ranches in the territory. Maybe *the* best. Ask anyone."

"I don't like where this is leading."

Seth rose and walked to the window and leaned on the sill. "You shouldn't have come. The part of me you liked has been knifed in the back and buried by the part of me I never let you see."

Chick made another innocent comment. "Now you're talking nonsense."

Turning, Seth sat on the sill and folded his arms. "The great man knows everything, is that it? I open up to you and you think it's the bug juice talkin'."

"I'll make some coffee and we'll have you restored to your old sober self before supper," Chick proposed. "Then we can talk this Nowhere business over with clear heads."

"God, I hate you," Seth said.

Chick was too stunned to respond.

"You haven't listened to a word I've said. Not one word. You've got it sorted out in your head how things are and you can't see anyone else's point of view."

"You don't really hate me." Chick found his voice.

Seth came to the table, his eyes boring into Chick's. "Leave. Now. Before we reach the point of no return."

"I don't cut out on my friends when they need me," Chick said. "I wasn't kidding about the Circle C throwing in with the Bar J."

Straightening, Seth laughed. A short, cold laugh, more like a snarl, that ended with, "I never saw it plain until now. All these years you had me fooled. All these years of me lookin' up to you, and for what?"

"Seth?"

"I did, you know. Even though you're from the East and didn't know a bucket dogie from calf slobbers when you came out here, I always respected you. You learned fast, and you made the right decisions, and the Circle C prospered. And I thought to myself, 'What an exceptional hombre.' But you're not. You're ordinary. With no respect for anyone but yourself."

Chick was trying to keep his temper but the insults were piling one on top of the other and he was close to losing it. "I've always held you in the highest esteem, too."

"Strange you never mentioned it," Seth said. "But why should you when the Bar J has always been in the Circle C's shadow? Second fiddle is all we ever were. Second fiddle is all we'll ever be."

"I won't listen to this foolishness. I'm leaving." Chick stood and took several steps but suddenly Seth was in front of him. "Move."

"Not until I've had my say."

"You've said too much as it is." Chick put a hand on Seth's shoulder and lightly pushed but Seth knocked his arm away, and not lightly, either.

"You'll hear me out whether you want to or not. You wouldn't go when I asked you to so now you'll ride out the storm."

"You're drunk."

"So? Out of the mouths of drunkards come truths they would never say sober." Seth poked Chick in the chest. "Yes, I truly do hate you! You're too damned perfect. You don't have flaws like the rest of us."

Chick tried to go around but again Seth Jackson barred his way.

"I came to you for help, if you'll recollect. A little loan was all I needed. Enough to set me straight with that gambler."

"I couldn't," Chick said.

"Hell, no!" Seth spat. "Not for something as sinful as gamblin'! Not even for an old compadre!"

"Calm yourself. You get mad too easy."

Seth was twitching in fury. "I'm just overflowin' with flaws, aren't I? You never get mad, huh? You never admit to yourself that you're no better than the rest of us."

"Enough of this." This time when Seth tried to block him, Chick grabbed Seth's left arm, hooked a boot behind Seth's leg, and tripped him as slick as could be. Seth immediately went to rise but Chick stood over him with his fists clenched. "Don't you dare. I've taken all I'm going to take."

"Go ahead! Leave!" Seth barked. "You weren't there for me when I needed you, you uppity son of a bitch. So don't pretend you're here for me now."

Chick Storm walked on, but then paused to look back. "There's a line that should never be crossed and you've crossed it. Our friendship is over. It ends here. Don't ever set foot on the Circle C again."

The whole house shook when he slammed the front door.

Chapter Fifteen

Billy Braden strapped on his gun belt as he came out of a back room. Shasta called his name but he ignored her and jangled down the hall to the front of the saloon. The place was packed, as it always was these days, and liquor flowed by the gallon. All the seats at the card tables were taken, and Clell Craven and Jeb and Jed Ellsworth, who were pretty fair card slicks, were raking in pots from half-drunk and hugely inexperienced cowboys.

Billy shouldered to the bar and pounded it to get Dub Wheeton's attention.

The balding proprietor was a walking smile. "What will it be for you tonight, my young friend?"

"I ain't your friend." Billy set him straight. "Just give me a shot of rotgut and go count your money."

"Sure. Whatever you say."

Billy took a sip and turned. It delighted him, the greedy fool being so afraid. Suddenly someone jostled his shoulder, jarring him so hard he nearly spilled his whiskey. "Watch where you're going, you damned jackass!"

The cowboy responsible was barely old enough to shave. "Sorry, mister."

"I should put windows in your skull." Billy refused to let it rest.

"I said I was sorry," the cowboy repeated, and then tried to be friendly. "I'm fresh in off the range. From the Slash Creek outfit, way off southwest of here. Have a week to myself, and I heard tell they have some sportin' girls in this town."

"You're an idiot," Billy said. He would have said more but Black Jack had been watching and called out his name and motioned. "But you're a lucky idiot. You get to live." He swaggered to the corner table but didn't sit. "What is it now?"

Black Jack, Ike Longley, and two other members of Black Jack's gang were playing poker. Black Jack asked for two cards before flicking his dark eyes at Billy. "Is it me or are you on the prod? Again?"

"What if I am?" Billy retorted.

"No one gets shot without my say-so," Black Jack reminded him. "We have a good thing going here. Anyone who spoils it answers to me."

Billy had a sharp reply on the tip of his

tongue but he bit it off. "I'm just tired of hangin' around this dump."

"You can always go help ride herd on the cattle," Black Jack suggested.

"Cow shit ain't my idea of a bouquet, thank you very much."

Another member of their outlaw fraternity, Zech Frame, grinned and winked at the others. "Why would the kid want to watch over four-legged heifers when he's got a two-legged heifer right across the street?"

Frame would never know how close he came to having whiskey flung in his face and being gunned in his chair. But Billy didn't dare. Not with Black Jack right there. Not to mention Ike Longley. Billy was confident he could beat Black Jack but he didn't stand a prayer against the Texas hellion. "When I want your opinion of my personal life, I'll ask for it."

Zech Frame glared and started to slide his chair out.

"Enough," Black Jack snarled. "I swear. If I wanted to put up with bickerin' brats, I'd take me a wife and do it right. Zech, you simmer down. And Billy, you're off the prod, as of now. Go stick your head in a water trough and cool off."

Billy only made it halfway across the

room when he was intercepted by Shasta, whose expression was like that of a puppy who had been kicked.

"Why did you run off like that?"

"Did you expect me to write a thank you note?" Billy tried to go around her but she clung to his arm. "Let go."

"What's gotten into you? You're treating me worse and worse all the time. What did I do?"

"You haven't done nothin'." Billy tried to pry her fingers off but she could be persistent when she wanted.

"It's her, isn't it? Something about her is eating at you and you're taking it out on me." Shasta's fingers tightened. "Forget about the blonde. I'm the only woman you'll ever need. Take me away and I'll prove it."

"Listen to yourself," Billy said in disgust. "As if I'd tie myself down with the likes of you." He shoved her and barreled outside and was on the boardwalk sucking in the cool night air when he realized he still had the glass of whiskey. Upending it, he threw the glass against the wall and it shattered into shards. He was madder than ever and wanted to kill something. But he couldn't. And that only galled him even more.

The lights were on in the general store.

George Palmer stayed open late most nights now to accommodate the influx. Word had been spreading. Nowhere was now a smaller version of Beaver City. It wouldn't stay small for long, though. In the past three months it had acquired close to twenty new residents and two new businesses, and there was talk of a hotel springing up.

Billy hitched at his gun belt and crossed the street. George was behind the counter, waiting on an old man. Helen was busy with the old geezer's wife. Both smiled at him, and all he could think about was how much he yearned to pistol-whip them to bloody pulps.

"Howdy, William," George Palmer said. "She's in the back, if you want to go on in."

"I surely do," Billy said politely. His nightly visits had given him the run of the place. He found their trust amusing.

Helen came over and put a hand on his shoulder. She did that a lot. "I should warn you. Sally isn't in the best of moods. She's been irritable all day."

"I'm on the peckish side myself," Billy admitted.

"Be gentle with her," Helen advised. "Women have their moods, you know. Half

190

the time we can't control them."

"You're a peach, Mrs. Palmer," Billy said, and pecked her on the cheek. She liked when he did that. He could tell.

"Go on back," Helen coaxed. "The last I saw her, she was in the parlor, reading."

"She does too much of that," was Billy's assessment.

But Sally wasn't in her favorite chair, she was at the window. She didn't turn when he entered, merely saying, "Good evening."

"Is that any way to greet the love of your life?" Billy came up behind her and put his hands on her waist. "Give your man a kiss, hon."

Sally complied, but her fingers on his shoulders were stiff, and Billy sensed a certain aloofness. "What's wrong? Your ma says you've been mopin' around."

"My mother talks too much," Sally said. Disentangling herself, she moved to her chair. "Have a seat." She pointed at the sofa.

Billy patted the cushion next to him. "Come join me so we can snuggle."

"I'd rather talk."

"Uh-oh," Billy said.

"Be serious." Sally studied him with a newfound intensity. "We've been seeing each other for months now, and what has

191

come of it? Other than you pawing me every night and trying to get up my dress?"

Billy had never heard her talk like this before. "Whoa there. What's gotten into you? I'd expect talk like that from those saloon tarts but never a lady."

"Speaking of which," Sally said, "word has reached me that you've been seeing one of those tarts, as you call them, behind my back. Is that true?"

Billy was on his feet with his hand hovering over his Colt before he realized what he was doing. "Who told you such a baldfaced lie?" Sheer rage pulsed through him. "Give me their name and they'll be dead within the hour."

"It's not true, then?"

"Of course not. I go to the saloon for a few drinks and cards, but that's all. I promised you I'd be true and I have been." Billy sat back down but his blood continued to boil. "Who told you?"

"That's not important." Sally made a teepee of her hands. "What is important is that when we first met, you went on and on about how different you are from Randy Quin. About how you'd never keep a girl like me dangling. That when you saw something you wanted, you went right out and took it."

"So?" Billy was uncertain what she was getting at.

"So it's been months and I'm still not engaged. I thought you loved me. I thought you wanted to live the rest of your life with me. Or so you keep saying."

"And I mean every word. But we can't rush things."

"Randy Quin wasn't much for rushing, either, and look at where it got him," Sally mentioned. "I took a shine to you partly because you're forthright. You make up your mind quickly about things."

Billy dearly wanted to talk about something else. He hated it when women nagged. "Right now I've made up my mind to take you for a moonlit walk."

"That's all you ever think about," Sally complained. "But I'm not going anywhere until we've hashed this out."

Billy liked how her dress clung to her legs when she crossed them, particularly the swell of her thighs. "You want me to get down on bended knee?"

"Do you plan to one day? Really and truly?"

"How many times must I say the same thing?" Billy responded. "The only reason I haven't proposed yet is that I wanted to surprise you by winnin' enough at cards for us to buy our very own house. You'd like that, wouldn't you?"

"More than anything," Sally said. "But one step at a time. First we get engaged, then we have the wedding. The house can wait until after. My parents will let us live with them a while."

It would be hard for Billy to think of anything less appealing. "How about that walk now?"

Sally sighed, then rose and smoothed her dress. "I suppose if I don't, you'll pester me like you always do. But you're to behave. You hear me?"

Eagerly bounding to her side, Billy impishly asked, "Don't I always?"

"No. You don't. And your hands are becoming friskier by the week." Sally held out hers so he could take it, and when he pulled her close, she whispered, "I want you so. I really do. But I have my reputation to think of."

"How would givin' in to the man you're going to marry be bad?"

"Do you have any idea what my parents would say if they found out my virtue was no longer intact?"

Billy had never heard it referred to that way before, and he broke out cackling. "Your mother's virtue isn't intact. Why should they care if yours is?"

Sally put a hand to her throat, then

shared his mirth. "I swear! You come out with the most scandalous notions! My father would shoot you for saying a bawdy thing like that."

"I'd like to see him try."

"Temper, temper," Sally teased.

The instant they were outside and Billy had shut the door, he kissed her, hard. His long-suppressed hunger bubbled and frothed inside of him like scalding water in a pot, and he came near to tearing off her clothes and having his way right there.

"Oh, Billy," Sally breathed when they parted for breath. "You make my head swim when you do that."

"I'd like to do a whole lot more."

Sally giggled. "I bet you would."

Billy wrapped an arm around her slim waist and she put her head on his shoulder and they moved off across the prairie where they could be alone. Darkness mantled them like a blanket. "You know, a man can only hold so much in," he remarked.

"Do you think women don't have the same feelings men do?" Sally rejoined. "You think we don't have the same wants, the same needs?"

"Then why hold back?"

"I want our wedding night to be the night. So it will be special. So I'll remember it fondly the rest of my days. Is that too much to ask?"

Yes, it was, but Billy choked down his anger and led her farther from the store than they had ever gone. They walked until the buildings resembled small shacks and the tinny tinkling of the saloon's piano faded to silence. Then he faced her and roughly pulled her close.

"We should go back," Sally said.

"Not on your life. I have you all to myself and that's how I like it." Billy roughly glued his mouth to hers and let his hands roam, and when the kiss ended, she was breathing heavily and her hair was mussed.

"Enough. Please."

"No."

"Billy Braden, you take me home this instant." Sally took a step back. "You're becoming entirely too willful."

"I thought you liked me that way." Billy pulled her to him yet again and would not relent even when she pushed and squirmed.

"Stop that!"

"No."

Sally mewed like a frightened kitten and broke loose and tried to run but Billy grabbed her and threw her to the ground on her back. Before she could think to rise, he straddled her legs and pinned her wrists.

"I'll scream!" Sally warned.

"Go ahead. No one will hear. Even if they do, so what? I'll shoot anyone who butts in. That includes your folks."

"You wouldn't!"

Billy slid his hands to where he wanted them, one high, one low. "I'm through waitin'. I'm through pretendin'."

"Stop!" Sally swatted at his arms and sought to buck him off, fear gleaming in the whites of her eyes.

Rearing back, Billy cuffed her. Not hard enough to mark her but hard enough to jolt her, hard enough to get her attention. "You want it as much as I do. Nothin' you can say or do will stop it. So you might as well enjoy yourself." He tugged at his belt buckle.

Tears gushed, and Sally tried a final appeal. "I beg you! Don't. Not like *this*. Wait until we're married."

Billy had had enough. "You dumb cow. I wouldn't marry you for all the gold in the Rockies." He hiked her dress higher. "This is all I've ever wanted. And now I mean to have it."

Chapter Sixteen

Randy Quin was a monument to misery. He went about his daily work wearing the face of a man sentenced to swing on the gallows. He never smiled, never grinned, never spoke unless spoken to. It got so, Amos Finch commented to Lin Cooley, "If I hear him sigh one more time, I'll shoot him."

On a hot, dusty weekday, the Circle C foreman and his partner were scouring heavy brush in the southwest section of the ranch, searching for strays. It was tough, tiresome work. The thickets were thorny mazes that posed a constant threat to horse and rider alike. Both Lin and Randy wore chaps and had their ropes in their hands.

After rounding up nine steers before noon, Lin drew rein to rest their horses. "You know, if your chin were any lower it would scrape the ground."

"Don't start," Randy said. "It's bad enough I have to put up with grousin' from everybody else. You'd think the sun rose and set on my say-so."

"You've got to admit you haven't exactly been a jackrabbit of late," Lin said, and came right out with it. "Five months is a long time to mope."

"You've been in love. You know how it feels." Randy let out with one of those sighs that were driving Amos Finch to distraction. "I reckon I'm the laughingstock of the whole territory."

"Not yet. Men who have been through what you did know it's no laughin' matter, and those that haven't don't think it's funny because they don't want it to happen to them." Lin took out the makings and commenced to roll a cigarette. "But if you keep on sulkin', you're in danger of being branded daunsy."

"I can't help feelin' like I was stabbed in the gut."

"No man can," Lin said. "But maybe it's time to pull the knife out, sew up the wound, and get on with your life."

"How do I perform this miracle?" Randy demanded. "Short of stickin' a pistol in my mouth and squeezin' the trigger?"

"Go see her."

Randy hooked a leg over his saddle horn. "It's finally happened. The strain of ramroddin' has gotten to you. You've gone loco."

"Tell me you don't want to," Lin challenged him. "She's all you think about. All you dream about. You can't look at the sky without seein' her face. If it weren't for your pride, you would have gone in to see her long ago."

"I've no hankerin' to make a fool of myself."

"You never know," Lin said. "Maybe she's changed her mind. Women are right fond of doing that."

Randy shook his head. "It's been pretty near half a year. She's forgotten about me. Last I heard, she was seein' that Braden character every damn night. I'm surprised they're not hitched."

Lin struck a match and took a few puffs. "That should tell you something. If it was serious, he'd have proposed by now." He blew a smoke ring. "Something you should know. The word is that he's stopped seein' her. The boys say he spends all his time at the saloon nowadays. They never see him over to the general store."

"Oh?"

"You need to do *something*," Lin said. "The plain truth is, the boys are tired of your mopin'. Kip Langtree says you're worse than his sister. And Charley Lone is ready to slip rat poison in your food."

"It's that bad?" Randy had no idea.

"*You're* that bad," Lin corrected him. "So go to her. Talk to her. Get it settled once and for all."

"There's nothin' to settle," Randy said.

But when the weekend came and Chick Storm gave his consent for as many punchers as wanted to go paint the town, Randy was first in line at the washbasin. Most of the punchers were bound for Beaver City to hear Lilly Nightingale, a singer fresh in from Denver. Since Lin had to stay and go over the latest tally with their employer, Randy figured he would have to ride in alone, until Kip Langtree and Moses Sikes mentioned that they were bound for Nowhere, too.

"Agnes Wilson is to blame," Kip said.

"You're in love with a married woman old enough to be your mother?" Randy remarked, with a wink at Moses. He had found his sense of humor and was honing its edge.

"Go sit on a rattler," Kip said. "It's those pies of hers. She makes them like my ma used to."

Randy's nerves were a wreck. The whole ride in, he couldn't stop thinking about Sally, about how much she once meant to him — and still did. He had tried to forget about her and get on with his life. But like a burr stuck to his clothes, he couldn't be shed of her, no matter how hard he tried.

"Remember the speech Lin gave us," Moses commented when Nowhere appeared in the distance. "We're to keep our revolvers holstered and be on our guard."

"Unless my pie attacks me, I'm safe," Kip Langtree said.

The buildings took shape, and with them the horses at the hitch rails and the people roving the street.

Now that the moment was almost upon him, Randy was having second thoughts. Sally had made her sentiments plain. She might laugh in his face, might denounce him right there in the store in front of others. His sense of shame was bad enough without adding to it. Another lance to the heart would about do him in. Right then and there he almost reined around. Only the presence of Kip and Moses stopped him.

Randy was so worried, he thought for sure people would point at him as he rode by and whisper and laugh. But no one paid him the least little attention. There were a lot of new faces, townsmen and cowhands alike.

Kip and Moses were hankering to visit

the restaurant but Randy went on to the stable so he had an excuse to pass the general store. A glance showed the store was doing brisk business. He caught a glimpse of Sally's father and mother but not Sally.

"Well, look at what the barn owl dragged in," Old Man Taylor greeted him. He was whittling and rocking, as perennial as the dust. "You surprise me, boy."

"I surprise myself." Randy stayed in the saddle. "There's been a lot of changes."

"Too many," Old Man Taylor said. "A crow my age gets set in his ways. He doesn't like the nest rebuilt."

"Any gossip worth sharin'?"

The stable owner crooked an eyebrow. "Particular or general?"

"General will do," Randy said.

"Well, let's see." Taylor scratched his chin with the point of his knife. "Dub Wheeton is thinking of sending for a mail-order bride. Now that he's a man of substance, he's been bragging how he can afford one."

"He's been linin' his pockets, has he?"

"It's those hens Shelton brought in. Every gamecock for a hundred miles has to come and stroke their feathers. Some lose their gumption and content themselves with buying the ladies drinks and sniffing their lilac water." The stableman chortled. "It's downright pitiful what we'll stoop to where women are concerned."

"Thanks." Randy took that as a personal slight.

"I didn't mean you, for God's sake. I admire how you handled the situation. Being bucked like that for a flashy no-account must have stung considerable."

"We were talkin' gossip."

"That we were." Old Man Taylor gestured toward the blacksmith shop. "Svenson nearly got into a fight with one of the new crowd. A mouthy maggot by the name of Dingus Mechum wanted his horse shoed but wouldn't pay full price. Mechum had a hand on his six-shooter and Svenson was holding that big sledge of his when Marshal Lunsford happened by and broke it up."

"Anything else?"

"Seth Jackson was in here a week ago and damn near drank himself under the table. First time he's ever done that, to the best of my recollection."

Randy made a mental note to tell Lin when he got back. "That's surprisin'!"

"Not nearly as much as who Seth was drinking with. Jack Shelton."

Another tidbit for Randy to relay. "Well,

I reckon I'd better leave you to your carvin'."

"There's one thing yet might interest you," Old Man Taylor said.

When it was not immediately forthcoming, Randy said, "Are you waitin' for winter?"

"No. I'm watching the Renfro woman cross the street."

Randy saw her, and snickered. "You need spectacles. Her backside is as broad as a barn."

"Some of us like barns." Old Man Taylor watched until Mrs. Renfro went into the barbershop. "Anyway, I see a lot sitting here. I know the comings and goings and habits of everyone. I know, for instance, that Agnes Wilson sweeps the boardwalk in front of the restaurant each morning promptly at six. I know that Dub empties the spittoons at seven. That Lafferty has a weak bladder and makes ten trips to the outhouse a day."

"I needed to know that?"

"What you need to know is that day after day, week after week, I saw Billy Braden strut across the street to visit the Palmers. He never missed a day until a couple of months ago. Then he stopped."

"So it's true," Randy said, hope flaring

anew. "You're sure he hasn't been going over lately?"

"Not unless he's doing it in the middle of the night when I'm sawing logs," Old Man Taylor said. "And here's another nugget. I haven't seen Sally Palmer in weeks."

Randy thought his heart stopped. "She's left town?"

"No, you infant. She never steps foot outside anymore. I used to see her taking walks and shaking out rugs and the like, but she's become a hermit."

"That's mighty strange."

Old Man Taylor picked up his folding knife and the block of wood. "I'm plumb talked out. Visiting with you is a trial for my ears. So scat."

Grinning, Randy wheeled his horse and rode to the general store. His grin quickly died. He almost went past the hitch rail, but reined up and alighted.

George Palmer was totaling a customer's purchase. Helen Palmer was showing a bolt of cloth to Svenson's wife, Greta. Other people were browsing.

Squaring his shoulders, Randy looked straight ahead and walked to the shelf lined with canned goods. His jingling spurs gave him away, and to his immense consternation, Helen Palmer squealed and flew toward him like a hummingbird toward a feeder. He was even more bewildered when she wrapped her arms around him as if he were her long-lost kin.

"Randall! How great to see you again! Let me look at you." Helen stepped back. "Why, you haven't changed a bit."

"Folks generally don't at my age," Randy mumbled for lack of anything better to say.

The next moment George Palmer was there, pumping Randy's hand and clapping him on the shoulders. "You're a sight for sore eyes, son. You stayed away entirely too long."

"It wasn't my idea," Randy said, and their smiles froze on their faces.

"Well, yes, there's that." George coughed and frowned. "Things happen. But the important thing is that you're here."

"I want to buy a can of peaches."

"Peaches. Sure." George selected a can and plopped it on the counter. "Our treat. How would that be?"

Randy produced his money. "I pay my own way, thanks." Flustered by their antics, he took the can and turned to go, then remembered why he was there.

"Surely you're not leaving already?" Helen Palmer saved him. "Sally will be heartbroken if she finds out you stopped by and didn't say hello."

"Go on back," George urged. "Stay as long as you want."

There was something about the way they stared that sent a ripple of unease down Randy's spine. "Thanks," he said. His courage nearly failed him as he walked down the hall. But he had made up his mind to see it through, and that's what he would do.

The living room was dark as night. The curtains had been drawn and none of the lamps were lit. A familiar silhouette filled a chair by the mantel. Her head was bowed, the luster of her golden tresses dulled by the gloom.

"Sally?" Randy said, taking off his hat.

Sally's head snapped up and she started to rise but then she just as quickly sank back down. In a small, trembling voice, she said, "Randy? Is it really you?"

"As real as I get." Randy moved toward a lamp. "Why don't I light one of these so we can see each other?"

"No!" Sally's shout was more like a scream. "Please! My eyes have been bothering me. I'd rather it stay like it is."

"Whatever you want." Randy moved closer. "Have you been to the doctor in

Beaver City? How bad are they?"

"They'll be fine. It's nothing to fret about."

Randy longed to see her face. "How have you been otherwise?"

"I can't complain."

"How are things with him?" Randy had to find out. The suspense was tearing him apart.

"It didn't work out," Sally said in a subdued tone. "He and I have gone our separate ways."

Randy almost said, "I'm sorry to hear that," but caught himself. "I think of you now and then," he told her, and wanted to kick himself. He thought of her all the time.

"And I think of you. Of how I wronged you."

"You didn't —" Randy began.

"Don't!" Sally interrupted. "Let's not sugarcoat it. What I did to you was terrible. Completely and utterly unforgivable. For what it's worth, I'm deeply, sincerely sorry."

Her words pumped new life through Randy's veins. He took another step and reached out to touch her.

"That's close enough."

Randy honored her request even though

he yearned to take her into his arms. "How about if I sit on the sofa and we talk a spell?" Taking it for granted she would agree, he moved toward it.

"No."

"Then how about we go eat at the restaurant later today?"

"I can't."

"Maybe you'd like a buggy ride," Randy desperately suggested. As he recollected, she adored buggy rides.

"I can't do that, either. I'm sorry. It's best if we don't see each other ever again."

"Oh." Randy twisted his hat into a knot. "I thought maybe —"

"You thought wrong."

Randy spun and got out of there. His worst fear had come true. She called his name but he had made a big enough fool of himself. A red haze filled his vision, and he was through the store and out in the street before his mind caught up with his legs.

"Randall?" Helen Palmer called.

Unwrapping the reins, Randy stepped into the stirrups. His neck felt hot and he couldn't wait to get back to the Circle C. Whatever Sally and he had was gone for good. It was about time he accepted the fact. A jab of his spurs, and off he rode.

He only looked back once.

Chapter Seventeen

Marshal Paul Lunsford started the day with five cups of piping hot black coffee. He shaved, used the washbasin, and combed his hair. Taking the broom from the corner, he swept out his office and opened the window to air out the liquor smell. He had cleaned his white hat and black suit the day before. After he dressed, he went to the gun cabinet. His scattergun was dusty from disuse. He cleaned it, then opened the top desk drawer and took out a box of shells. A handful went into his vest. Two more went into the scattergun.

It was early morning and Nowhere lay quiet. Store owners were opening up and Svenson was firing up his forge.

Lunsford saw Old Man Taylor come out of the stable and sit in his rocking chair. The scattergun in the crook of his left arm, he walked over. "Morning."

Taylor was eyeing his suit. "Is it Sunday and I've lost track?" He snapped his fingers. "Oh. That's right. We don't have a church."

"I thought it wouldn't hurt to spruce up," Marshal Lunsford said.

"Has an elderly widow moved to town? Or a pretty spinster maybe?" Taylor pretended not to hear. "You could walk down the aisle in duds like that."

"I need a favor."

"So long as it doesn't involve lending money, I'm all ears." Taylor groped in a pocket for his folding knife and opened it.

"I want you to keep me informed on the comings and goings of Black Jack Shelton and his crowd."

Old Man Taylor took a plug of tobacco from his breast pocket, offered it to the marshal, and when Lunsford shook his head, Taylor bit off a piece and chewed a while before asking, "What are you up to, Paul?"

"My job."

"Ever hear of going up against a stacked deck?"

"I have my equalizer." Lunsford patted the scattergun.

"You don't have eyes in the back of your head. And unless you've forgotten how to count, there are a lot more chicken hawks than one rooster can deal with."

"Will you or won't you?"

Taylor shrugged. "I do it anyway."

"Thanks." Marshal Lunsford went up the street to the saloon. It, too, was uncommonly quiet. Dub Wheeton was drying off the bar and the Renfro boy was sweeping. Only one table was occupied, by the very man Lunsford wanted to see. He walked over and said without preliminaries, "I want you to leave town."

Black Jack Shelton looked like he had just woke up. His hat was pushed back on his head and his eyes were half open and he was starting his day with a glass of whiskey. He woke up fast, though, and set down the glass. "I must be hearin' things."

"Leave by noon," Lunsford said. "You and all your vultures."

"Well, now. This is interestin'. You didn't drink all your backbone away like I figured." Black Jack pushed a chair with his foot. "Have a seat. Let's talk about this."

"There's nothing to talk about." But Marshal Lunsford sat. He placed the scattergun across his lap and molded his left hand to the hammers and the triggers.

"Nice cannon you've got there. Ben Towers favors a cannon, too, only his is longer." Black Jack grinned. "Care for a drink? On me?"

"All I want is you and your kind gone from my town."

"When you bite into a chunk of meat, you don't let go," Black Jack said. "Did I break some law? Or did one of my boys get out of line?"

"I know who you are."

Black Jack did not act surprised. He tilted his chair back. "You're definitely not the walkin' whiskey vat some claimed. How long have you known?"

"Since the day you showed up."

"And you waited all this time to put on your Sunday-go-to-meetin' clothes and march in here and pretend that badge means something?" Black Jack's dark eyes twinkled with amusement.

"So long as you behaved, I couldn't do anything. Texas and Kansas and Oklahoma Territory statutes don't apply here."

"Then what's changed?"

"I found out about the Bradshaws."

"Who?"

Lunsford would swear the outlaw didn't know. His brow knitting, he said, "Farmers. A man and his wife on their way from Wichita to Amarillo in a covered wagon. They disappeared."

"Ah. And you think I had something to do with it?" Black Jack shook his hairy head. "I didn't."

The lines on Marshal Lunsford's forehead deepened. "You sold a Conestoga to George Palmer."

"That I did."

"That wagon belonged to the Bradshaws. I've been in touch with their brother. He described some of their belongings, and they match what you sold to George Palmer."

"The Conestoga wasn't mine. I admit it."

"You do?"

"But I had nothin' to do with what happened to the Bradshaws. They were dead long before I laid claim to their effects."

Lunsford was a fair judge of when someone was telling the truth and when they were lying, and damned if he didn't think Black Jack was telling the truth. "What happened to them, then?"

"You'd have to ask them and right about now their bones are bleachin' white out on the wasteland."

"Whether you killed them or not isn't the issue anyway," the lawman said. "I still want you out of town."

"No."

Marshal Lunsford shifted the scattergun so the twin muzzles were pointed squarely at Black Jack's barrel chest. "It's not like you have a choice."

"On the contrary." Black Jack was smug as ever. "I have all kinds of choices. Three of them are behind you."

Slowly twisting. Marshal Lunsford saw Ike Longley, Ben Towers and Clell Craven. They had spread out to have clear shots and make it that much harder for him to slip past them.

"I have sixteen choices in all," Black Jack boasted. "Each one a trigger waitin' to be squeezed."

"That was a threat."

Black Jack lowered the front of his chair to the floor. "I'm not that childish, Marshal. I never bluster. I just say how things are." He drummed his fingers on the table, then said, "How about if I explain how things are with you?"

"I'm listening," Marshal Lunsford said. He couldn't keep an eye on Black Jack and the three killers at the same time so he concentrated on Black Jack.

"You want to throw a noose around my neck for the Bradshaws but for once I'm innocent. And the hell of it is, you believe me."

"If it wasn't you, then it was one of your curly wolves."

Black Jack shrugged. "I won't do your job for you. As for me, unless I step out of line here in Nowhere, there's not a damn thing you can do. You said it yourself. Laws elsewhere don't apply."

Marshal Lunsford couldn't hide his anger. "I'll find something."

"You're welcome to try." Black Jack laughed. "And when you do, put on those pretty clothes of yours and bring your cannon and look me up. I won't be hard to find. Neither will they." He motioned toward Longley and the others.

"You think you have it all worked out," Marshal Lunsford said as he stood. "But life has a way of tripping us up."

Black Jack raised his glass in sham salute. "Come again soon, you hear? Later in the day when the girls are workin'. I'll fix you up with one. Being as you're a cripple, we'll let you ride her for half price."

Their laughter followed Marshal Lunsford out. Fury rendered him blind to his surroundings and he collided with Dingus Mechum, who was on his way in.

"Watch where you're going, you gob of spit!" Dingus bawled. "I don't care if you are wearin' a badge. It doesn't give you the right to knock people over."

Any other time, Lunsford would have let it go. Not today. He rammed the scattergun's barrels into the pit of Dingus's stomach, and when Mechum doubled over, clipped him across the back of the head with the stock. The scrawny cutthroat wound up on his hands and knees, sputtering for breath. "Insult me again and you lose teeth."

For a few glorious moments Lunsford was twenty years old again. He was young and healthy and in his prime. Back before Gettysburg. Back when he was a whole man instead of a shattered replica. Back when he never took guff off of anyone.

People were staring but Lunsford didn't care. Let them jabber behind his back, he thought. Let them wonder if he was worthy of wearing the symbol of their trust. He would show them all.

Old Man Taylor hadn't moved from his rocking chair. "This day is starting out right entertaining. But from now on I wouldn't turn my back to that weasel, were I you."

"Saddle my horse for me."

"You're leaving town? I can't recall the last time you did that. Must be a special occasion. Mind saying why?"

"Yes." Marshal Lunsford hurried to the jail before he changed his mind and packed his saddlebags and rolled up his blankets into a bedroll. His roan was waiting when he came out. One-handed, he threw his saddlebags on and shoved the scattergun into his bedroll. Taylor stepped forward to help him mount but he shook his head. "I'm not an invalid yet."

"What do we do if there's trouble while you're gone?"

"Hide."

"Seriously," Old Man Taylor said. "Suppose someone is shot?"

"Bury them." Lunsford reined to the north.

"You should appoint a deputy. It isn't right for the town to be unprotected. Not with that wild bunch in our midst."

"I appoint you," Marshal Lunsford said in jest. "Until I get back, keeping the peace is your job."

"Me? I've never packed a gun. Pick Svenson. He's big and strong. Or Lafferty. He was a soldier in the war, wasn't he? Paul? Paul?"

Lunsford wasn't listening. He wanted to be shed of Nowhere, wanted to breathe air not fouled by the stink. For half a mile he rode at a trot, then slowed to spare the roan. It had been ages since he was in the saddle and he had forgotten how good it felt; the rolling gait of a good horse under him, the wind and the sun on his face, the feeling that he was master of his life's direction.

He had left early enough to arrive at the Circle C ranch house by sunset but he wasn't in any hurry to get back to Nowhere so he made camp several miles out, and that night the yip of coyotes lulled him to sleep instead of the tinny clink of a piano. He was on the go early and by along about nine several Circle C punchers spotted him and came to investigate. Once they were assured of who he was, they informed him that he had strayed west of where he should be. Kip Langtree volunteered to take him direct to the ranch house.

Lunsford hadn't been to the Circle C in years. Little had changed. The house had shutters now and there were more flower gardens and the canal had been expanded.

Only a few hands were around. The rest, Lunsford's escort explained, were busy scouring the length and breadth of the Circle C for cattle.

"It's not roundup time, is it?" Lunsford had never ranched but he knew enough to know there were two roundups, one in the spring when calves were gathered and branded, and another in the fall to collect beeves for market and brand any calves missed in the spring. Here it was October, well past the second roundup.

"It's a special gather the boss wants done," Kip Langtree said.

They were near the house and the man in question stepped out to meet them, his wife at his side. "Marshal Lunsford! This is unexpected. To what do we owe this visit?"

"Oh, honestly," Dixie said. "Your questions can wait. Our guest must be tired after his long ride." She came down the steps. "Paul, it's a pleasure to see you again."

Lunsford squeezed her hand and she led him inside and seated him at the dining room table near a wide window.

"Would you like some ginger beer? Or maybe lemonade would be more to your taste?"

"Water will do me fine. I don't want to put you to any bother."

Dixie grinned. "Lemonade it is."

Chick sat at the head of the table. "Don't feel put upon. She's been telling me what I want since I said 'I do.' "

Out in the garden a wren was warbling and over at the chicken coop hens were pecking in the dust. Farther off, cattle grazed.

"Is your foreman around?"

"Lin's off making a tally of our herds

and won't be back for days yet," Chick said. "Is there something I can help you with?"

"The night Joe Elliot was shot, I asked Cooley to talk to you. I never heard back, and I'd like to know why he didn't."

"He did," Chick said.

"Then why didn't you send word whether the Circle C will back me if I go up against Black Jack and his killers?"

"No answer was answer enough."

"So you won't help me?" Lunsford couldn't keep the accusation out of his tone. "You'll let Nowhere go to the mongrels?"

"The plain and the short of it?" Chick said. "It's not our fight. Nowhere let the vermin in. Nowhere should sweep the vermin out."

Lunsford flexed his good hand. "It's hard for me to sweep with one arm."

"Have you asked Seth Jackson for help?"

"Seth didn't ride in with guns blazing when Black Jack's lobos shot Joe Elliot and those other two Bar J hands," Lunsford mentioned. "I doubt he'll want to do it now that he gets to sit at Black Jack's personal table when he's in town."

Chick said, "It's come to that, then."

"They're on the best of terms. Once a

week Seth is in town, guzzling red-eye like a fish. He does more staggering than walking these days. The other night I saw him try to climb on his horse five times before he made it. I went over and suggested he stay in town and sleep it off. Do you know what he said?" Lunsford didn't wait for Storm to answer. "He said he didn't need help. That he could find perdition all on his own."

"He was a good man once."

"I can't think poorly of him, not when I had my own mouth glued to a bottle's teat for so long." Lunsford extended his arm. "Chick, I'll be honest with you. The Circle C is my last hope of cleaning the buzzards out."

"My men are punchers, not gunnies. I'd be getting a lot of them killed. My conscience won't let me."

"But it will let you sit here sipping lemonade while Nowhere sinks deeper and deeper into quicksand? What happened to the days when we were our brothers' keepers?"

"There are plenty of able-bodied men in Nowhere. Swear them in and give them guns and do the job yourselves."

"I'd be better off deputizing your cows."

Into the dining room came Dixie Storm.

"Here you go. With a spoonful of sugar."
She set a glass of lemonade in front of him.
"Is there anything else you need, Paul?"
"If you only knew."

Chapter Eighteen

The trouble started with two cowboys drifting north from Dallas. Pete Weaver and Arvil Bickam were on their way to Denver. Pete had come into some money when an uncle died and they planned to spend it making the rounds of every whorehouse in the Mile High City.

Along the way they heard about the three girls at Dub Wheeton's, so Pete decided a detour was in order. On a wild and festive Saturday night they arrived in Nowhere and immediately repaired to the saloon to wash down the dust of miles of travel. The place was packed wall to wall. Cowhands, drifters, townsmen, all drinking and playing cards and laughing and smoking. Men doing what men loved to do.

The three winsome forms moving among them were not having nearly as good a time. For Belle James, Susie Metzger and Shasta Cunningham, Saturday was the hardest night of the week. They didn't get a moment's rest from sundown until after midnight. When they weren't trolling the room encouraging customers to buy more drinks, they were in the back rooms. It was long, tiresome work, and by ten all three were dragging their heels — even the veteran of their trade, Belle James. She was at the bar when Pete Weaver and Arvil Bickam bought her a drink and proposed that she take both of them at the same time.

Belle shook her head. "The rule is one gent at a time, boys. Two or more always makes for grief, and that I don't need."

"But we're best friends!" Pete declared, clapping Arvil on the back.

"Hell, yes!" Arvil wholeheartedly agreed. "We partnered up five years ago and get along like two peas in a pod."

"I really can't," Belle said, with a glance toward the corner where Black Jack was engrossed in a card game.

Pete flashed a wad of bills. "We'll pay you twice the going rate. How would that be?"

Belle wavered.

"Three times the going rate!" Arvil offered. "And we won't tell a soul so you can keep the extra for yourself."

As larcenous as the next dove, Belle

caved. "I want the money in advance. And you two better not act up."

The last room on the right was the one Belle regularly used. She went right to the bed and began undressing. "Shuck them clothes, boys. I ain't got all night."

Pete and Arvil stood with their hats in hand, looking at her and at one another. Then Pete whooped and sprang but Arvil snagged his arm.

"Hold on. Who says you go first?"

"It was my idea," Pete said, tugging loose.

"So? I think we should flip for the honor. I don't much like having another man's leavin's."

"What difference does that make? I'm your pard, aren't I?" Pete reminded him. "It ain't like she's corn on the cob."

"I still think it's fairer if we flip," Arvil insisted. He dug a coin from his pocket. "Heads or tails?"

"Neither. I still think I should go first. It's my money payin' for this spree." Pete threw his hat on the bed and went to undo his belt.

"Hold on," Arvil said, stepping in front of him. "Just because it's your inheritance doesn't give you the right to take on airs. We've always shared and shared alike, haven't we?"

Belle James had her dress half off. It was sparse on buttons and stays so she could shed it like a second skin. "Enough silliness, you two. Make up your minds and get on with it."

Pete's jaw was thrust forward. "Now you listen here, pard. I aim to have her first and I'm going to have her first, and if you give me any fuss, you can forget comin' to Denver with me."

"That's the whiskey talkin'," Arvil said.

"No. It's me talkin'. I'm rarin' to take this gal and I don't much like you buttin' in."

Arvil thrust his jaw out. "All I'm doin' is sayin' we should flip a coin, damn it."

"I've changed my mind," Pete announced, pushing his friend aside. "Go get yourself one of the other girls. This one is mine."

"The hell you say."

"Quit cussin' at me," Pete warned.

"We cuss all the damn time, you jackass," was Arvil's response. He held the coin out. "Now do we flip or not?"

"Not," Pete said, and swatted the other's hand.

The coin sailed in an arc and fell onto the bed next to Belle James. She scooped it up, saying, "If you two don't quit your squabbling right this second, I'm not servicing either of you."

"No!" Arvil said. "It's not my fault he's being such a baby. Give me a minute and I'll talk some sense into him."

"Like hell you will." With that, Pete drew his revolver and shot Arvil Bickam in the stomach at a range of two inches.

At the blast Arvil staggered back, too shocked to do more than bleat. Pressing a hand to the wound and his smoldering shirt, he recovered his wits enough to blurt, "You knothead! You've done shot me!"

"And I'll do it again if you don't get out of my way," Pete said.

Belle James jumped up and backed against a wall. "No gunplay, boys!" she yelled. "No gunplay!"

"He started it," Arvil said, and drawing his own Colt, he shot Pete in the belly.

Jolted, Pete clutched himself and staggered into the hall. He snapped another shot at Arvil but missed.

By now shouts had arisen. Dub Wheeton came running from the front, an empty mug in his hand. "What is this? What is this?" he excitedly demanded. "I don't allow gunplay!"

"Allow this," Pete said, and snapped a

shot at him. The slug bit into the wall and Dub hastily retreated.

Out of the back room lurched Arvil. His shirt was stained red and he was huffing and puffing but he raised his pistol, thumbed back the hammer, and fired. He hit the ceiling.

"Damn you!" Pete said. "Quit shooting at me!"

"You started it!" Arvil repeated.

Pete staggered into the saloon. Men were scurrying to give him room, pushing and shoving in their haste to avoid taking stray lead. Pete waved his revolver at them and bellowed, "Out of my way, you mangy sons of bitches!"

Arvil came through the doorway, waving his own artillery. "This is a private spat! Anyone who butts in will regret it!"

Pete turned and fired at him and hit the jamb.

Arvil cursed and fired and a man across the room cried out, clutched his chest and pitched to the floor.

Over in the corner, Black Jack took a cigar from between his clenched teeth. "Those yacks are spoilin' my game." He nodded at Ike Longley, who rose and came around the table.

Pete aimed at Arvil but this time there

was a metallic click. "Damn," he said. "A misfire."

"Now will you listen to reason?" Arvil asked.

Longley stepped from the crowd with his hands on his Remingtons. His right arm blurred and a Remington spat smoke and lead and Pete Weaver melted in a heap with a hole between his eyes. Longley's other arm moved and the other Remington cracked and this time Arvil Bickam did a slow pirouette into eternity.

The gleaming Remingtons were twirled into Longley's studded holsters, and a collective sigh of relief was exhaled.

Then the batwing doors parted and in rushed Old Man Taylor holding an equally old squirrel rifle. "What's all the shooting about?" He spied the bodies and halted.

Ben Towers stepped from among the onlookers. "What's it to you, old man?"

"The marshal left me in charge while he's gone," Old Man Taylor said, and stepped to the mortal remains of Pete Weaver. "Who are these boys?"

"Who the hell knows?" someone said.

Dub Wheeton was wringing his apron. "One of them mentioned something about being from Dallas."

Old Man Taylor saw the third figure on

the floor. "Isn't that Sam Ketch from over to Bowdry? Why'd he get shot?"

"He made the mistake of standin' in front of a bullet," a drinker said, which sparked some laughs.

"What started it?"

No one could answer until Belle James stepped from the back. She had dressed and brushed her hair. "They were fighting over me."

Old Man Taylor examined the bodies. "They're all dead, sure enough. Three lives lost over a sage grouse. I guess it's fitting the Texas boys killed themselves."

"I killed them," Longley said.

"You?"

"He had to," Dub Wheeton said.

"No one is allowed to take the law into their own hands," Old Man Taylor said. "I'll have to ask him to come to the jail and stay there until the marshal gets back."

"Ask all you want," Longley replied. "It will never happen."

Old Man Taylor leveled the squirrel gun. "I'm afraid I must insist. I'll let you keep your guns and I'll make your stay at the jail as pleasant as I can."

Longley stood stock still. "Old man, you'd best think this out. I can draw and put two slugs into you before you squeeze that trigger. Take your antique and go back to your whittlin' and leave the law to the cripple."

"He asked me to do him a favor."

"Did he ask you to die for him?"

Black Jack's chair scraped as he rose. "Taylor, what in hell's gotten into you? Quit makin' a nuisance of yourself. Leave Longley with me. I give you my word he's not going anywhere. When the marshal wants him, he'll be here."

Old Man Taylor slowly lowered his rifle. "I reckon that will have to do. No hard feelings, I hope?"

Tension drained from the room and eager drinkers were bellying to the bar when Lafferty, the owner of the feed and grain, declared loud enough for everyone to hear, "I guess we have two sets of law in Nowhere. One for ordinary folks and one for gun sharks."

"That was uncalled for," Dub Wheeton said.

"Easy for you to say," Lafferty argued, "when they're the ones lining your pockets. You've forgotten you're a part of this community."

Black Jack came toward the center of the room. "I'd quit jabberin', were I you."

Lafferty had nearly drained a large glass

of rye. He shook it at Longley, saying, "Why should he be treated special? If I shot someone, no matter what the provocation, I'd be behind bars until my hearing."

Dub nervously put a hand on the thin man's shoulder. "Will you cut it out? The marshal will handle everything when he gets back."

"Don't patronize me," Lafferty said. "I have every right to speak my peace. I live in this town, don't I?"

"You should go home," Black Jack said.

"And you should realize there are some people you can't boss around. If I want to stay here drinking, I'll stay here and drink. You might intimidate these others but I'll never back down to the likes of you."

"What do you mean by that?"

Old Man Taylor stepped between them. "Lafferty, please."

"Someone has to say it." To Black Jack, Lafferty said, "Do you think we're blind? That we don't see what's been going on right under our noses? You've taken over this town to the point where you dictate how the law is applied."

Dub tried to push him toward the batwings. "You've had too much to drink. Go sleep it off."

"I'm perfectly fine. I've been saying all

along that Nowhere is no place for his ilk. We should run them out of town while we can still claim to have a shred of dignity left." Lafferty scanned his listeners. "Who's with me? Who thinks we should clean up Nowhere?"

No one spoke.

Black Jack put his big hands on his hips and laughed. "Looks to me like you're preachin' to empty pews."

Lafferty startled everyone by walking up to Black Jack and poking him in the chest. "Mock me all you want. But I brand you for the sinful oaf you are! And your scalawags as gunsmen scum!"

A hush fell. A hush so total, the ticking of the pedestal clock behind the bar was unnaturally loud.

"Get out of here." Dub tried one last time.

It was too late. Black Jack's right fist swept from his hip to Lafferty's jaw — a short yet immensely powerful blow that crunched Lafferty's teeth and lifted him off his feet to crash to the floor, unconscious. Black Jack raised a boot to stomp his face.

"Don't!" Old Man Taylor cried, and jerked his squirrel gun.

There was a sound like thunder and Thomas Taylor's chest exploded. Ben

Towers had fired a single barrel from his twelve-gauge shotgun into the stableman's back. The buckshot left a cavity the size of a cannon ball.

Black Jack was furious. "What did you go and do that for, damn it?"

"He was fixin' to drill you," Ben Towers said.

"He wouldn't have fired." Black Jack nudged the body with a boot and sighed. "Well, what's done is done. Clell, get a bunch of these boys to clear out the mess. The rest of you, the drinks are on me."

A chorus of whoops and cheers rose to the ceiling.

Chapter Nineteen

Marshal Lunsford still had half a mile to go when he heard gunfire — shot after shot, some singly, others in sporadic volleys. Alarmed, he brought his horse to a trot. He was a lot closer when he heard shouts and laughter. Closer still when he heard glass shatter.

The lawman couldn't hold the scattergun and ride at the same time, so he had to leave the scattergun in the bedroll for the time being even though every nerve screamed for him to arm himself. He slowed when he came within sight of those doing the shooting, then stopped entirely.

Sunset wasn't far off, and long shadows dappled Nowhere from end to end. Every hitch rail was filled. Other horses were bunched wherever there was space. It was the busiest Saturday yet, and a rowdy crowd of cowboys, numbering close to thirty, were drinking and hollering and firing their pistols in the air. As yet they hadn't noticed him.

Lunsford swung wide of town and passed behind the buildings on the east side of the street until he came to the stable. After tying his horse to a rail, he cat-footed to the front. The rocking chair was empty. "Tom?"

A partially whittled block of wood lay in the dust. So did the stableman's folding knife.

"Tom Taylor?" Marshal Lunsford entered the stable. "Are you in here?"

A pair of legs was sticking from a stall.

Hoping the old man was taking a nap, Lunsford edged closer. He thought there would be one body. There were four; Taylor and Sam Ketch and two men Lunsford never saw before. To go by the flies and the smell, they had been there all day, or longer.

Shock gave way to anger. Just then Lunsford heard footsteps, and dashing under the hayloft, he cocked his scattergun.

A hand poked inside the livery, then a head, and George Palmer asked, "Marshal? Are you in here?"

Marshal Lunsford showed himself.

"I thought it was you!" George was so happy, he gripped the lawman's good arm and pumped it. "You won't believe what we've been through! It's been hell! Pure hell, I tell you! We've all been afraid for our lives. To say nothing of the lives of our wives and children."

"Suppose you calm down," Lunsford said. He indicated the stall. "Start with them and fill me in."

"I don't know all the details," George answered. "There was shooting in the saloon the night you left. Taylor went running in, and then there was more shooting and after a while men came out carrying the dead."

"And since then?"

"Everything was all right until a few hours ago. Several drunks came out of Dub's and started shooting into the air and generally making nuisances of themselves. Svenson tried to get them to stop but they made him dance a jig by firing at the ground near his feet. When they tired of their sport he went back into his blacksmith shop and hasn't been back out since."

"What did the rest of you do? Wilson and Renfro and Lafferty and the others?"

"Lafferty is laid up. Something to do with a fistfight with Jack Shelton. I told you. We've been through hell."

"It ends now." Lunsford moved to where they had a clear view of the street. The cowboys were down in front of the restaurant, shooting holes in a water trough.

"My wife is terrified," George said. "She made me close the store. I was hiding behind the pickle barrel, watching, when you showed up."

"I want you to go to Svenson, Renfro and Wilson and have them meet me at my office in fifteen minutes. I'll arm and deputize you."

"Us?" George had the look of someone who had swallowed a cactus. "But we're not peace officers. I've never fired a gun in my life."

"Odds are you won't have to. Crowds are only as wild as their leaders. Once we arrest the ones causing the ruckus, the rest will disperse."

"You're asking too much."

Lunsford grasped Palmer's arm. "Damn it, this is your home, too. And I can't do it alone."

George backed toward the doorway. "That's what we pay you for. To stop things like this. I'm sorry. I would help you. Really I would. But I wouldn't be of any use. All I would do is get myself killed." He scurried to the general store.

The cowboys were having too much fun to notice.

Ducking out, Lunsford stayed close to the buildings until he reached the saloon. Only a handful were left. Among them, Black Jack and three of his underlings; Ben Towers, Clell Craven and Ike Longley.

"Look who's back, boys!" Black Jack declared. "Where have you been, Marshal? Word was, you pulled up stakes and skedaddled."

"I need deputies," Lunsford said.

The four killers looked at one another.

"You heard me," the lawman said. "I can try to restore the peace alone. But to avoid bloodshed it's best to have deputies backing me." Lunsford nodded at each of them. "I hereby appoint you four."

"Us? Deputies?" Black Jack threw back his head and roared. "Are you drunk?"

"It's in your best interests," Lunsford noted. "You want this town to grow, don't you? Most folks won't stay if there's no law and order. How long will Nowhere last without the general store, the blacksmith, and the restaurant? You'd have to ride clear to Beaver City for supplies."

"So?" was Ben Towers's response.

"Go peddle your patent medicine somewhere else," Clell Craven said. "We're not sippin'."

Longley didn't say a word.

But Black Jack did. He laughed and thumped the table and declared, "By God, you tickle me! You truly do! And you're right. A dead town ain't any use to me. So how about it, boys? Want to have a little fun?"

"Me a deputy?" Ben Towers said. "Now I've heard everything."

"Leave it to me." Longley rose and hitched at his gun belt and strode toward the batwings.

Marshal Lunsford hurried after him but couldn't match the tall man's stride and was a few steps behind when Longley moved to the middle of the street and advanced on the rowdy revelers. A few saw him and nudged others. Most were watching four inebriated cowboys ventilate the sign above the restaurant.

Black Jack, Ben Towers and Clell Craven tagged along, Black Jack chuckling and tittering like he was having the time of his life.

Longley was ten yards from the crowd when he stopped, his hands close to his Remingtons. About half were aware of him by now and had turned into a forest of human trees. The four cowboys emptied their revolvers and began to reload, and in the quiet that ensued, Longley said, "Enough."

Marshal Lunsford had never seen so much fear in so many eyes.

All but one of the four cowboys imitated a scarecrow. He had his back to Longley, and was the drunkest of the bunch. "Who said that?" he demanded, turning on wobbly legs. "We'll show you what we —" His mouth dropped open. "You! They told us about you!"

"Holster your hardware," Longley instructed them.

Every man who had his revolver out promptly obeyed.

"No more yellin', no more shootin'," Longley commanded. "You want to drink, you drink in the saloon. Anyone who objects, step up and say so."

No one stepped up.

"Scatter," Longley said.

They scattered — some to the restaurant, some to their horses, most toward the saloon.

Marshal Lunsford stepped to Longley's side. "I want to thank you. I could never have done that."

"You're right. You couldn't." Longley wheeled and stalked off.

Ben Towers was still incredulous. "I never thought I'd live to see the day when a lawman asked *us* for help. Too bad that old stableman wasn't more like you. I wouldn't have had to kill him."

"What?" Marshal Lunsford said.

"Maybe we should be deputies permanent," Clell Craven proposed. "That way no one would ever cause a lick of trouble."

"I like that notion," Black Jack said.

Marshal Lunsford pointed his scattergun at Ben Towers's belly. "Shed that shotgun. I'm placing you under arrest for the murder of Thomas Taylor."

The three killers instantly grew somber.

"What's this?" Ben Towers said. "What sort of game are you playin'?"

"My job." Marshal Lunsford thumbed back a hammer and they all clearly heard the distinct click.

"Careful with that thing," Ben Towers cautioned. "At this range you'll blow me in half."

"I use slugs," Marshal Lunsford said. They didn't blow a man apart like buckshot, but slugs allowed for greater range and still had enough wallop to knock a man down.

Clell Craven looked at Black Jack. "What do we do? Say the word and there will be one less cripple in the world." His gun hand was twitching but the scattergun prevented him from doing anything rash.

Black Jack asked, "Are you sure you want to do this, Lunsford?"

"Your man will have a fair hearing. In cases like this, we send over to Beaver City for Judge Arnold. He's the closest thing No Man's Land has to a circuit judge."

"I know who he is. He was a judge in Iowa or some such once, and he's always gabbin' about how No Man's Land needs law and order."

"He's also big on stretchin' necks," Clell Craven commented.

Ben Towers hadn't done as Lunsford directed and still held his shotgun. "You're not takin' me anywhere, tin star. Pull that trigger and I swear I'll pull mine before I go down."

"Then we both die." Lunsford set himself. "Which will it be? Jail for a while or a pine box for eternity?"

Towers looked at Black Jack. "If he kills me, empty your revolver into the bastard."

"No need," Black Jack said, abruptly smiling and at ease. "I want you to do as he says."

Towers blinked. "What in hell has gotten into you? First you let him deputize us. Now this?"

"He's right about both of you being blown to bits, and I don't want you dead.

245

Go with him," Black Jack said. "Everything will work out. You'll see." He took Towers's shotgun. "I'd take good care of your cannon."

Marshal Lunsford backed off a few steps. "I'm glad you're being reasonable." To Ben Towers he said, "Walk ahead of me and keep your hands where I can see them. My left arm might be useless but there's nothing wrong with my trigger finger."

"I'll remember this." Ben Towers headed for the jail. People stopped to stare but he looked straight ahead, his spine as stiff as a broom handle.

More of Black Jack's owlhoots were in front of the saloon. Zech Frame came to the edge of the street and put a hand on his hogleg but he didn't draw. Dingus Mechum looked fit to bust.

Marshal Lunsford didn't feel safe until he swung the jail door shut behind them. He ordered Towers into the cell, then closed the door and locked it. Placing the scattergun on his desk, he sat in his chair and reached for the drawer that contained his flask. But after staring at it, he slid the drawer shut again.

"What do you hope to prove?" Ben Towers was on the cot, one knee bent.

"Black Jack won't let anything happen to me."

"I keep telling you. It's my job."

"Do you really think the sheep in this town will give a good damn when you're feedin' worms?"

"They don't figure into it. I took an oath."

Several small boys had their faces pressed to the window.

"Get out of here!" Marshal Lunsford cried, and rose to shoo the sprites off. Up the street, Black Jack and Clell Craven were huddled with Zech Frame and Dingus Mechum.

"You had impressed me as savvy but I guess I was wrong," Ben Towers said. "When you're gone, I'll ask Black Jack if I can fill your boots. That would be fittin', don't you think?"

Marshal Lunsford moved to the bars. "How many men have you killed?"

"What's that got to do with anything?"

"I'm curious. Longley, Craven, Black Jack, you. I've never had to deal with killers of your caliber before."

"Killin' isn't anything we brag about," Ben Towers said. "It's just something we do when we have to." Towers removed his hat and rubbed his bald head. "The first was an uncle who abused my sister. The second was a man who tried to rob me. The third, a sheriff who tried to arrest me for the uncle." Towers placed his hat on his knee. "After that, I was branded for life."

"And the others?"

"Craven started out killin' darkies. His pa was a Confederate major who died in the war, and he hates them worse than anything. Black Jack shot a drummer when he was ten for money to buy gumdrops and he's been killin' ever since. Longley, I can't say. He never talks about his past."

"I wish you'd picked some other town," Lunsford said.

"Your only chance is to let me loose and light a shuck."

Marshal Lunsford stood and cradled his scattergun. "I have to see about some burials. Later I'll bring you supper from the restaurant."

"Don't bother being nice. It won't save you."

The street was quiet. The sun had gone down and lamps were being lit. Marshal Lunsford stayed in the middle of the sheet where he could see trouble coming. He doubted Black Jack would try anything so soon, but as he went about gathering townsmen to help load the bodies onto a buckboard, he felt a growing sense of fore-boding.

Barring a miracle, his days, if not his hours, were numbered.

Chapter Twenty

Another grueling day of searching the chaparral.

Lin Cooley and Randy Quin threaded through the dense brush with a skill that came of experience. Lin was in the lead, raking the ground for signs, the morning sun warm on his chest and legs.

"Are you sure this is the smart thing to do?" Randy Quin asked. "I can ride back and fetch some of the others."

"We need to know," Lin said.

"I still can't believe it. I never thought anyone would have the gall."

Glad he was wearing his buzzard wing chaps, Lin avoided thorns as long as his thumbnail. He rose in the stirrups but for as far as the eye could see there was nothing but brush, brush and more brush.

"How did they know to come this way?" Randy asked. "How did they know there would be a trail?"

"They made their own," Lin said. The chopped vegetation had been scattered about but the chopped ends were plain to see.

"As much work as it took," Randy said, "they'd have it easier raising cattle honest."

For the next hour they hunted in silence except for the plod of hooves and the creak of saddle leather. Then Lin rounded a stand of scrub oak and immediately reined up. Before them the brush had been cut and flattened to form a sizeable clearing. Beyond, a wide trail, pockmarked with tracks, led south.

"Here's where the cows were bunched," Lin deduced, "before they were taken." He made a circuit of the clearing, Randy close behind. "I figure seventy head, or thereabouts, and four riders."

"Only four?" Randy said. "Let's go after them ourselves then."

Lin smiled. "You're as fickle as a spinster. We'll report to the big sugar and let him decide. My hunch is he'll want to catch the whole outfit."

"You think there are more than four?"

"Could be," Lin allowed. "Let's follow a little ways and hope they change direction. If they don't, the boss will have even more cause to be upset."

Miles later the tracks were still pointing south. Reining up, Lin announced, "This is far enough. We'll go break the bad news."

"What is this world comin' to?" Randy asked.

"It's always worse when it's someone you know who strays too far over the line," Lin said.

It took most of the afternoon to reach the ranch house. Lin took his tally book and went up the steps and knocked.

Dixie came to the door with a pair of scissors and a comb in her hands. "I'm trimming his hair."

"I'll come back then."

"You'll do no such thing. His ears work just fine."

Chick was in a chair in the kitchen, stripped to the waist, a towel over his shoulders. "Do you have the final tally?"

"That and more," Lin said. "And you're not going to like it."

Dixie said, "Don't keep me in suspense."

Lin placed the tally book on the table. "The Circle C is missin' close to five hundred head. Most from south and east of the Coldwater. They use the heavy cover and move the cows at night. The last time was about a week ago."

"They take the cows south?" Chick asked.

Lin nodded.

Chick started to stand up but Dixie pushed him back down. "Sit still. The rustlers can wait until I'm done." She ran a comb through his hair and snipped with the scissors. "How will you handle it?"

"I'll go straight to Seth and demand he return the cattle or he makes restitution," Chick said.

"Hold still." Dixie cut close to his right ear. "That's not enough, Chickory, and you know it."

"What else?"

"Range law is plain. It's not written down in a law book but every rancher from here to the Rio Grande lives by it." Dixie shifted to trim his other ear. "Let him off easy and you lose respect. Worse, the Circle C will get a reputation as a weak-sister outfit and we'll have every brand artist in creation thinking they can help themselves."

Chick squirmed in his chair. "It wouldn't be as bad as all that."

Dixie stepped in front of him and wagged the scissors in his face, "Don't you dare. Didn't you learn anything when you were over there last? You said yourself that he told you he hated you."

"He was drunk."

Dixie put the scissors and the comb on

the table and clasped her husband's chin in her hands. "Listen to me, and listen good. You're the most decent man I know but you're too softhearted. Remember those squatters? You wanted to let them stay when that woman looked at you with tears in her eyes because they had eight or nine kids. I had to run them off myself."

"I remember," Chick said.

"And that time those old buffalo skinners helped themselves to four of our cattle and you were willing to let them off with a warning because they were half starved? I had to get the boys to make an example of them."

"Seth is a friend."

"Seth is a rustler."

"What you want me to do will mean the end of the Bar J."

Dixie straightened. "Would you rather it meant the end of the Circle C? Would you rather all our years of toil and sweat came to nothing?"

"Of course not," Chick responded.

"Then you have to be strong. You have to treat Seth Jackson like you would anyone else you caught stealing. Show the world that the Circle C protects its interests. At the end of a rope if need be."

Lin interjected his opinion. "I agree with

your missus, Mr. Storm. A ranch is like a man. Any sign of weakness and the buzzards will take that as a personal invite."

Chick had grown sullen. "I don't want his blood on my hands."

"It's not like it's the first time," Dixie said, "and it probably won't be the last either.

"So you get up and you get dressed and you send riders to bring in every hand who can be spared and then you go do what needs to be done." She stroked her husband's cheek. "Make me proud."

Chick went to fetch his shirt. Lin turned to leave but Dixie put a hand on his arm.

"What I said when you paid Jackson a visit last time goes double now. Don't let anything happen to my man."

"I'll do my best, ma'am."

"All my friends call me Dixie."

By noon the next day twenty-two riders were set to follow Chick Storm into the fiery pits of hell if need be. Another eleven were due to show up before the day was done but Chick refused to wait. "They can catch up," he told Lin Cooley. "Randy will stay and bring them to that clearing you found. They can follow our trail from there."

"The more guns we have, the better," Lin said.

"If twenty-two of us can't whip a bunch of brand blotters, we deserve to come back with our tails between our legs." Chick addressed the others. "All of you know about the rustling. All of you know what's at stake. But no one is to shoot unless I give the say-so. Is that understood?"

At their collective nods and yells of assent, Chick smiled at Dixie and touched his hat brim, then brought his bay to a trot.

Lin wasn't fond of the idea of leaving before the rest of the Circle C punchers showed up but he was foreman and he was paid to back his employer. That night he saw to it that the horses were picketed and sentries were posted. When he returned to the campfire, Chick was nursing coffee and gazing morosely into the crackling flames.

"I hate this. Hate it more than I can say."

"We have it to do," Lin said.

"I know, I know." Chick sighed. "You would think I should be happy we found out before they stole me blind. But I liked Seth Jackson once. Hell, I still do, even after how he treated me."

"What made you so suspicious that you wanted a new tally?" Lin inquired. "Those tracks we found that time on the Bar J?"

"That, and how Seth behaved. Plus, it's

pretty well known that Black Jack is a rope-and-ring man."

"You're one savvy hombre, Mr. Storm."

"I wish I could claim all the credit but Mrs. Storm had a lot to do with it," Chick said. "Nothing gets past that woman. Ever."

Lin filled a tin cup with steaming black coffee. "Mr. Jackson and the outlaws in cahoots. Who would have thought it? Why did he do such a thing?"

Chick added a branch to the fire. "Some men make a wrong decision here, a wrong decision there, and before they realize it, they've gone too far to turn back."

"When the time comes, you're welcome to leave it to me," Lin offered. "No one should have to hang a friend."

"You're a good man, Lin Cooley, but some things we do ourselves or we can't look in the mirror ever again."

For three days they pushed on. Twice the rustlers had tried to erase the tracks by brushing them with broken branches but the brush marks were as plain as the tracks.

On the fourth morning Chick sent Lin on ahead with Moses Sikes — "so we can fight shy of nasty surprises. We'll drag our heels until we hear from you."

Lin had been through that region a few times but not enough to know it as well as he did the Circle C. He rode with caution, his eyes on the highlines. The land was broken by bluffs and cut by gullies, ideal for hiding a large number of cattle.

Moses was doing the same. "I should ask in case we're not as clever as we think and they know we're comin'. Do we shoot to kill if we have to?"

"We do, although Mr. Storm is partial to a hemp social."

Moses shuddered. "I never could stand the sight of a strangulation jig, myself. All that kickin' and gurglin' and soilin' themselves."

"Maybe we'll be lucky and they'll try to shoot it out," Lin hoped.

Half an hour later the lowing of cows reached their ears. Leaving their horses concealed, the two cowboys shucked their rifles and crept up a bluff. At the flat summit they dropped onto their bellies and snaked to the brink.

"I thought you said five hundred?" Moses whispered.

The number of cows was in the thousands, spread along interconnecting canyons that radiated outward from a central gorge like the spokes on a wagon wheel radiated outward from the hub. A stream and ample grass ensured they wouldn't want for forage or water.

"Where are the rustlers?" Moses asked.

Lin was wondering that same thing. The cattle appeared to be unattended but there had to be someone keeping watch. Tendrils of smoke gave him a clue. He pointed, and Moses grunted.

"Sloppy operation. They're too sure of themselves."

"Or so lazy they'd rather sit on their backsides than ride herd," was Lin's guess.

Chick Storm listened with keen interest when they returned, then picked half the men and announced, "When we reach their hideout, you'll go with Lin. The rest will stay with me. Walk, don't ride, and keep your horses quiet. Get as close as you can and wait for me to make our play."

Lin was tempted to ask that Moses Sikes or Amos Finch be given charge of the other half so he could stick close to Chick but Chick might want to know why.

The rustlers were camped on a grassy strip of bank overspread by leafy boughs. Five men lounged in the grass, but appearances were deceiving. Their horses were saddled and within quick reach, and their rifles were at their sides. Two Lin recog-

nized. The Twins, everyone called them —
Jeb and Jed Ellsworth, Southern boys as
deadly as sidewinders.

Fifty yards out, Lin had his men leave
their mounts in the care of Kip Langtree,
whose muttered curses showed what he
thought of being left out.

Lin spied some Circle C punchers
sneaking in from the other side, and he
hoped the rustlers weren't as sharp-eyed.
Then one of the twins sprang erect and
cried out, and in the blink of an eye, both
the Ellsworths had leaped to their horses
and were in the saddle.

"Halt!" Chick Storm shouted, stepping
from behind a tree. "We have you covered!
You can't possibly get away."

The other rustlers froze but Jeb and Jed
applied their spurs. In a twinkling they
were down the bank and splashing across
the stream.

"Drop them!" Chick commanded.

A ragged volley crashed but amazingly
neither twin was hit. Lin was covering the
others in case they tried to gun Chick, a
wise precaution as it turned out, because
the next instant a heavyset rustler stabbed
for a pistol. Lin shot him through the
shoulder and the man was spun around
like a child's top.

More shots boomed but by now the Twins were in among the cows and had swung onto the sides of their horses, Comanche-like, to make themselves harder to hit.

"After them!" Chick shouted, and pointed at half a dozen punchers. "Bring them back on their saddles or over them!"

Moses Sikes was first to his horse and first across the stream. The Circle C hands behind him whooped and hollered.

Lin strode into the open, his rifle fixed on the heavyset rustler. "The next one will be through your brainpan."

At Chick's say-so, several punchers disarmed the rustlers. Once that was accomplished, Chick walked over to the one Lin had shot and without any forewarning whatsoever, he punched the man in the mouth. The rustler flopped about like a stricken chicken, blood pouring from his crushed lips.

"Damn your hide, mister! You busted some of my teeth!"

Chick bent and gripped the man's shirt and hauled him off the ground. "That will soon be the least of your worries, friend. Or haven't you heard how your kind are treated in these parts?"

Some of the rustler's bluster evaporated. "I don't know what in hell you're talkin' about. My pards and me were hired to tend herd."

"You're a liar," Chick said, and punched him again.

Amos Pinch stepped forward, drawing a boot knife. "Let me at him, boss. I'll have him squealin' like a stuck pig."

The rustler was on his back, spitting more tooth fragments. The other two had gone pale but so far were being brave about their fate.

"I have an offer for you," Chick informed them. "I'll only offer it once." He paused. "Tell me who you work for. Tell me Seth Jackson's part in this." He paused again. "Tell me everything and I'll let you live."

"We don't know Seth Jackson from Adam," one replied.

"And I suppose you don't know this is the Bar J?" Chick countered. "I wasn't hatched yesterday."

The man with the broken teeth sat up. "You're in for it, mister," he said, blood bubbling from his mouth. "You made the biggest mistake of your life when you came after us."

"This is getting us nowhere," Chick declared. He surveyed the nearest trees and pointed at a stout limb twenty feet off the ground. "Break out the ropes, boys. It's time for a lynching bee."

Chapter Twenty-one

Billy Braden was in the saloon, working on his third whiskey, when someone touched his arm and he turned to see George Palmer with hat in hand, mad as hell but trying mightily not to show it. "Son of a bitch! I can't ever recollect you steppin' foot in this den of iniquity, George."

"It's Mr. Palmer to you."

Billy made no attempt to hide his contempt. "I haven't called anyone mister since I was twelve and I sure ain't startin' with you."

"You've changed, William. You're not like you were when you started courting my daughter."

"Shows how much you know," Billy said. "What you see is how I am and how I've always been. You thought otherwise only because you saw what you wanted to see. You and your whole family."

"We treated you decent," George Palmer said.

Billy grinned. "So I should be in your

debt, is that it? I should treat you as decent as you treated me? Think again. I never asked for you and your wife to welcome me into your house. I never asked for you to be so obligin' about your little girl."

George was a study in scarlet. "I'm not here to squabble. She wants to see you, William. It's important."

"So she sent you to fetch me?" Billy's hand drifted to the pearl grips on his Colt. "I never go anywhere I don't want to."

"I'm asking you, not telling you," George said. "All she wants are ten minutes of your time. You owe her that much."

"I don't owe her a damn thing," Billy disagreed. "All those weeks I was comin' over, she never once asked me to stop."

"Why did you? All of a sudden like that?"

"You ask too damn many questions." Billy turned to the bar. "Go back and tell your precious pride and joy she and I are quits."

"Please, William," George pleaded. "She's been quite distraught. What can it hurt? It won't take much of your time."

"Don't flatter yourself," Billy growled.

George took exception. "A civil tongue and respect for others take a person a lot further in life than a pistol and an attitude."

Spinning, Billy jabbed him in the chest. "What the hell do you know? What have you ever done that's so great?"

"I own my own business. To you that might not seem like much, but it's an honest living. And I have a wife and a daughter any man would be proud of. That has to count for something."

"Your wife and daughter," Billy said scornfully. He drained his glass and gazed around at the half-empty saloon. "Hell. What else do I have to do? All right. I'll go have a talk with her."

"You will?" George was elated, and dogged Billy's footsteps on the way out.

A couple of Conestogas were parked in the street. They carried newcomers to Nowhere, two of them an elderly couple. Billy stopped dead at sight of them.

"Is something wrong?" George asked.

"No."

Helen Palmer was waiting on a customer. But when Billy marched in, she clasped her hands to her bosom and dashed over to take one of his hands in hers. "You came! I knew you would. I knew you're not as vile as everyone claims."

"Oh?" Billy lightly ran his forefinger across her palm. "And I knew I could count on you to think the best of me."

"I think the best of everyone," Helen said.

"That's why you're so special." Billy winked and reached down as if to pat her posterior but instead went down the hall to their living room. "Why are the curtains drawn?"

"I like it better this way," Sally Palmer said. She was in the rocking chair, a vague outline against the dark. She made no attempt to rise and greet him.

Walking over, Billy hunkered and covered one of her hands with one of his but she slid it out from under. "I thought you wanted to see me?"

"It wasn't my idea." Sally's golden hair had not seen a brush in days, and her dress lay in loose folds over her belly. "I already know what you'll say. But my parents insisted. My mother in particular. Even after what you did, she thinks the world of you."

"You told her?"

"No. She would tell my father and he would come after you and you would kill him, and I love my father too much for that."

"How sweet." Billy reached up to give her cheek a playful pinch but she pulled back. "What's gotten into you? You're

266

actin' like I'm one of those old prospectors who never take a bath."

"I can't stand to have you touch me," Sally said. "It makes me sick to my stomach. I would just as soon shoot you."

"I came over here to be insulted?"

"All that trouble you went to crossing the street, huh?" Sally's sneer was laced with hate. "You're here because my parents want me to appeal to your better nature. What they don't know is that you don't have one. There isn't a shred of goodness in your depraved soul."

Billy rose. "I've killed people for less."

"Go ahead." Sally thrust her chin at him. "Hit me. Beat me. Batter me so I can't stand. Kick me when I'm down so I bleed inside."

"Has anyone ever told you that you're a few bales shy of a wagon load?" Billy gave a little wave. "You've wasted enough of my time. Adios."

Sally rose half out of her chair, then said, "Before you run off, there's something you should know. You're going to be a father."

Billy slammed into an invisible wall. "What?"

"I'm pregnant."

Slowly turning, Billy stared at her stomach. "You don't say." He broke into a grin. "How do I know it's mine?"

Even in the dark, the tears that filled Sally's eyes glistened wetly. "You're the most despicable man who ever lived."

"Oh, please," Billy scoffed.

"You're the only one I've ever been with. The only man who ever —" Sally choked up and lowered her head but then raised it again, anger transforming her from soft and vulnerable to hard and spiteful. "You're the one who raped me."

Billy was at the chair in a twinkling, his hand clamped to her chin. "What did I warn you about that?" he hissed. "You're never to mention it. Not here. Nor anywhere. Not even to yourself when you're alone."

"Or what? You'll kill me?" Sally spat. "Go ahead! I dare you! You would be doing me a favor."

"How so?"

Sally placed a hand on her belly. "Do you think I *want* this baby? Do you think I want your seed taking root inside me? If I could, I'd cut it out and bury it so no one would ever find out."

"Do your folks know? It doesn't look like you've swelled that much."

"It's early yet. Another couple of months and I'll be a melon. I suspect my mother knows. I've been sick most mornings of late and that's a sure sign."

"What about your father?"

"He thinks I've been pining after you." Sally's laugh was as brittle as thin glass. "Little does he know I'd love to stake you out and have ants eat you alive."

"I don't want any part of this," Billy said.

Sally suddenly snatched his hand and pressed it to her. "Feel the new life in there? Life you helped create. If you were half the man you think you are, you would do the right thing."

Billy stepped back. "So that's what this is about. You expect me to marry you now that I know about the kid?"

"My mother is hoping you'll accept responsibility," Sally said, "but I know better. I finally figured it out."

"Figured what out?"

"That you never loved me. Not for a minute. All you ever wanted was to get up my dress. All those nice things you said, all the compliments about how pretty I was and how you couldn't stand to be apart from me and how I was the most wonderful woman you ever met, was all a pack of lies."

Billy grinned at his cleverness. "You can

catch more flies with honey than you can with vinegar."

"And once you caught this fly, you didn't want anything more to do with it." Sally's bitterness oozed from every pore.

"I've had better gals. All you did was lie there like a log."

Sally gripped the arms of the chair until her knuckles were white. "I hate you. I hate you so much, I want to scream. But as much as that is, there's someone I hate more. Someone I hate with every particle of my being."

"Who would that be?" Billy asked.

"The reflection that stares back at me from the mirror. The fool who trusted you. The wretch who believed she was special in your eyes, and who let you entice her into compromising herself. Into committing the worse deed a single woman can commit."

"Where's my bandanna when I need it?" Billy taunted, dabbing at his eyes with his sleeve. "Don't blame me for your mistakes. You're a grown woman."

"I agree there," Sally admitted. "I gave up a man who adored and respected me for a piece of trash."

"Be careful," Billy said.

Sally walked up to him, her chin jutting

in defiance. "Haven't you been listening? You don't scare me anymore. Hurt me as bad as you want. I don't care."

"How about your ma and pa? Don't you care about them either?" Billy gripped her left wrist and twisted it sharply but she didn't cry out. "I'd just as soon hurt them as you."

"How could I have been so stupid?" Sally asked. But she wasn't speaking to him.

"If there's one thing I know about women," Billy said, "it's that they only hear what they want to hear." He pushed her away and stepped to the hall. "If I'm still around when you have the kid, send word and maybe I'll stop by to see what it looks like. I'm sort of curious."

"Come anywhere near me after today and I'll shoot you."

Billy laughed. "You don't have the guts." He walked to the door into the store and had his hand on the latch when he abruptly turned and crept back. Sally's head was bowed and her shoulders were quaking, but when she raised her face, she wasn't crying. She was shaking with rage. Smacking her fists against her legs, she moved to an oak cabinet. She opened it, rose on the tips of her toes and reached as far back as she could reach on the highest shelf. She was after a bundle that she carried to the table and slowly unwrapped.

Billy's eyes narrowed.

A short-barreled revolver lay exposed, an Allen and Wheelock model. In the same bundle was a box of cartridges. Sally opened the box and began loading it. When she was done she held the revolver in both hands and stared at it. "Do I dare?"

Billy almost yelled for her to go ahead and do it. His skin prickled and he scarcely breathed.

Sally stepped to the mirror. She pressed the barrel to her temple. She took a deep breath and pulled back the hammer. "This is what I deserve."

Lit by anticipation, Billy inched forward.

"I'm sorry, Mother," Sally said to the mirror. "I'm sorry, Father." A tear trickled down her right cheek. "But most of all, I'm sorry about you, Randy. I wronged you. I hope you can find it in your heart to forgive me."

Billy quivered with anticipation. He saw her finger curl around the trigger but she wasn't quite ready yet.

"This is best for everyone. It will spare me the shame. Spare my parents the humiliation. Spare Randy the heartbreak."

Billy waited. And waited some more. She held the revolver steady but it was soon apparent she didn't have the courage, or the will, to do the deed. He crept toward her, staying to one side so she wouldn't notice his reflection until it was too late.

"I love you, Randy," Sally said. "I know that now, when it's too late. When I've lost you."

Billy had to skirt the sofa. Taking off his hat, he bent at the knees. Five or six feet and he would be next to her.

"My grandmother used to say that pride goes before a fall," Sally rambled on. "It's true in my case. I was too proud for my own good. I thought that if Randy truly loved me, he would propose like I wanted."

Billy flexed and unflexed his fingers.

"All that mattered to me was *me*." Sally continued to justify the decision she had made. "I couldn't be patient a while longer. I had to give in to temptation, just like Eve in the Garden."

Another short step or two and Billy would be close enough. Suddenly she half turned and he froze, afraid she would spot him.

"But is this the right way out?" Sally asked the mirror. "Or is this the last resort of a coward?"

Billy coiled his legs. He had to act soon. Her mother or father might walk in and spoil everything.

Sally looked at the revolver, at the muzzle an inch from her face. "What will people say about me after I'm gone? How will I be remembered?"

"As a stupid bitch," Billy said. She tried to turn but he was behind her, sliding his hand over hers, his trigger finger over her trigger finger. At the last split second their eyes met. She divined his intention and started to lower her arm but all he had to do was squeeze.

The revolver went off with a loud boom. Flesh and brains and bloody strands of golden hair splattered over the mirror and the wall, and Sally Palmer collapsed, her eyelids fluttering like a butterfly's wings.

Billy Braden laughed.

Chapter Twenty-two

Randy Quin had never seen anyone hanged before but he had heard all the grisly details. Lynching was a lot more common back in the early days when vigilantes were the only law and order.

Certain crimes, those considered the vilest, always merited swift justice. Harming a woman, for instance, was considered the vilest of the vile. So was horse stealing. In a land where a horse was essential for getting around, taking a man's mount left him stranded and vulnerable. Cattle rustling also resulted in a lot of hemp socials. Cattle, after all, were a source of livelihood for ranchers and a source of badly needed milk and cheese for farmers.

Randy and the Circle C punchers with him arrived on the bank of the creek just as three ropes were being thrown over a stout limb. He dismounted and hurried to Lin Cooley, who was covering the rustlers while Amos Finch and Ely Soames bound their wrists. "Was this all there were?"

"The Twins lit a shuck," Lin said. "Moses and some of the boys are after them."

Other punchers led three horses to the oak and positioned them under the ropes.

"It gets ugly now," Lin said.

One of the outlaws was resisting, a heavyset man whose mouth and chin were smeared bright red. "You ain't stringin' me up! No sir, you ain't!"

"Want to bet?" Amos Finch said, and slugged him across the head with the butt of his revolver. Not hard enough to knock him out but enough to daze him so Amos and Ely could bind his wrists.

The youngest of the rustlers was glancing this way and that, like a terrified puppy anxious to bolt for its life.

Chick Storm stood with his arms folded across his chest. Surveying the scene like a general surveying troops, he said, "Get them on their horses. We don't have all day."

"No!" the youngest rustler squealed, and fled. A two-legged jackrabbit, he bounded past several Circle C hands and was almost in the clear when a leg flicked out and caught him across the shins and down he tumbled.

Randy felt sorry for them but they had brought it on themselves. Every male over the age of six knew rustling was a hanging offense.

Amos and Ely boosted the dazed rustler onto a saddle and held him steady while another Circle C cowhand on horseback applied the noose.

The young one kicked up a fuss but four punchers seized him by the arms and legs and bodily carried him to the second horse. He screamed as they hoisted him up, screamed louder as the noose was slid over his head and tight around his throat. "You can't do this! Please!"

The third man offered no resistance, but sat the saddle in sad resignation.

"Anything any of you want to say?" Chick Storm asked.

"I don't want to die," the young rustler responded.

"No one ever does, boy. You might want to make peace with your Maker before it's too late."

The young one's face was slick with sweat. "Let me go and I'll never rustle again as long as I live."

"It's too late for that," Chick said.

"Please, mister," the young rustler begged. "I have a mother and three sisters back in Ohio. I only left because I wanted to see the world. I never planned to hook up with Black Jack."

"Little mistakes lead to bigger ones. You

should have stayed home."

The rustler with the bloody mouth had recovered sufficiently to begin cursing a mean streak and trying to slip his head from the noose but without the use of his hands it was hopeless.

Chick said, "Lin, you know what to do."

Lin Cooley walked behind the three horses and elevated his Winchester. He fired twice, as swiftly as he could work the lever. Simultaneously, Amos Finch whipped off his hat and hit one of the horses, bellowing, "Yeehaw!"

Randy involuntarily flinched as the horses swept out from under the rustlers and the waddies were jerked from their saddles. Their bodies snapped taut, then all three were kicking and twisting and vainly striving to stave off the inevitable, all the while gasping and gurgling and uttering the most obscene sounds. Randy wanted to tear his eyes away but couldn't.

The young one was the most violent. In his wild flailing his right leg swung out and his spur caught in the shirt of the rustler with the red mouth. Both men thrashed harder but only for a few seconds. Gradually growing weaker, their movements became more and more sluggish until finally they ceased and the three hung as limp as empty grain sacks. The young one's tongue jutted from his mouth and his eyes had rolled back in his head.

"Lord Almighty," a Circle C hand breathed.

"Do we cut them down and bury them, Mr. Storm?" Amos Finch asked.

"We do not." Chick had turned away. "We'll leave them there as a warning to the rest."

Hooves pounded on the other side of the stream, and out of the brush galloped Moses Sikes and the five who had gone with him. They forded and drew rein, and Moses reported, "They got away, Mr. Storm. I'm awful sorry. Those horses of theirs were as fast as antelope."

Chick wasn't upset. "Rustlers always keep the best horses for themselves. Don't worry. They'll get theirs."

"Where to now, boss?" Randy inquired. "The Circle C?"

"We're not done yet. Everyone mount up. We're paying Seth Jackson a visit."

"What about all these cattle?" This from Lin. "Some are ours."

"They'll keep," Chick said. "But I suppose it won't hurt to leave ten of our men here to keep watch. You pick the ten. Be sure they stay hidden, and if more rustlers show up, to give them lead poisoning."

When the time came to ride out, Randy rode beside Lin. They were a grim, determined bunch, no one more so than Chick Storm. Randy had never seen his employer so stone-faced, so severe. "What do you reckon he'll do to Mr. Jackson?"

"There's only one thing to do when you find a rattler in your bedroll," Lin said. "You shake it out and stomp it to death."

The ride took hours. Four Bar J riders spotted them and came to see who they were. One was grizzled Hap Evans. He took one look and then the four flew toward the ranch house at a gallop.

"Shouldn't we stop them?" Randy asked Lin. "Now Mr. Jackson will know we're comin'."

"It doesn't matter. There is nowhere he can run."

Close to fifteen Bar J hands were clustered near the corral when they arrived. Among them were Joe Elliot, back on his feet after taking all that lead; Hap Evans, his cheek bulging with tobacco; Toby Gill, Deke Scritch and others, all sensing this wasn't a social visit and wearing their worry on their sleeves.

Chick Storm reined up near the front porch. No sooner did his boots touch the ground than the front door opened and out swayed Seth Jackson, holding a half-empty whiskey bottle.

"I thought I made it plain I never wanted to see you again," Seth said.

The Bar J hands were drifting over but stood to one side.

"Fan the wind," Seth commanded, "or I'll have my boys throw you off the Bar J." When Chick didn't say or do anything, Seth shook the bottle at him. "Why the hell are you lookin' at me like that?"

"I was wondering how it came to this," Chick said. "How two men who were once so close drifted so far apart."

"I'm not the one who turned his back when the other needed a helpin' hand," Seth snapped. "If you ever came to me for money I would have given it to you, no questions asked."

"Is that what brought all this on? The money?"

"Brought what on?" Seth demanded.

"The rustling, for starters."

In the hush that followed Randy was conscious of several factors: the Circle C punchers with leveled rifles or their hands on their revolvers; the Bar J punchers looking at one another and at their Circle C brethren as if uncertain of what to do; and the raw, blistering hatred on the face of Seth Jackson.

"How dare you! You show up on my spread with a small army at your back and make wild accusations?"

Randy had the impression Chick Storm did not want to do what they were doing, and that was why Chick spoke much more kindly to Jackson than most anyone else would have.

"You deny knowing about the four thousand head of rustled cows hidden on your ranch?"

Seth Jackson stalled by taking a swig of whiskey. "You've seen these cows with your own eyes?"

Chick nodded. "Seen them, and made human fruit of three of the rustlers."

At this the Bar J cowboys began talking among themselves in low tones.

"What makes you think the cattle were rustled?" Seth asked. A wariness had come over him. That, and something else, something Randy could not quite identify.

"There were ten brands or more," Chick patiently answered. "Including my own."

Seth took a step back as if he had been punched. "Circle C cattle have been taken?"

Randy was puzzled by the Bar J owner's reaction. Jackson's surprise was the genuine article.

"It's been going on for months," Chick

said. "I conducted a special tally and came up short. We found where the rustled cows were being bunched and followed the sign here."

"That can't be," Seth said.

"I can take you to see the cattle if you want," Chick offered. "I don't recognize all the brands but enough of them to know the rustlers have ranged all over."

Seth Jackson asked a strange question. He said, "Not just from Kansas?"

"No," Chick replied.

Seth leaned against a porch post as if he needed the support to stay upright. "So that's the way it is."

"The way what is?"

Straightening, Seth swallowed more coffin varnish. "I thank you for bringin' this to my attention. It will be dealt with. I promise you."

"Yes, it will," Chick said.

"You can take your boys and leave."

Chick stayed where he was.

"Didn't you hear me?" Seth stepped to the edge of the porch. "Get on that horse of yours and ride."

"It's not that easy," Chick said gently. "I didn't come all this way just to let you know."

"What are you sayin'?" Whether it was

the alcohol, Randy couldn't say, but Seth Jackson hadn't grasped the terrible truth yet.

Chick motioned at a towering maple tree that shaded the ranch house. "That will do nicely."

Seth glanced up and the blood drained from his face. The whiskey bottle thudded at his feet. "You can't mean that."

"You know range law as well as I do."

"But I had nothin' to do with it," Seth said. "Neither me nor any of my hands."

Chick faced the Bar J punchers and spoke slowly, choosing his words. "The rustlers couldn't run an operation that big and no one know about it. They had to be working hand in hand with someone here. Someone who could keep the rest of you away from where the rustled cows were being held." He looked at the Bar J's foreman.

"And you reckon it was me?" Joe Elliot said indignantly. "Hell, if I'd known, I'd have hung them out to dry myself."

Chick turned to Seth Jackson and reiterated, "There had to be someone."

Joe Elliot wasn't done. "Some of us have had suspicions, Mr. Storm. We saw signs, for one thing. And we were told to keep away from the northwest sector." He raised his right hand as if he were in court and about to swear on the Bible. "But I give you my range word none of us knew for a fact what was happening until now."

A hush fell. All eyes were fixed on Seth Jackson, who was glowering like a mad bull.

"I've heard you had become mighty friendly with Black Jack's crowd," Chick said to him. "I didn't want to believe it. It's not easy thinking the worst of someone when you've always thought the best."

"So I played cards with them a few times," Seth said. "What does that prove?"

"A man is known by the company he keeps."

Seth ran a hand across his mouth and glanced down at the whiskey bottle. "These wild accusations don't prove a thing."

"Then why did you tell your punchers to shy away from where the cows were being held?" Chick softly asked. He nodded at Lin Cooley, who walked to his horse and took his rope from his saddle.

"You can't," Seth said.

"Sometimes a man has to do things regardless," Chick said. "I'd have given anything for us not to come to this. I always imagined us twenty years from now grey-haired and wrinkled, sitting in our rocking chairs and reminiscing about the good old days."

"My hands won't let you," Seth said. "They're loyal. As loyal as yours." He gestured at the Bar riders. "Show the high and mighty Circle C that we don't take kindly to being falsely accused."

None of the Bar J men moved.

"Come along, Seth," Chick coaxed. "No need to make it harder than it is."

"God," Seth said, and groaned. He looked at the whiskey bottle again, and bent down, saying, "The condemned is always granted a last request, and I want to finish this." When he unfurled, he had the whiskey bottle in one hand and his revolver in the other and he fired twice.

Quick as thought, Lin Cooley drew and answered in kind. His slugs rocked Seth Jackson on his boot heels and Seth tottered for a few moments, then crashed to the porch, two holes in his shirt above his heart.

Randy was gaping at two other bullet holes. At one in his employer's forehead, and one where his employer's right eye had been.

Chick Storm was dead.

Chapter Twenty-three

There had been a lot of days of late when Marshal Paul Lunsford wished he had never pinned on a badge. This was another. He stood next to the blanket draped over the crumpled body of Sally Palmer, and his insides churned. "So you're telling me she took her own life?"

Helen Palmer's cheeks were slick with tears. George had an arm around her shoulders and was doing what he could to comfort her. "She — she had been — despondent of late," Helen said. "She wouldn't leave this room. Would hardly ever eat. Wouldn't keep herself and her clothes as clean as she used to."

"Do *you* think she killed herself?" Marshal Lunsford asked the father.

"It's possible," George said, struggling not to cry. "More than possible, to be honest. I don't know what was eating at her but something was. I thought maybe it had something to do with her breaking up with him." George nodded at the smirking figure in the chair.

Marshal Lunsford had never wanted to hit anyone as much as he wanted to hit Billy Braden. "You couldn't have stopped her, boy? You didn't have a chance to take the gun away from her?"

Billy had found a hairpin somewhere and was picking at his teeth. "Hell, Marshal, I had no idea she had that pistol until she pressed it to her head. And then all that blood and her brains splatterin' all over. It was terrible."

Helen moaned and sagged against George.

"Spare us the details," Lunsford said. To keep from bashing Braden with his scattergun, he went into the store. Many of Nowhere's residents were present, anxiously awaiting news. "It's true," he announced. "Sally has committed suicide."

It was Agnes Wilson who brought word to him. She had been in the store at the time, and George sent her to fetch him. She then imitated Paul Revere and went up and down the sheet informing everyone.

"Why would she do such a thing?" Renfro wondered. "She was young and beautiful and had everything to live for."

"Who knows why people do what they do?" Marshal Lunsford responded. "The important thing now is to spare the Palmers as much misery as we can. Svenson, I need you to make a coffin. There are some planks lying over by the stable you can use. Renfro, you and your son help. We'll bury her within the hour. No sense in dragging it out."

The blacksmith and the barber went to leave but only took a few steps, then stopped in disbelief.

Marshal Lunsford turned, as shocked as the rest to hear cheerful whistling.

Out of the hall sauntered Billy Braden, his thumbs hooked in his gun belt. "Do you need me for anything else, Marshal?"

"You'll want to help with the burial, I suppose," Lunsford said.

"Why?" Billy made for the street. "She and I were through months ago. It's bad enough she got blood on my shirt."

The resentful stares cast his way had no effect. Pausing in the doorway, Billy snickered. "Would you rather I lied and said she meant the world to me when she didn't? That wouldn't be honest."

"You must have liked her a little," Mrs. Renfro said.

"Lady, the only one in this world I honest-to-goodness give a damn about is the handsome cuss I see in the mirror.

Everyone else, and I do mean everyone, can go stand in front of a stampede for all I care." Touching his hat brim, Billy laughed and left.

Mrs. Renfro crinkled her nose. "I never!"

"He's despicable," Mrs. Lafferty said. "That whole bunch is a blight on our town. They should be driven out."

Now it was Marshal Lunsford who bore the brunt of their stares. "I'd be more than happy to oblige, ladies. One of you come to the jail and file a formal complaint and I'll demand Black Jack and his coyotes leave. I'll also need volunteers to back my play if Black Jack refuses."

No one took him up on it.

"I didn't think so," Marshal Lunsford said wearily. "Off you go, Svenson. I'll stick around until the coffin is done." He shooed everyone out and shut the door and hung the CLOSED sign up. Then he perched on the stool behind the counter and absently flipped through an old newspaper.

A knock brought his reading to an end. Charley Lone, the Circle C cook, was at the door, shaking a sheet of paper with scribbling on it, and beckoning.

Marshal Lunsford walked over. "Can't you read?" He pointed at the CLOSED sign.

"Can you?" Charley shouted back, and wagged that sheet again. "Palmer sent word my order is in and I've come clear from the Circle C to fetch it." He shielded his eyes with his other hand and peered about the store. "Where's George, anyhow? Why are you mindin' the fort?"

Lunsford threw the bolt and opened the door. "I take it you haven't heard?"

"Heard what? I rolled into town not two minutes ago." The cook indicated a buckboard.

"Sally Palmer shot herself." Lunsford didn't elaborate. "George and Helen are in the back and I'd rather not disturb them, if you don't mind."

"Oh." Charley scratched his beard. "I reckon I can wait around a little while. But I need to be back at the Circle C quick as I can. Those boys starve without me."

"The funeral is in an hour. After it's over you can get what you need." Lunsford returned to the stool. "Don't you usually order from the general store in Beaver City?"

Charley nodded, and grinned. "It's the kid. Randy Quin. He wanted me to order from here now and then so he'd have an excuse to come in with me and see his girl." Charley grunted. "Damn. I bet he's

291

heartbroke when he hears the news."

George Palmer came out of the back, his face pasty, his eyes wide and unfocused. "I can't believe it. I just can't believe it."

"What's wrong?" Lunsford asked.

"She just told me," George said.

"Told you what?"

"Helen has known all this time and she just now broke down and told me." George looked wildly about.

"What are you talking about?" Marshal Lunsford didn't like the strange, disturbing gleam that had come into the store owner's eyes.

"Ask Helen." Leaning on the counter, George uttered a low, mewing whine while gnashing his teeth as if he were in great pain.

"George?" Lunsford slid off the stool and put his hand on Palmer's shoulder but Palmer shook it off.

"*Ask her!*" George practically screeched. "Just you go ask her!"

Bewildered, Marshal Lunsford hurried to the living room. Helen was in the rocking chair, doubled over, her arms clasped about her legs and her entire body in the grip of convulsive sobs. He was loathe to intrude on her grief but he said, "Helen? What's wrong with your husband?"

The answer came in a whimper. "I told him. I shouldn't have but I couldn't keep it inside. Not after what's happened."

Lunsford placed his hand on her shoulder, and she looked up, blinking back tears. "What could you possibly say that has him so upset?"

"She was with child."

A chill started at the base of Lunsford's neck and rippled down his spine to his feet. "Sally was pregnant?"

Helen nodded, too overcome to speak.

"Who was the father? Not — ?" Lunsford couldn't bring himself to say the name. He would rather it were Randy Quin. Or some other puncher. Anyone but —

"Billy Braden, yes," Helen said. "My baby wouldn't tell me the particulars but I suspect she was forced."

Marshal Lunsford didn't hear the rest. He ran down the hall and burst into the store. Charley Lone was still there but not George Palmer. The front door was wide open and so was a drawer behind the counter — the drawer where George kept a revolver in case anyone ever tried to rob them. "Why didn't you stop him," Lunsford said to Charley as he snatched his scattergun off the counter.

"What for? What's going on?" the Circle C's cook asked.

The blazing afternoon sun caused white dots to dance before Lunsford's eyes as he crossed the street. He dreaded what he might hear but he reached the batwings without shots ringing out.

Black Jack, Longley and Clell Craven were at their customary corner table, Billy Braden beside them. They were frozen in place, as was everyone else.

In the middle of the room stood George Palmer, the revolver held in trembling hands. He wasn't trembling because he was afraid. He was trembling because of the seething fury that twisted his features.

". . . hold on there, hoss," Billy Braden was saying. "I have no notion what you're talkin' about."

"*You — you — you — !*" Palmer couldn't bring himself to say it.

Black Jack was as confused as everyone else. "What is this, storekeep? Why did you barge in here wavin' that hogleg?"

"He knows!" George screamed. "Ask the boy! Ask that filthy slug what he did to my Sally!"

"We heard she died," Black Jack said. "Are you sayin' he killed her?"

George took a couple of slow, deliberate steps. "He might as well have! It's all the same!"

Marshal Lunsford slipped inside un-
noticed. "That will be enough, George," he
said quietly. "Lower the gun and come
with me."

Palmer spun but instantly whirled back
toward Billy Braden. "This has nothing to
do with you, Paul!"

"On the contrary," Lunsford said. "We're
friends, aren't we? What sort of friend would
I be if I let you make a mistake like this?"

"It's no mistake!" George declared. "If
you knew what I know, you would understand. He deserves to die! He's scum! Pure
rotten filth! And these are his last moments on earth!"

"Murder is murder, George," Lunsford
noted.

"There isn't a jury alive who would con-
vict me. A man has a right to protect his
own. A father has a right to see that justice
is done."

Lunsford sidled toward him. "Justice is
one thing, revenge another. You won't be
able to live with yourself if you do this."

"I won't be able to live with myself if I
don't." George cocked the revolver. "How
does it feel, boy? Are you scared yet?"

Billy was smiling. "Mister, I've never
been afraid once my whole life long. Other
men, maybe, but not me."

"What makes you so special?" George asked.

"It's simple. I don't care whether I live or die." Billy spread his arms wide. "So go ahead. Shoot."

"Don't!" Marshal Lunsford cried.

Indecision caused George to hesitate. He took aim but his arms were shaking so badly, he couldn't hit the broad side of the saloon.

"What are you waitin' for?" Billy baited him. "Want me to make it easy and pull the trigger for you?"

"Damn you!" George wailed. "Damn you to hell." Beads of sweat dotted his face as he tried to steady his aim.

Longley had turned his chair so he was facing the middle of the room, and now Clell Craven did the same.

In a sudden spurt of speed Marshall Lunsford reached George Palmer and swung his scattergun. He connected with Palmer's wrists and Palmer yelped and let go of the cocked revolver. It hit the floor and went off with a loud *bang*. Nearly everyone ducked, but the slug had buried itself in a wall.

"Don't try to stop me!" George shouted, and lunged at the six-shooter.

Marshal Lunsford was a hair faster. He

sent it skidding with a well-placed kick while at the same time he hollered, "Dub! Grab it and don't let him have it!"

With an ungainly bound, Dub Wheeton scrambled over the bar and got his pudgy hands on the gun a heartbeat before George.

"Give it to me!"

Lunsford rushed to separate them but he need not have worried. George was too distraught to do more than ineffectually flail at Dub's shoulders and neck. "Enough, George. It's over."

Weeping now, Palmer sank to his knees and covered his face with his hands. "It's not fair! It's just not fair!"

"Help me," Marshal Lunsford said to the Renfro boy, and together they helped George to his feet and guided him across the street.

Helen was in the front of the store. Mrs. Svenson and Mrs. Wilson were comforting her. She ran to George and flung her arms around him and the two of them gave rein to their despair and sobbed in great racking heaves.

Lunsford sent the Renfro boy back and bent his weary steps to the jail. From the blacksmith shop came loud hammering and the rasp of a saw. He didn't stop. Once in his office, he shut the door and sat behind his desk.

"What's all the fuss about?" Ben Towers asked.

"Nothing that concerns you." Marshal Lunsford opened a drawer. His silver flask gleamed dully. He took off his hat and placed it beside his scattergun, then wearily rubbed his eyes and stared longingly at the flask.

Lunsford slammed the drawer shut and rested his forehead on his good arm. He felt tired. So very tired. He didn't mean to doze off but he did. The sound of his door opening awakened him, and he sat up.

Black Jack, Longley and Clell Craven were filing into the jail. Black Jack sat on the desk, and smiled. "You've had him long enough," he said, with a nod at Towers. "I need him."

"The judge hasn't been here yet."

"Too bad." Black Jack picked up the scattergun, thumbed back both hammers, and pointed it at him. "You have two choices."

The key was on a large metal ring on a hook. Marshal Lunsford opened the cell and stepped back, only to have his scattergun jammed against the base of his spine.

"One out, one in," Black Jack said, taking the key. He laughed as he locked the door. "Make yourself comfortable."

"When I get out I'm coming after you," Marshal Lunsford promised.

Clell Craven thought that was funny. "We'll be tremblin' in our boots until then, cripple."

Chapter Twenty-four

The reason Black Jack needed Ben Towers had to do with the arrival of the Twins on lathered mounts they had nearly ridden into the ground.

Black Jack sent word to his men to meet in the stable an hour after the funeral. With Taylor dead, hardly anyone ever went there except to tend to the horses. He ordered the Twins to close and bar the double doors so no one could walk in on them.

They were all there: quiet, deadly Ike Longley; Ben Towers, happy to be out of jail, fondling his shotgun as if it were a lover; Billy Braden, sulking for some reason, as the kid often did; Jed and Jeb, as alike as shadows, as vicious as they came; Clell Craven, the scent of blood in his nostrils and relishing the prospect; Dingus Mechum, twitching and grinning; Zech Frame, who once slit a Sioux woman's throat and drank her blood. And the rest of them, another half dozen, the ones nobody had ever heard of because they had yet to make a name for themselves: Maddox the Kentuckian and Tine the West Virginian, Rebs through and through; Tom Anis, Chester Park, and Bob Waxman, backshooters all; Jeff Dean, almost as young as Billy and so shy he never spoke and never looked anyone in the eye unless he was killing them.

The women were there, too: Belle James, looking a lot the worse for her profession; Susie Metzger, as tough as any of the men and proud of it; and Shasta Cunningham, making moon eyes at Billy Braden.

Black Jack started right in. "You've all heard the news. The Circle C found our rustled herd and by now has likely hung Sam, Coker and Stillman. My guess is they went on to the Bar J."

"Maybe the two outfits will take to swappin' lead," Clell Craven speculated. "Less of them for us to worry about."

"I'm not countin' on it," Black Jack said. "No, sooner or later they'll show up lookin' for us." He let that sink in. "We have to decide what to do."

"What else?" Billy Braden said. "We kill every last one of the sons of bitches."

A few of the others grinned or nodded.

"There's nothin' I'd like better," Black

Jack said, "but there are a lot more of them than there are of us, and I don't want to lose any more of you."

Dingus Mechum voiced that dry, wheezy cackle of his. "Why, Black Jack, we never knew you cared."

"How would you like my boot up your ass?" Black Jack growled, and when Dingus shriveled, he went on. "The way I see it, we have two choices. We run or we fight. We can collect our things and be saddled and ready to ride in half an hour, if that's what you want."

"I don't much like turnin' tail," Ben Towers said.

Zech Frame bobbed his chin. "Folks will hear of it and think we're yellow."

"What other choice do we have?" Susie Metzger asked. "How can we fight all those cowboys?"

Black Jack pushed his hat back on his curly thatch. "We tree the town and set a trap and when the cowboys show up, we blow them to hell and back. Then we ride out with our heads high."

Laughter and nods greeted the proposal.

"Now *that* I like," Billy Braden said. "Especially the treein' the town part. Why, we do it right, we'll be plumb famous. Every newspaper in the country will write us up."

"Who cares about fame?" Clell Craven said. "This town is burstin' with money, and all of it can be ours."

"Anything else we want, besides," Zech Frame said.

Belle James, always one of the shrewdest, cleared her throat. "Seems to me there's a third choice. Why not tree the town and leave *before* the cowboys get here? That way we all make it out alive."

Black Jack had an answer ready. "Because I don't like turnin' tail either. We let these cowpokes run us off, then every cowboy from Mexico to Colorado will think they can do the same. It'll be that much harder to rustle cattle from now on." He looked at the deadliest of them all. "What do you say?"

Ike Longley was leaning against a stall, his body relaxed, his slender hands on his Remingtons. "We stay. We tree the town. We kill the cowboys. We go."

Whoops filled the stable, and Black Jack raised his arms. "Quiet, damn you! We don't want them suspicious until it's too late for them to fight or run." He paused. "Ben, you take Tom, Maddox and Tine, and Chester and Bob, and start at the other end of town. We'll fan out from this end. Deal with the men first. The women can wait."

"Like hell they can," Dingus joked, and gripped his crotch.

"Use your heads," Black Jack advised. "Find out where they've hid their pokes before you slit their throats."

Shasta Cunningham raised her hand as if she were in school. "What about the children? Surely we won't harm them?"

Everyone stared at her.

"She has a point," Black Jack said. "Killin' kids will rile up everyone within a thousand miles. We'll herd the younguns in here and roll a wagon against the doors so they can't get out."

"Aw, shucks," Dingus grumbled.

"We're forgettin' the tin star," Ben Towers said. "I want to deal with him myself."

"Why waste the lead?" Black Jack responded. "We've spread word he had to leave town and no one knows he's locked in his own jail. Another couple of days and he'll die from starvation or thirst."

"I'd still rather do him myself."

"Then save him for last. Let him sit in there listenin' to the screams, knowin' we're treein' his town and there ain't a damn thing he can do about it. It will tear him apart."

Ben Towers chuckled. "You're a man after my own heart."

"One thing," Clell Craven said. "How long before you reckon the cowboys show up?"

"Not until tomorrow at the earliest," was Black Jack's guess. "Plenty of time for us to have all the fun we want. So let's get to it." He was first out of the stable and made straight for the blacksmith shop, several others tagging along.

Svenson was shaping a red-hot horseshoe, his muscular arms rippling as he swung his big hammer with methodical precision. "I vill be wif you in a moment," he said in his thick accent.

Black Jack walked to a bench covered with tools. He picked up a file, then put it down in favor of a pair of long metal tongs.

A few more strokes of Svenson's hammer, and the brawny blacksmith set it down and turned to them, wiping his huge hands on his apron. "How may I help you?"

"Your poke," Black Jack said, as Clell Craven and Zech Frame moved to either side without being obvious about it.

"My what?" the Swede said.

"Your poke. Your money. Your savin's," Black Jack made it clearer. "Since there isn't a bank within sixty miles, you must have it stashed somewhere handy. In your house, I reckon." The house was next to the shop.

"You vant my money?" Svenson smiled like it was a joke.

"We vant your money," Black Jack mimicked him. "Make it easy on yourself and tell us where it is."

It sank in that they were serious, and Svenson balled his massive fists. "You cannot haf it. Leave, or I vill hurt you."

Black Jack nodded at Clell and Clell drew his revolver and shot Svenson through the right thigh. The blacksmith lurched against the anvil, tried to run toward the side door to the house, and fell. Before he could rise, Clell and Dingus had him by the arms and Zech jammed his revolver against the Swede's ear.

"Now then," Black Jack said, using the tongs to grip the fiery red horseshoe. "Where's your money?"

Blood stained Svenson's overalls and he was puffing like a fish out of water but he shook his head and said, "I vill never say."

"Why is it," Black Jack said to Clell, "that so many people are so damn stupid." He undid the blacksmith's apron and started on the overalls.

"No!" Svenson started to resist but

stopped when Zech thumbed back the revolver's hammer. "You can't!"

"Your money," Black Jack said. When the Swede glared, Black Jack thrust the horseshoe down his pants. There was loud sizzling and an odor reminiscent of fried bacon filled the shop. Svenson howled, his face the same color as a beet, every vein in his neck bulging.

"The money," Black Jack said again.

Tossing his head from side to side, Svenson sputtered and spat but wouldn't say.

"I can do this all day." Black Jack walked to a pile of horseshoes and gripped one and placed it in the furnace. "There won't be much of you left down there, but that's your decision."

"Enough!" someone cried.

Black Jack wheeled. Svenson's wife, Greta, was in the doorway, holding a large brown leather pouch.

"I saw you come in. I heard what you said." Her English was a lot better than her husband's. "This is all we have. Take it and go."

The pouch contained three hundred and fourteen dollars. "It's a start," Black Jack said, and motioned for the others to precede him out. Once they had, he drew his

Smith and Wesson and shot Svenson through the head.

"You devil!" Greta Svenson shrieked, and hurled herself at him, her nails hooked to rend and rip.

Black Jack smashed her across the temple, twice, and she sprawled in the sawdust and dirt beside her husband, whose body was still convulsing.

Nowhere was in an uproar. Shots rang out up and down the street. Helen Palmer came running out of the general store, screeching hysterically. George Palmer was a few steps behind her, his face bloodied, limping but trying to keep up. He glanced back and extended his arm. "Don't!"

Billy Braden grinned. "Where do you think you two are going?" He stroked the trigger of his pearl-handled Colt and part of George Palmer's skull went flying.

Terrified, Helen halted and wept as Billy came up to her, seized her wrist, and hauled her back into the store. The door slammed shut, and a high-pitched wail keened.

Heads were poking out of windows and doorways. Lafferty stepped from the feed and grain, armed with a rifle. He never saw Longley. But he had to feel the twin slugs that ripped through his chest. He was dead before he struck the boardwalk.

Black Jack strolled past building after building, liking what he saw.

In the barbershop, Renfro was on the floor, curled into a ball, while Jeb and Jed kicked and kicked and kicked, staving in rib after rib and reducing one of the barber's ears to a smear.

In the restaurant, Maddox was pistol-whipping Tim Wilson while his wife gaped in horror, held fast in Tine's grasp.

In the new millinery, Belle James was slapping the owner into unconsciousness while Susie Metzger and Shasta ripped dresses to shreds.

"We should tree towns more often," Black Jack said. He saw Dub Wheeton and the Renfro boy come from the saloon. Dub promptly retreated indoors but the boy raced toward the barbershop.

"Pa! Pa! They're killing people!"

"And you're next," Ben Towers said. He brought the boy down with a twin blast from his shotgun that exploded the boy's head like a ripe melon and left a stump where the boy's neck had been.

"Yes, sir," Black Jack said, angling toward the saloon. "I haven't had this good a time since that night we hurrahed Salina." He halted well short of the batwings and hollered, "Dub! It's me. I'm comin' in."

"No!" Wheeton shouted. "I'll shoot! I swear!"

"What's gotten into you?" Black Jack stalled as Ben and Clell hurried around the side.

"I saw what you're doing to everyone! I won't let you do it to me!"

"How long have we been friends now? How long have I been drinkin' your whiskey and givin' you a share of the money my girls make? Do you really think I would hurt you?"

Up the street a pistol cracked and a woman screamed.

"Hear that?" Dub said. "I don't trust you, Black Jack. I don't care what you say. Don't step foot in here or you'll be sorry."

"And I don't take kindly to threats." Black Jack had to keep him distracted. "We should talk this over face to face. Come on out where I can see you and I give you my word you won't be harmed."

"Do us both a favor and go away."

The sounds Black Jack had been waiting for, the *thump* of a heavy blow and the *thud* of a body striking the floor, galvanized him into rushing inside. Dub Wheeton lay at the end of the bar holding a hand to his head, with Clell standing over him.

"Now then," Black Jack said, "about that money I've been sharin'. I've changed my mind. I want it back."

"I won't give it to you."

"Think so?" Black Jack gestured, and Clell and Ben pinned Dub to the floor, holding the saloon owner's arms so he couldn't move them if he tried.

"What are you doing?"

Black Jack was next to Dub's pudgy right hand. He raised his boot. "This is your last chance."

"Do your worst," Dub blustered.

Black Jack brought his boot crashing down. Bone crunched and blood spurted, and Dub Wheeton was overcome by paroxysms of torment. He thrashed and howled and blubbered.

"I can do this all day or you can tell me where the money is."

Dub tried to say something but couldn't.

"I can't hear you."

"It's in a tin behind the second keg!"

The total turned out to be over a thousand dollars. Black Jack placed it in the brown leather pouch and patted the pouch. Drawing his Smith and Wesson, he bent over Dub. "Didn't you say to do my worst?"

Black Jack stroked the trigger.

Chapter Twenty-five

The Circle C hands were halfway home. Lin Cooley and Randy Quin were in the lead. Several riders appeared in the distance and Lin raised a hand, bringing everyone to a stop — including Moses Sikes, who was handling the team pulling the buckboard that bore the mortal remains of Chick Storm.

In addition to the Circle C punchers, half a dozen Bar J hands had tagged along, among them Joe Elliot, Hap Evans and Toby Gill. Elliot brought his horse up next to Lin's.

"Who do you reckon it is?"

"The one in the middle is a woman or I'm a sheepman," Lin said.

Randy was as intent as a hunting hawk. "Why, it's Mrs. Storm! She came all this way to meet us."

"I shouldn't have sent Kip and Amos on ahead to tell her about Chick," Lin said, glancing at the canvas that covered the bed of the buckboard. "I should have known a woman like her wouldn't be content to wait."

"Has a lot of spunk, does she?" Joe Elliot asked.

"No more than a grizzly." Lin swung down. The canvas had bunched up, exposing an arm. He smoothed it and took off his hat and turned.

Dixie Storm wore range clothes; a man's hat, a man's shirt, a man's pants. Around her waist was a gun belt, in the holster a Bisley revolver with ivory grips and a nickel finish. Without saying a word, she brought her pinto alongside and nodded at Lin.

Lin pulled back the canvas.

"Damn." Dixie bowed her head, but only for an instant. When she raised it again, her jaw was set like a steel trap. "Tell me how it happened."

"Didn't they — ?" Lin began, motioning at Kip and Amos.

"I want to hear it in your own words," Dixie said. "You're foreman. I entrusted his life to you." As she said that last, her hand dropped to the Bisley.

Lin complied, leaving nothing out, quoting as best he could the things Chick and Seth had said. In the silence that ensued he waited for the Bisley to clear leather and to feel the burning sensation of a bullet as it ripped through his body.

Dixie's gun hand rose to her reins. "So. Chick talked when he should have pulled iron. I warned him. I told him he was a better friend to Seth than Seth could ever be to him. Now he's dead and I'm a widow and the bastards who made me one will pay." She shifted toward Moses. "Mr. Sikes, I will be grateful it you'll take my husband to the ranch and put the body in the springhouse. It's cool there. He'll keep there until I get back."

"Yes, ma'am."

"The rest of you," Dixie said, facing them, "are welcome to ride with me or not. Chick was my man. None of you are obligated."

Lin placed his hat back on. "That was uncalled for. We work for you as well as him, and we're loyal to the brand." He swung onto his mount. "I'm with you, ma'am, come what may."

A chorus of agreement confirmed that not a hand among them would bow out.

Randy Quin was loudest of all. "We'll wipe those varmints out or be buried ourselves!"

Dixie looked at him, her face softening. "Randy. I was so caught up in my loss, I almost forgot about yours."

"Ma'am?"

"We ran into Charley Lone on our way here," Dixie said. "He was on his way back from Nowhere." She did a rare thing for her. She hesitated. "I don't know how else to say it so I'll come right out with it. Sally Palmer is dead. She shot herself. I don't know all the particulars but it had something to do with that Billy Braden character."

Randy was mute with shock.

"I'm sorry to break it to you like this. If you would rather not ride with us, I'll understand."

"That's a poor joke, ma'am." Randy found his voice. "I have as much reason as you do now. Count me in."

"Then let's ride!"

Lin had questions to ask but he decided they could wait. He trotted on Dixie's right, aware that she glanced at him now and again.

Joe Elliot came up on her left. "I hope you don't mind us helpin' out, ma'am." Joe had to raise his voice to be heard above the rumbling hooves. "But the Bar J has a stake in this, too." When she didn't respond, he said, "I'm right sorry above your husband. Mr. Storm would do to ride the river with."

"Mr. Storm was a man," Dixie said, and

did not say anything more after that for a long while.

They pushed on past sundown. Lin thought she would call a halt about eight but on they rode. By the stars it was close to midnight, and the lights of Nowhere were twinkling on the horizon, when Dixie Storm drew rein. "This is as far as we go until morning! Bed down if you want but keep your horses close. And no fires. We don't want them to know we're coming."

Lin had to hand it to her. Being in charge came naturally.

Dixie turned to him. "I want you to take fifteen men and circle to the other side of town. We don't want Black Jack's coyotes slipping out on us."

"No, ma'am," Lin said.

In the act of swinging down, Dixie unfurled. "I beg your pardon? With Chick gone, you'll do as I say."

"I'm not going anywhere."

"Explain yourself, Lin Cooley, and make it good."

"I let you down once already, ma'am," Lin said. "I let Mr. Storm die. But I won't make the same mistake twice. I'm stickin' to you until this business is settled. Send Joe Elliot to the other side of town."

"Mr. Elliot doesn't work for me."

Joe immediately said, "I would if you asked me."

"Then as of this moment you're on the Circle C payroll," Dixie said. "You, and any Bar J hand so inclined. Which means you take orders from me. And my first order is to take the Bar J punchers and five or six others and camp on the other side of Nowhere. We go in at first light."

Joe Elliot was the happiest man in all creation. "You heard the lady," he said to Hap and Toby and the rest.

Climbing down, Lin watched them trot into the night. He stretched to relieve a kink in his back, then noticed Randy Quin was missing. Roving from puncher to puncher, he found the younger man off by himself in a patch of night so black, Lin wouldn't have known Randy was there had Randy's horse not nickered. "Here you are. I thought maybe you'd gone into town by yourself."

"I'd like to be alone, pard," Randy said, squatting. "To think about Sally and all."

"Sometimes it helps to talk."

Randy toyed with his belt buckle. "I killed her, Lin."

"And I shot Abe Lincoln."

"I'm serious. If I'd got up the gumption to ask for her hand in marriage all those months I was courtin' her, she'd never have looked twice at Billy Braden and would be alive right this moment."

"Are you fixin' to take credit for every settler the Comanches have killed and those the flood drowned last year?"

Randy rotated so his back was to Lin. "You've never been cruel until now."

"I see it as doing you a kindness. We can't be blamed for things we can't control. Sally was a sweet gal and I liked her but she didn't know a good man when she had one or she would have waited for hell to freeze over for you to propose."

"I won't have you paintin' her as less than she was."

"Fair enough." Lin stood. "But is it right to paint yourself as less?"

Randy didn't say anything.

"You courted her proper. You treated her like a lady, with respect and courtesy. Whatever Braden did to cause her to kill herself had to be something you would never have done because you loved her too much to ever hurt her."

"I loved her more than anything."

"You didn't kill her. She brought it on herself, with help from that slug."

"Billy Braden," Randy said.

"So quit whippin' yourself over this." Lin

ended his argument. "And come and have some coffee."

"If you don't mind," Randy said, "I'd still like to be by myself."

"It's your grief. But don't forget I have two ears." Lin smiled and returned to find the saddle had been stripped from his horse and his bedroll had been spread out. When he saw who had done it, he was rooted in surprised. "Ma'am?"

Dixie Storm had spread out her blankets next to his and sat facing Nowhere, her legs bent, her hands around her knees. "I've been waiting for you. We need to talk."

"We do?" Lin said uncertainly. He eased cross-legged onto his blanket. "Shouldn't we get some sleep? Mornin' will be here before we know it."

"I loved Chick, Lin."

"He loved you," Lin said, unsure where this was leading.

Dixie seemed not to hear. "I loved him, but he's gone now, and I have to get on with my life. That might sound cold but I've never been one to twiddle my thumbs when things needed doing."

"No, ma'am, you sure haven't."

"I can run the Circle C by myself. I'm as good a rancher as Chick, maybe better, bless his soul. But I'm fairly young yet and the nights are long and I don't much like the idea of spending the rest of them alone."

Lin glanced to both sides but none of the punchers were close enough to hear. "You can't be sayin' what I think you're sayin'."

Dixie looked at him. The starlight lent a radiance to her features that heightened her femininity. "Why can't I?"

"With respect, ma'am, your husband isn't in the ground yet."

"You think I'm being too forward? Would you like it better if I waited a month? Six months?"

"Folks might think it more fittin'," Lin said.

"I don't live my life by what others think." Dixie paused. "How old would you say I am?"

Lin had no notion. Guessing the ages of women, he had discovered, was like trying to lasso the wind.

"All right. Don't answer. I'm ten years younger than Chick, which makes me nine years older than you. That's not much of a difference, and the women in my family preserve well."

"Are you proposin'?" Lin came right out with it.

"No, that's yours to do if and when you're so inclined. I'm only asking you to consider it. You never would on your own. You're too much the gentleman and you had too much respect for my husband."

"This will take some sortin' out," Lin admitted.

"Not really. We'll wait a year for propriety's sake, then you can formally ask the question and we'll be married with all the trimmings and spend the rest of our lives together, the Lord willing."

"You have this all worked out."

"Most of it. I'm still young enough to give you kids if you want them, if that's a consideration."

Lin said, "You make it sound like a business proposition."

"Instead of a romance?" Dixie saw right through him. "It's been my experience that when you put two people together, love will generally bloom. Especially if they want it to. You need to work out in your head whether you want it to."

"This is all so sudden."

"I'm sorry," Dixie said.

Lin had one more question. "Why me?"

"Why not you?" Dixie rejoined. "You're handsome. You're bright. You're as good as men get."

"I'm flattered. I think." Lin chuckled. "Ma'am, you take the whole cake."

"I speak my mind. Always have. Always will. And from here on out, I would like for you to call me Dixie."

"Some boots need to be worn a spell before they're comfortable," Lin commented.

"Granted," Dixie said, and was quiet a bit. Then, "You've been our foreman for three years. I know you as well as I've ever known anyone, and you have many qualities I admire. Chick had a lot, too."

"He was one of the nicest men I've ever met."

"Too nice, and it got him killed. You're a shade wiser. You would never talk yourself into an early grave like he did."

"Mr. Storm was being considerate," Lin said.

"There's a fine line between consideration and weakness." Dixie disputed him. "Chick was too willing to give others the benefit of the doubt. Me, I wait for them to prove they deserve it. Same as you, I suspect."

Lin was uncomfortable speaking ill of his recently departed employer, and made a comment to that effect.

"My apologies. I should have taken your feelings into account. I'll shut up now. All I ask is that you give my idea some thought and if it sits well with you, give me a sign to put my mind at ease." Dixie whispered the next. "I want you to know, if not you, there won't ever be anyone."

"I'm not the only male in these parts," Lin half joked.

Dixie's eyes found his in the dark. "Males are plentiful. *Men* are rare. Men like you are rarer still."

"I put on my britches a leg at a time like all the rest."

"That I'd like to see one day." Dixie smiled and took off her hat and lay on her side with her back to him. "Thank you for hearing me out."

"My pleasure," Lin said. For long minutes he sat staring at her, working it out in his head.

"You should try to get some sleep. Morning will come all too soon."

"Yes, ma'am."

"And Lin?"

"Yes?"

"Try not to get yourself killed tomorrow."

Chapter Twenty-six

Billy Braden sat up with a start. For a few seconds he didn't know where he was or how he got there. Then he felt the bed under him and saw his clothes strewn about and he groped for his Colt and found it under his pillow. The bedroom window was open. Rising, he padded over. The street was deserted except for the bodies and the debris. It would be dawn in an hour.

Billy quickly dressed. He was strapping on his gun belt when a tiny whimper issued from the throat of his bed partner. "So you're awake," he said.

Helen Palmer's wrists were tied to the bedpost and she had a gag in her mouth. Dry tears streaked her cheeks and fresh ones were pooling in her eyes. She tried to say something but the words were muffled.

"You weren't bad," Billy said. "A lot more lively than your daughter."

Helen strained against the ropes, her body bent like a bow.

Coming around the bed, Billy sat beside her. "Don't pretend you didn't like it. You wanted me from the start!"

Helen broke into racking sobs.

"Not again," Billy sighed. Reaching across, he picked up his pillow. "All this blubberin' is why I gagged you."

Twisting away from him, Helen tugged and yanked and twisted her wrists back and forth.

"It won't do you any good," Billy said. "When I tie knots, they stay tied." He held the pillow in both hands. "You know, it just hit me. You'll make four. The daughter. The baby. The father. Now the mother."

Tears poured from Helen's bloodshot eyes.

"That's right. It wasn't suicide. I helped Sally along by squeezin' the trigger. She wanted to but I don't think she had the sand." Billy positioned the pillow above Helen's face. "Ever pull the tails off lizards? Or pluck the legs off bugs?" He lowered the pillow and pressed, grinning when she bucked so violently the bed shook. Bit by bit her resistance grew weaker until her legs were barely moving. Lifting the pillow, he let her breathe. "Not yet."

Helen noisily sucked in breaths.

"Close, wasn't it?" Billy said. "There's a

knack to knowin' when to let up. One time in Indian Territory it took me six hours to kill a buck. I cut out his eyes and ripped out his tongue, and worse. He was a tough one."

Helen was staring at the pillow.

"I'd like to see how long you can last," Billy told her. "But the sun will be up soon and I have a lot of miles to put behind me." He lowered the pillow again and this time he did not raise it until her body had been still a while.

Billy left by the back door and stuck to the rear of the buildings until he came to the stable. Slipping inside, he hurried to the stall his horse was in. He had hold of his saddle blanket and was turning when a shadow separated from the surrounding darkness.

"Going somewhere?"

"Black Jack!" Billy draped the blanket back over the side of the stall and stepped into the aisle. "You're up early."

"I haven't been to bed." Black Jack slowly advanced. "You're up early yourself, kid."

"I couldn't sleep either."

"You?" Black Jack smirked. "You could kill your own mother and not lose a wink of sleep." He gazed out the open door.

"How is Mrs. Palmer, by the way?"

"Fine, last I saw her."

"Liar." Black Jack halted. "You never answered my question. Where are you fixin' to go?"

"My horse could use some exercise," Billy said.

"Another lie," Black Jack declared. "I doubt you'd know the truth if it jumped up and bit you on the ass."

"I resent that."

"Resent it all you want. So long as I don't turn my back on you, you won't do a damn thing about it." Black Jack oozed confidence. "Doesn't it make you wonder? Why I've kept you around, knowin' you for what you are?"

"I'm no worse than any of the others." Billy wished the other man would let down his guard for just a second. That was all it would take.

"Three lies. You're ten times worse. I never have to worry any of the others will put a slug between my shoulder blades."

"The Twins are backshooters," Billy noted. "And you can't tell me Ben or Clell or Dingus haven't shot anyone from ambush."

"Bushwhackin' is only common sense," Black Jack said. "With you it's different.

You like it. You get the same pleasure from killin' that you do from makin' love."

Billy had put up with enough. "What's all this leadin' up to?"

"Nothin'. Nothin' at all. I just wanted you to know that you never pulled the wool over my eyes like you did over the Palmers'. Pity about that girl. From what I hear, until you came along she was as pure as snow."

"Gettin' sentimental, are you?"

Suddenly Black Jack was next to him, a brawny fist cocked. "Watch how you talk to me, pup. I would kill you where you stand for tryin' to run out on us but we'll need all the guns we have any minute now."

"What are you talkin' about?"

"Oh. That's right. I never sent word to you, did I?" Black Jack chuckled. "The cowboys are here. Some north of town, some south. I imagine they're waitin' for first light."

"We're hemmed in?"

"Careful or you'll wet yourself," Black Jack advised. "Maddox and Tine are off keepin' watch. They'll let us know when the cowboys start in."

Billy licked his lips. "How many are we up against?"

"Upwards of forty, I reckon."

Billy glanced at his horse. "That's twice as many as there are of us. I don't like the odds."

"Don't worry. Half those cow nannies will be dead two minutes after they ride into town. The rest, well —" Black Jack shrugged. "We kill for a livin' and they don't, so we have the edge."

"You hope," Billy said.

"Better get to the general store. And remember, no one fires until we spring our surprise." Black Jack walked toward the double doors.

Billy's hand dropped to his Colt.

"Comin', Ike?" Black Jack asked without looking back.

Ike Longley materialized out of empty air. He was staring at Billy's right hand, his own hands on his Remingtons.

Uncurling his fingers, Billy grinned and held his arms out from his sides. "You must be part Comanche."

"And you're part yellow," the fastest of them said.

Black Jack had stopped. "The only reason he didn't gun you, kid, is because I asked him not to. I'm savin' you for myself."

"Why pick on me?" Billy wondered.

"I don't like you."

Longley backed out and the pair melted into the predawn grey.

Swearing, Billy strode to the horse stall. "I'll show them. I'll do what I damn well please." But he didn't pick up his saddle blanket. He didn't even touch it. Swearing some more, he wheeled and stomped outside. Dark figures were darting from doorway to doorway, taking positions. He headed for the general store, his rage boundless. "After this is over I'll see to him. Just wait!"

Out of spite Billy slammed the door with such force, the window cracked. As he passed the counter he swept everything on it to the floor. He upended a table, scattered the contents of a shelf. He was making so much noise, he didn't hear the door open.

"What the hell has gotten into you, boy?" Dingus Mechum had a Henry rifle in one hand and a jug in the other. "You're makin' enough racket to raise the folks we killed."

Billy grabbed a pile of neatly folded blankets and scattered them in all directions. "I ain't in the mood."

"Fine. Then I won't warn you." Dingus chugged from the jug and turned to go. "Here I thought we were friends."

"Hold on," Billy said. "Warn me about what?"

"Black Jack has spread word you're on your own. If you get into trouble, none of us are to help or we answer to him."

Billy thought his head would explode, he was so incensed.

"I told him that's not right," Dingus said. "That so long as you're one of us, we should treat you the same as everyone else."

"What did he say?"

"He took hold of my throat and said that if I didn't do as he wants, I'll be breathin' dirt." Dingus's scrawny neck bobbed. "What did you do to get him so riled, anyhow? He has it in for you."

Billy said, "Tell me something I don't know."

"Watch yourself." Dingus stepped out onto the boardwalk and looked up and down the street. "Clell thinks this will be like shootin' fish in a barrel but cowboys don't die easy." He jogged north, leaving the door open.

Billy moved to close it just as a lithe form in a blue shawl entered. "Go away," he said. "This is no place for you."

Shasta Cunningham slid the shawl down around her slim shoulders. "I can be where

I want, and I want to be with you."

"Haven't you heard? I'm not supposed to live out the day." Billy slammed the door a second time.

"More reason for me to stay," Shasta said. "Someone has to watch your back." She brought a stool over and straddled it. "Is there anything you need? Anything at all? I'll get it for you."

"Quiet would be nice."

Shasta indicated the saloon. "Belle and Susie are all set. They were giggling like little girls when I left and betting how many they would kill."

"You're better off with them." Billy tried one more time.

"You're the one I love," Shasta said. "You're the one I want to spend the rest of my days with. Not that you'll have me."

Billy studied her. "You puzzle me no end. I treat you like the whore you are. I tell you time and again you're nothin' special. Yet there you sit, professin' your love."

"Women are ruled by their hearts, not their heads. I can no more deny how I feel about you than I can stop breathing."

"But I don't love *you*," Billy stressed.

"So?" Shasta brushed her bangs back. "It's who we care for, not who cares for us. You should be grateful. I'm the one person in this whole world you can trust."

Billy made a *ppfffttt* sound. "I don't trust anyone. Ever. A person lives longer that way."

"You'll change," Shasta predicted. "The day will come when you'll want to settle down and a wife and a home will start to look good. I only pray I'm around when that happens."

"Set your sights on someone else and you'll be a heap sight happier," Billy said. He saw the Twins jog past, trailed by Zech Frame and Jeff Dean. "There's the one you want. He'd dig in roots wherever you say and wait on you hand and foot."

"Jeff Dean is as dull as a stump," Shasta said. "You're the one who makes me smile. You're the one I dream about at night, the one I think about when I'm with all those other men."

"Stop," Billy said.

"They don't mean anything to me. Not a one. Most of the time, I don't even look at their faces."

"I said to stop."

"Sorry." Shasta slid off the stool and placed her hand on his arm. "You're the one I love." She brushed a hand across his cheek. "I wish you could see yourself through my eyes. Then you'd know how I feel about you. You wouldn't look at girls like Sally Palmer ever again."

"Talk about something else."

"You never loved her. You wanted her, is all. Just like you wanted that woman up to Wichita that time. And once you had her, you lost interest."

"Go behind the counter and stay there. I don't want you takin' a stray."

Shasta clasped her hands and cheerfully exclaimed, "Then you do care! I knew that deep down you did. I see it in your eyes sometimes when you're too drunk to pretend you don't."

"Women are the only critters in creation stupider than cows," Billy remarked. "All you've ever been to me is an excuse to wear out a mattress. A man can take a poke without it being true love."

"You're just saying that because you don't like to admit your true feelings. Men are like that."

Billy moved to where he could see the entire length of the street. The eastern sky was rapidly brightening. Drawing his Colt he verified cartridges were in all the chambers. Some men liked to keep the chamber under the hammer empty for safety's sake, but not him. "Why aren't you behind the counter yet?"

"I'm staying by your side," Shasta said. "To cover your back, remember?"

"Do what you want. But I won't watch yours. I look out for me and only me," Billy let her know.

Suddenly Shasta pointed. "Look there! Over by the barbershop. Why is he doing that?"

Black Jack had stepped from between buildings and was waving his hat back and forth.

"It's the signal," Billy said.

The cowboys were coming.

Chapter Twenty-seven

"I'd rather you didn't," Lin Cooley said.

Dixie Storm dismissed his request with a wave of her hand. "It's my husband who was sent into the next world. It was Circle C stock they rustled. So I'm going in with you, and that's my final say. Savvy?"

"Yes, ma'am." Lin reluctantly gave in. When she gigged her horse toward Nowhere, he was quick to catch up and stay next to her.

Slate grey clouds filled the sky. It would rain before the day was done but right now the wind was still and the clouds were motionless, as if the world were holding its breath waiting for something to happen.

Nowhere was cast in preternatural twilight, its buildings jutting skyward like so many squat tombstones. An ominous pall of impending violence hung over the land like a burial shroud.

Lin Cooley loosened his Colt in its holster. His was nickel-plated with pearl steerhead grips, and he'd had it engraved with a leaf scroll design by a master gunsmith in El Paso.

"I hope Mr. Elliot has started in," Dixie commented. "We don't want any of them getting away."

"Joe is a good man," Lin said.

"Coming from you that's high praise." Dixie rose in her stirrups and looked behind them. "The men have all checked their guns?"

"I saw to it personally. Whatever is waitin' for us in there, we're going in with our eyes open."

Randy Quin had come up beside Lin. "I'd go in alone if I had to. Sally would still be alive if not for those —" He glanced at Dixie and settled for saying, "No-accounts."

"Strong feelin's can make a man careless," Lin cautioned.

"I don't much care what happens to me," Randy said. "It's Braden I want, and Braden I'll have, and God and the Devil be hanged."

Lin was alert for the telltale silhouettes of riflemen on the roofs or at windows but he saw none. "Mighty peculiar," he commented. "They could pick a few of us off before we got there if they tried."

"Maybe they lit a shuck," Randy said. "The Twins were bound to tell Black Jack we tumbled to their rustlin' scheme."

"Black Jack is as mean as they come," Dixie said, "but no one has ever accused him of lacking a backbone."

"True," Lin said. He had a hunch the outlaws would make a fight of it and his hunches were seldom wrong — although in this instance it might be better if he were. "Some of his bunch are as gritty as fish eggs rolled in sand." Longley, Towers and Craven alone had a string of thirty kills to their credit, and if they went down, it wouldn't be with bullets in their backs.

"Nowhere looks deserted," Dixie commented. "You'd think people would be up and about by now."

There wasn't a soul to be seen.

Lin scoured the roofs and windows again. He was willing to swear unseen eyes were on them.

"There's Joe," Randy said.

Joe Elliot and the rest were approaching from the north, riding four abreast, most with their rifles shucked. Elliot spied them and waved.

Lin returned the gesture, then motioned for Joe's riders to fan out. Joe nodded in understanding. Within moments Hap Evans and three punchers were swinging to the east while Toby Gill and three more looped west.

Shifting in his saddle toward Amos Finch and Kip Langtree, Lin said, "Amos, take three men and link up with Hap. Kip, you do the same with Toby. We'll enter Nowhere from four sides at once."

"On my way," Amos said, using his spurs.

Lin slowed so the encirclement would be complete before they moved in. He noticed something he hadn't noticed before; sprawled forms scattered here and there. "Look at all those bodies."

"Land sakes!" Randy exclaimed in honor. "They've wiped out the townsfolk."

"We should send someone on ahead," Dixie proposed. "Maybe get them to show their hand."

"I'll go," Lin volunteered.

"You're the ramrod," Dixie said. "We can't afford to lose you. Any one of our hands will be glad to go in your stead."

Randy said, "I know I would."

"You'll stay with Mrs. Storm," Lin directed. To her he said, "I'd never ask a puncher to do something I wouldn't do myself." He motioned for his contingent to halt, then signaled to Joe Elliot and the riders coming in from the east and west to stop where they were.

"You do a woman proud," Dixie said.

"Mr. Storm isn't buried yet," Lin reminded her, and cantered forward until he was fifty yards from the stable, at which point he slowed to walk, his right hand on his Colt. The stable doors were closed, as was every door in sight. His skin prickled as he came abreast of the blacksmith's shop. He thought he heard a sound so he drew rein but it wasn't repeated and after a minute he rode on.

The general store, the feed and grain, the barbershop, all were closed. A Conestoga down the street had been left unattended, its tongue in the dust.

Lin noticed that the inner doors to the saloon were open and one of the batwings was moving ever so slightly, as if someone had peeked out and then ducked back when they saw him coming. The feeling of being watched was stronger. He peered from under his hat at every shadowy nook and recessed cranny but still saw no one.

Lin's gaze alighted on the marshal's office. On an impulse he kneed his horse over. The door was unlocked, the air stale and musty. "Lunsford?" he said, and when there was no reply, he started to back out.

"Cooley? My God, is that you?" A pale shape assumed substance behind the cell bars and a pale hand groped between them. "Don't go!"

"Marshal?"

"Let me out of here! The key is on the desk."

Lin took it over. "Here you go. But what are you doing locked up in your own jail? Was it Black Jack?"

"Who else?" Lunsford was haggard, his clothes a mess. Jamming his hat on his head, he brushed past Lin, picked up the scattergun, and broke it open. Then, without a word, he strode toward the door.

Lin beat him there. "Hold up. What's your rush?"

"I have a score to settle. You best ride back to the Circle C. Your boss will be upset if you get involved."

"Mr. Storm is dead," Lin revealed, and brought the lawman up to date, concluding with, "You're the only living soul I've seen."

Marshal Lunsford was stuffing extra shells into a pocket. "Yesterday I heard a lot of shots and screams and people yelling for help." He shouldered out the door and despite the clouds, squinted at the nearest body. "It was a slaughter. They counted on me to protect them and I let them down."

"You're only one man."

"Don't sugarcoat it." Lunsford stalked toward the saloon. Wedging the scattergun between his bad arm and his body, he pulled back the twin hammers. "I failed. I've been failing all my life but this is the worst. And the last."

"Let's wait for the others," Lin suggested, but he wasted his breath. The lawman barged through the batwings and stood glowering like a mad old bull but there was no one to shoot.

"Dub?" Lunsford called out.

"Let's try the general store," Lin said. "Someone is always there." He wheeled and had taken a couple of steps past the overhang when a noise from above brought him around in a crouch, his right hand stabbing for the Colt.

Belle James and Susie Metzger were on the roof, only their heads and shoulders visible above the false front. "Hey there, cowboy," Belle James said.

Marshal Lunsford had trained his scattergun on them. "What are you ladies doing up there? Where's Black Jack and the rest of his butchers?"

"They burned the breeze for safer pastures," Susie Metzger said. "We didn't want to go so we hid."

"That won't wash," Lunsford responded.

"I want the truth, or so help me, it won't make a lick of difference that you're a woman."

Belle James used language no church-going lady ever would, then said, "Why is it so hard to believe? Do you think we liked Black Jack bossing us around? Do you think we liked all the killing?"

"I never saw shackles on your ankles," Lunsford said.

"His threats were enough," Belle James said. "When a man like Black Jack tells you he'll blow out your wick if you try to run off, you take him seriously."

Lin was more interested in something else. "Where are the rest of the townspeople?"

Susie Metzger covered her face with her hands. "It was awful. Ben Towers and Craven and the rest went from door to door on a killin' spree. No one stood a prayer."

"The women and kids too?" Lin asked. He had been taught to hold womanhood in the highest esteem, and harming a child was unthinkable.

"Black Jack took some of the ladies with him," Susie said. "I have no idea what he did with the half-pints."

Belle James was staring at the scattergun.

"I wish you wouldn't keep pointing that thing at us. It makes me nervous."

Lowering it, Lunsford said to Lin, "We need to search the whole town. For that we need help."

Lin stepped to the middle of the street and beckoned to Dixie and then to Joe Elliot. He couldn't see the riders to the east and west but Amos and Kip would start in when the others did.

Marshal Lunsford hadn't taken his eyes off the fallen doves. "Come on down from there. You're safe now that Black Jack is gone."

"If you don't mind," Belle said, "we'll wait until you're sure. We *heard* them ride off. We didn't actually *see* them."

"Now you tell us," Marshal Lunsford trained his scattergun on the other side of the street.

Lin's skin crawled but nothing happened, and presently the clomp of hooves heralded the arrival of the Circle C hands and their allies. The cowboys converged on the saloon, jamming the street from side to side.

"Well?" Dixie asked, with a nod at Belle James and Susie Metzger. "What did the tarts have to say?"

"Now see here, lady," Susie said.

"Dearie, the day anything you say matters more than a pile of dog shit to me is the day cows sprout wings and fly."

The color of Susie Metzger's face matched the color of her hair. "I've half a mind to come down there and box your ears."

"Feel free to try."

Susie had more to say but Belle James nipped it in the bud by barking, "Enough! We're on their side now, remember? We can't ask their help unless we stay in their good graces."

"Our help?" Dixie said.

"We want to go back East," Belle said. "Somewhere people aren't always killin' one another. But we need a stake."

Marshal Lunsford mentioned what was on Lin's own mind. "All the money you made in those back rooms and you don't have enough to get you there?"

"Black Jack barely gave us enough to live on. He kept ninety percent of what we made for himself."

Randy Quin had dismounted. "Why are we jawin' with them when there's a town to search? Billy Braden might be here somewhere and he has a lot to answer for." He moved toward the general store.

Lin had it in mind to divide the men in

half and conduct the hunt from opposite ends of town. Then he saw Dixie threading her paint toward him, and he waited to hear what she had to say.

The next instant, up the street, a rifle crackled. Lin's instincts shrieked at him to hunker and seek the source but instead he ran to the paint and reached up to help Dixie down. She was lighter than he thought she would be and she clung to him a few seconds longer than he thought was necessary.

"Thank you," she whispered.

Amos and some of the other hands had reined in close, forming a protective ring. "Is anyone hit?" the old puncher hollered.

Everyone was looking at everyone else. No one was wounded or down and none of the horses had been shot.

"Where did it come from?" Joe Elliot bawled. "Did anyone see?"

Belle James and Susie Metzger had dropped from sight.

Marshal Lunsford was close to the batwings, and to gauge by his expression, he was as puzzled as Lin.

The paint began acting up and Dixie held tight to the reins. "Joe! Kip! Go find the shooter!"

It was an order Lin should have given.

He had to stop thinking about her and concentrate on the reason they were there. "The rest of you spread out! We're too bunched up!"

Both Elliot and Langtree had to work their way through the press of horsemen. They had barely begun when Lin caught movement out of the corner of his eye, on the roof of the saloon.

Belle James and Susie Metzger had reappeared and were leaning out over the false front. Each held one end of a wooden keg.

For a few seconds Lin couldn't make sense of what they were up to. Sparkling sprinkles of light gave him a clue.

Sticking out the top of the keg was a lit fuse.

Chapter Twenty-eight

Grabbing Dixie around the waist, Lin Cooley propelled her toward the other side of the street. Belle James and Susie Metzger had already let go of the keg of black powder. Raising his Colt, Lin snapped a shot on the fly. Not at them. It would do no good. He shot at the keg in the hope that detonating it in midair might spare a few punchers and their mounts. Then Lin fell flat, pulling Dixie with him. He was looking over his shoulder and saw the result.

A tremendous explosion blew apart the saloon's false front and sent chunks of Belle James and Susie Metzger arcing through the air. A few riders were also blown apart. Six or seven were punched from their saddles. A horse lost its head in a spectacular spray of blood while others were slammed onto their sides or reared and plunged.

To Lin it was like being rammed by a longhorn. He had tried to spare Dixie by shielding her with his body but she involuntarily cried out. The world faded to silence and Lin thought his eardrums were ruptured. Chaos swirled on all sides but he couldn't hear it. Dixie was saying something to him but he couldn't hear her. Amos Pinch was firing his pistol but he couldn't hear the shots.

A cloud of smoke and dust coalesced outward, swallowing everyone. "Cover your mouth and nose!" Lin shouted to Dixie, and couldn't hear his own words.

The cloud slowly dispersed. Lin rose on his elbows and beheld cowboys sprawled in the street, a few with missing limbs, one with half his face gone. A horse had a jagged spear of wood imbedded in its neck and was thrashing in a panic, posing a threat to other riders and animals.

Heaving to his knees, Lin winced as a cacophony of sound assaulted his senses. Men were shouting, cursing, screaming; horses were nickering and squealing; guns were firing on all sides.

Dingus Mechum was in the Conestoga down the street, firing a Henry over the seat. Clell Craven was in the doorway of the barbershop, working a Winchester's lever. Other outlaws were firing from other vantage points.

"It's a trap!" Dixie cried. She had drawn

her Bisley and was banging shots at someone near the stable.

A Circle C puncher clutched his ruptured throat and toppled from his saddle.

Another fell to a slug that cored his head from front to back and left bits of his brain clinging to his mount's flank.

Gripping Dixie's left arm, Lin hauled her toward the jail, and cover. A young outlaw came running around the corner, fired from the hip, and missed. Lin's answering shot did not.

Somewhere a shotgun thundered. Somewhere else a man screeched his death cry.

Amos and Kip and Joe Elliot and Toby Gill were firing like madmen.

Pandemonium ran riot.

Marshal Paul Lunsford was crouched near the batwing doors, watching Circle C cowboys drop right and left, and helpless to prevent it. Then the saloon window abruptly shattered and the twin barrels of a shotgun poked out. It went off, a cannon among peashooters, and twenty feet out, Amos Finch's head disappeared from his shoulders in a spray of gore.

A long stride brought Lunsford to the batwings. He dived under them and rolled on his good shoulder and came up on one knee with his scattergun level, but Ben Towers had seen him and was running toward the back rooms. Lunsford resisted the temptation to rush his shot and gave chase. He wanted to be sure.

Towers was reloading. He had removed the spent shells and was inserting a new one. Suddenly he stopped and whirled and fired.

A doorway was to Marshal Lunsford's right. He flung himself through it and was spared but came down hard. As he rose, he saw one of the newcomers to Nowhere, the man who had planned to open a hotel, on his back on the bed, gaping lifelessly at the ceiling.

The slam of the back door spurred Lunsford into flying down the hall. Without thinking he grabbed the latch but in a flash of insight realized his mistake and threw himself to the floor. The door exploded inward, leaving a hole as big around as a watermelon. He rose high enough to see out and spotted Ben Towers running north.

Flinging what was left of the door open, Marshal Lunsford pumped his legs as he hadn't pumped them in more years than he cared to remember. He was terribly out of shape, and had been since he lost his arm and much of his zest for living. But now he dug deep down inside himself, deep into the reservoir of stamina he possessed when he was decades younger, and found the spark he needed to keep running.

Ben Towers darted into a space between the barbershop and a house.

Lunsford slowed so as not to make another blunder. Removing his hat, he risked a quick peek. Towers wasn't there. He sprinted toward the street and almost too late saw the business end of Towers's shotgun jut past the corner. It went off as Lunsford hurled himself at the ground. He felt a stinging sensation in his side and a warm stickiness under his shirt, and then he was up and running again, out into the seething herd of bedlam. Outlaws and cowboys were engaged in a mad melee of lead swapping. A riderless horse galloped past, nearly bowling Lunsford over.

Ben Towers was in front of the restaurant, taking deliberate arm.

Lunsford brought up his scattergun but Towers fired first just as a horse galloped past. The horse took the brunt of the twin barrels, and staggered. Lunsford squeezed one trigger and then the other. His slugs lifted Towers off his feet and cartwheeled him into the restaurant window, which shattered into a thousand shards.

Off to Marshal Lunsford's right, Joe Elliot and Kip Langtree were swapping shots with two outlaws. To his left, Randy Quin was charging the general store, firing as he ran.

Hurriedly reloading, Lunsford reentered the frenzied fray.

In the initial confusion, Randy Quin was racked by brief indecision. He had never been in a gunfight, never killed another human being in his life. But when he saw his friends being blasted from their saddles and heard their screams and the buzz of leaden hornets seeking his own life, he drew his revolver and squeezed off shots at targets as they presented themselves.

More hornets buzzed him and Randy sought the source. His blood ran cold when he saw Billy Braden in the general store, shooting out the doorway. Caterwauling like a panther, Randy rushed him, firing as he ran.

Billy spun and vanished among the display goods.

Randy figured Braden would expect him to come in through the door so he did something Braden wouldn't expect; he launched himself at what was left of the front window. He didn't give any thought to being cut by the glass, or the consequences of having his neck or wrist slashed open. He wasn't thinking of anything except revenge. Sweet, glorious revenge.

Sharp pain lanced Randy's left forearm and his right leg but he surged to his feet and fired at a shadow. The shadow replied and new pain flared in Randy's side. He squeezed the trigger but all he heard was a sharp *click*. Dashing behind the counter, he began reloading as slugs chewed the wood to splinters. His fingers were unaccountably stiff.

Out in the street the conflict was at its fiercest. Guns blasted in riotous cadence. Out of the confusion Toby Gill appeared, his shirt discolored, weaving as if he were drunk. Randy tore his gaze from Gill and raised his eyes to the top of the counter. Almost immediately a pistol cracked and slivers stung Randy's cheek.

Ducking, Randy crabbed to the end of the counter. He heard rustling but he couldn't isolate where it came from. Cautiously peeking out, he spied Billy Braden slinking toward the spot he had vacated. Billy's back was to him.

Randy had time to aim. He intended to

shoot Braden in the head but at the exact moment his Colt spat lead and flame, another shadow flew from behind a table piled with bolts of cloth.

"Billy! Look out!"

It was Shasta Cunningham. The slug meant for Billy struck her instead, square in the bosom. She fell against Billy, blood gushing from her mouth and nose, and Billy threw her aside like a dirty rag.

Randy had a clear shot but he didn't shoot. He couldn't. The monstrous horror of what he had done paralyzed him. He saw Billy's fancy Colt rise, saw smoke puff from the end of the barrel. Searing agony jolted his left shoulder, but it also jolted him out of his daze. Rising on his knees, he fired as Billy Braden fired again, fired as Billy doubled over, fired as Billy keeled headfirst to the floor, fired again and once more and then the hammer clicked on a spent cartridge and Randy felt himself melting, inside and out. His last thought was of Sally Palmer. His last sight was of Lin Cooley out in front of the store, a pistol in both hands, blazing away.

A minute earlier Lin had been in the jail, watching the tide of battle turn. He saw cowboy after cowboy go down, wounded or slain. Something had to be done or the gunfight would become a slaughter.

Lin dashed to the desk. He opened each of the drawers but did not find what he was looking for. A cabinet in a corner, though, proved a trove of weapons; several rifles and four revolvers. One was a Colt the same model as his, only plainer, and it was already loaded. He ran to the doorway. "Stay here."

"Where are you going?" Dixie responded. "We're safe here."

"Those are my friends out there."

Dixie clutched his arm. "Please," she said.

Lin smiled and nodded, and then he was outside and racing up the street into the gun-smoke-filled jaws of earthly hell. Circle C hands were sprawled in the dust, some groaning or holding themselves.

Dingus Mechum was firing at the wounded, trying to finish them off.

Lin fired twice and Dingus pitched across the seat, half in, half out, his Henry falling from fingers gone limp.

Other outlaws appeared, one on a roof, another in the doorway of the feed and grain. Lin shot one and spun and shot the other. Clell Craven cut loose from the barbershop and Lin spun and banged off two shots and Craven stumbled and looked down at himself and died.

A slug nipped at Lin's side, another at his shoulder. He turned and discovered the Twins were rushing him from behind, laughing as they fired, thinking they had him. But the backshooters reckoned without the Colts in his hands and when it was over he had been shot but they were dead.

Down the street two figures ducked into the stable.

Lin lurched toward it, his right leg giving him trouble. He reloaded his Colt and then the other and he was almost to the stable doors when they were flung wide, framing Black Jack and Ike Longley with the reins of their horses in their hands. "Going somewhere?" Lin asked.

Black Jack grinned. "Well, well. The Circle C pistolero. Do you want him, Ike? Or should I?"

Longley let his reins drop and lowered his hands to his Remingtons. "You and me, cowpoke. What do you say?"

Lin said nothing.

"Holster those six-shooters and we'll see which one of us is best," Longley proposed. "How about it?"

"Go to hell," Lin said, and squeezed both triggers. It was kill or be killed and he had a lot to live for. Longley's Remingtons streaked out and Longley answered him. Lin was jarred but not down, not yet, not until he banged off four more shots and Longley's face smacked the dirt.

Lin's legs folded and he lay staring at the grey sky and wondering how much longer he had to live. A bearded face filled his vision, and hollow laughter pealed as if from the depths of a well.

"I reckon I do the honors, after all," Black Jack said, and leveled his revolver.

There was a shot. Just one. A hole appeared high on Black Jack's cheek and his face disappeared. Another replaced it. A face far fairer. A hand gently touched Lin's shoulder.

"Don't you die on me!" Dixie Storm said.

In the sudden silence, Marshal Lunsford's ears were ringing so loud, he barely heard his name being called. He walked to where Joe Elliot lay in a spreading red pool.

"Did we get them?"

Lunsford surveyed the carnage. Memories of Gettysburg washed over him; the blasted bodies lying in droves, the dead and dying horses, the sickly sweet smell of blood and the stench of ranker odors. "We got them."

"Good." Joe smiled. He tried to lift a hand but couldn't. "Damn. This just ain't been my year. If you see Lin, would you tell him I regret I won't be able to work with him?"

"I'll tell him," Marshal Lunsford said, and the light of life faded.

Kip Langtree was over by the restaurant, tendrils of gun smoke curling from his revolver. "I never," he said as the lawman walked over. "I just never."

"No one does until they live through it," Lunsford remarked. He gave the cowboy's arm a sharp shake. "Snap out of it. I need you to ride to Beaver City and fetch the sawbones. If he won't come, you by-God make him. Do you understand?"

Kip nodded. "He might be bruised some but he'll be here." Off he ran.

Lunsford spotted Dixie Storm and started toward her but stopped when an outlaw came crawling out from between buildings, a crimson smear in his wake.

"Help me! Please!"

"Zech Frame, isn't it?"

"Yes. I'm hurt, hurt bad. I need a doc."

"So do a lot of others, you son of a bitch." Marshal Lunsford pointed his scattergun at Frame's head and fired both barrels.

A year later Lin Cooley and Dixie Storm were married. They had four children and their ranch prospered.

Randy Quin survived the bloodbath at Nowhere as it became known, largely thanks to the efforts of Greta Svenson, who nursed him back to health. They courted for several years until Greta finally tired of waiting for him to propose and she asked him. They had no children but lived to a fine old age.

So did Marshal Paul Lunsford. He was reelected to four more terms and saw Oklahoma become a state and Nowhere become a true and legal town. In his waning years he could be found on his porch in the rocking chair that once belonged to Tom Taylor, rocking and remembering, rocking and remembering.